Magical Bonds

MAGICAL BONDS

CECILIA AGETUN

Magical Bonds (Freya's Legacy, book 2)
Published by Cecilia Agetun
www.ceciliaagetun.com

ISBN: 978-1-7396488-3-1 (ebook)
ISBN: 978-1-7396488-4-8 (paperback)
ISBN: 978-1-7396488-5-5 (hardcover)

Book design:
Brittany Evans, https://bedesigns.ca/

Editor:
Sabrina Lozier, https://sabrinalozier.com/
Catherine Dunn, https://catherinedunn.co.uk/

To Sian and Ray Stephenson

For giving me a home away from home.

ACKNOWLEDGEMENTS

I'd like to thank the people in my critique groups; Elizabeth, Jordan, Mila, Noah, Heather, Branan, Trena – I couldn't have done it without you.

Thanks to my beta readers; Izabella, Haven, Kim, Maria, Brooke, Megan, Mary, and everyone else that provided me with feedback. A special thanks to Samantha, John and Clay for their honest and brutal critique – my book is so much better for it.

I want to thank Gudrun for going through my work, and Brittany for the amazing cover. I'd also like to thank Sabrina for fitting me in at short notice after issues with another developmental editor, and my copy editor Cathrine for being so understanding when the book got pushed back.

A special thanks to my other half Dave for supporting me on my writing journey.

And a massive thanks to the reader, for allowing me to share my world with you.

MAGICAL BONDS

SKY

My Life

The dark clouds loomed closer despite me willing them away. Maybe tomorrow would be different and I'd have the ability to move things with my mind.

'Sky, can you bring the washing inside? It looks like it's going to rain,' my mother called from inside the house.

'I'm busy. Why can't Dawn do it?' I shouted back, though I knew the answer. My mother never asked Dawn to do anything.

'She's studying.'

I sighed. 'Fine.' I glanced up at the sky one more time before I got up from my spot in the grass. I brushed the grass off my black trousers and went inside to get a bag for the clothes.

Tomorrow, things would be different. I'd be sixteen and my magic would awaken. I'd spent countless hours daydreaming about which affinities I would have and how it would feel to finally wield magic. Would my mother still make me do all the chores if I had three out of the four affinities like my sister? I shook my head at the thought. It didn't matter. As long as I wasn't chosen to sacrifice my magic, I'd be happy with just two.

The smell of impending rain hung in the air, and the wind swirled my raven hair as I took down the clothes and stuffed them into the bag. I walked back to the house and dropped the bag next to my mother, who was standing in the kitchen stirring a pot of pasta. 'Here's the clothes you asked for.'

She put down the spoon and wiped her hands on her apron before turning to face me with a raised eyebrow. 'And what do you want me to do with them?'

I shrugged. 'I don't know. You asked for them.'

She tilted her head and gave me an unyielding gaze.

With a groan, I swung the bag over my shoulder. 'Fine, I guess I'll put the clothes away too.'

'Thank you,' my mother said calmly. 'When you're done, would you mind setting the table?'

I went upstairs without answering, grumbling to myself. It wasn't fair that they treated me like a servant in my own home and expected me to do all the chores. Just because Dawn studied under the High Priestess didn't mean she couldn't help.

After putting the clothes away, I returned to the kitchen to set the table. I placed the bread and butter on the table and got the salad bowl out from the marble cooler.

'Anything else you want me to do?' I asked, folding my arms over my chest, struggling to hold in my scowl. My mother chose to ignore my mood as usual.

'Yes. Would you mind letting everyone know that dinner is ready?' She pulled a tray of meatballs out of the oven and placed it on the kitchen counter.

I didn't understand how she always seemed happy and content with just being at home. Before she had us, she was a skilled healer, or so I heard, but she never spoke about it. I wondered if she missed it.

I made my way over to the stables at the side of our house, passing a few empty stalls before reaching the area in the back where my father carried out most of his work as a farrier.

He was standing behind our horse, Lightning, with her hoof in his hands, questioning Night about the procedure while using his elemental magic for earth to bend the shoe into a perfect fit.

Even though my brother was only thirteen, he had been working with my father from a young age to learn the trade so he could carry on the family business. He didn't have much say in the matter, but at least he seemed to enjoy it.

'Dinner's ready,' I told them when I got a chance.

'Thank you, Sky. We'll be there in a moment,' my father answered.

I returned to the house and stopped at the foot of the staircase. 'Dinner's ready,' I shouted, hoping Dawn would hear me from her room so I wouldn't have to go all the way up to get her.

I took my seat at the wooden dining table and waited for the others to arrive. A few minutes later, Dawn came skipping down the stairs in a blue skirt and a white blouse with her hair neatly plaited in a braid. She smiled at our mother. 'It smells amazing.'

My mother returned her smile and brought the pasta and meatballs over to the table as my father and brother walked into the room. 'Sorry we're late. It took a bit longer than expected.' My father kissed my mother on the cheek before he joined us at the table.

Everyone busied themselves with eating until my father cleared his throat and looked over at me. 'How did the crystal test go, Sky?'

'I hope you studied hard like Dawn,' my mother chimed in.

I stifled an annoyed sigh. Of course I had studied. I'd always been good at school, but once we began learning about spells and elemental magic, I'd put even more time and effort into studying. It had always fascinated me to understand the reasons how and why a spell worked, and I dreamed of becoming a scholar in spell magic. That way, even if I couldn't earn my family's respect, I'd earn the respect of the villagers and finally be acknowledged. Maybe I could come up with some new technology that could help the village or even eradicate the need for the sacrifices.

'It went fine,' I answered, picking at my food.

My father turned to my sister. 'Dawn, how was your day?'

She looked up and swallowed the food in her mouth. 'It was good – really interesting, actually. We're learning about the Dark Moon Ritual, how it started and why Hecate sealed our village away from the human world and into its own realm.'

I crossed my arms at the mention of the Goddess, leaning slightly forward. 'She sealed the village two hundred years ago, so why are the sacrifices still needed? And why are only people with two affinities or less chosen?'

Dawn's jaw tightened. 'Don't you know demons are immortal? Hecate needs the magic to make sure our village remains hidden. If not, the demon will be back to destroy it.'

'How can you be so sure?' I uncrossed my arms and gestured with an open palm. 'Is it not possible the demon actually fell in love with Katie Whitelake, the High Priestess in training?'

Dawn grimaced. 'No. Demons can't feel love. He seduced her and forced her to carry his child. It's not natural. That's why she and the baby died during labour.'

I stared at Dawn across the table. 'If that was true, don't you think they would have banished or killed the demon before all of that instead of letting him hang around in the village until the baby was born?'

She narrowed her eyes at me. 'If it wasn't true, why

would the High Priestess and the Elders call upon the Goddess Hecate for protection?'

I had opened my mouth to argue further when our father spoke up. 'Girls, let's just enjoy the food. It would be nice to have one meal where you two aren't bickering.'

'Sorry,' I mumbled before picking at my food again. I never understood why Hecate hadn't just killed the demon if he was that evil. Sacrificing the magic of three witches each year to keep our village concealed didn't make sense. There had to be more to the story than what we had been told. Unfortunately, the only being still around who had been there when it happened was Hecate herself, and my gut feeling told me she had ulterior motives.

I turned to my father. 'Are you coming to my ceremony tomorrow?'

He gave me a sympathetic look. 'I wish I could, honey, but I need to work.'

Tears burned behind my eyes, but I tried to hide it by concentrating on my food. He had been at Dawn's ceremony.

Night, who was sitting next to me, placed a hand on my shoulder. 'I'll be there, and Mum too.'

'And I'll be in the temple already, so I'll see if I can get any free time to come too,' Dawn said with a soft smile.

I forced myself to return the smile. 'Thank you.'

I didn't have high hopes, but I wasn't bothered about Dawn. We had been close once, but everything had changed about two years ago when she'd discovered she had an affinity for three elements and started studying under Hecate and the High Priestess. Part of me was proud of her, but an even bigger part of me was jealous.

'What elements do you think you're going to be able to wield?' Night asked as his eyes lit up with excitement.

I had given it a lot of thought. Father could wield the elements of earth and fire, and my mother had an affinity for fire and water, but there was no guarantee I would have the same affinities as them, even though Dawn was gifted with all three.

I smiled at Night. 'I guess I'll find out tomorrow.'

My mother started to collect the empty plates, her eyes meeting mine. 'Speaking of tomorrow, what would you like to do for your birthday? It's your big sixteenth. I know your father won't be able to make the ceremony, but we could still celebrate with you in the evening.'

I shrugged. 'I don't know. Maybe just a quiet meal at home.'

She furrowed her brow. 'Are you sure? We should at least go out and celebrate.'

Dawn's eyes gleamed. 'Maybe we can go to the Cauldron Kitchen? They always have a lot of lovely stews and soups. Or maybe the Firepit. Their pizzas are amazing.'

'I'll think about it,' I replied shortly. It was common to have big parties and affinity reveals when turning sixteen, but I had always preferred the quiet and comfort of home.

After I'd helped my mother with the dishes, I went upstairs to my room. I used to share it with Dawn, but after she'd started studying in the temple, she complained about needing her own space, so my parents had quickly finished work on the house extension so she could have her own room. Luckily it had benefited me too.

My room was a mess. There were several books scattered over the floor, along with random pieces of clothing. A desk stood in one corner, which was actually tidy, and a single bed was located along the other wall. It wasn't a big room, but it was mine.

I picked up a fiction book from the floor and lay down on my bed. For a little while, I could escape reality and become someone else – someone who mattered.

'Sky, time to get up. We need to be at the temple in an hour,' my mother called.

I jumped out of bed and went to have a shower. When I came back to my room, I walked over to my wardrobe and looked through my clothes. I pulled out a flowery dress but hesitated. They would give me a robe to wear, so there wasn't any point in dressing up. Instead I picked a pair of black trousers and a blue top.

Half an hour later my mother, Night and I rode our bikes to the temple. We cycled past wheat fields being harvested and turned on to a gravel road. It was one of five main roads that led to the temple. The fields disappeared behind us and gave way to houses built closer together. We reached the town square, and the white stone temple towered before us with its large pillars supporting the roof.

We rounded the upper corner of the farmer's market and turned in to an area designated for parking, which was divided into stations for bikes and horses. I got off my bike and looked around, taking in the familiar view. From here my school was clearly visible, as well as the notorious university where people studied to become scholars.

Butterflies fluttered in my stomach as we walked towards the temple, and I had to slow down and wait for them to catch up on several occasions. There were two enormous staircases leading to the entrance of the temple, and between them was a waterfall pool with a statue of the Triple Goddess in the middle, a representation of Hecate in her maiden, mother and crone forms.

As we reached the bottom of the stairs, a woman in a white robe greeted us. 'Welcome to the temple. Are you here for the affinity ceremony?'

My mother nodded and pointed at me. 'Yes. This is Sky, who will perform the ceremony.'

The woman intertwined her hands. 'How lovely. Sky, please wait here until everyone has arrived.' She gestured to my mother and Night to continue up the stairs. 'Please enter the temple and take a seat.' Once they'd walked past us, the woman turned to me. 'Are we waiting for anyone else to arrive?'

I shook my head. The affinity ceremony was open to the public, but most of the time it was only family and close friends that attended it.

'Very well. Please follow me to the changing room so you can begin the cleansing.'

After she had shown me the room, located underneath the stairs, I changed into a temporary linen robe and made my way to the pool to perform the ritual of purifying my mind and soul so they would not affect the outcome of the ceremony.

I dipped my toe into the water, expecting it to be cold, but it was warmer than I'd thought. I waded to the waterfall and took a deep breath before stepping under it, visualising the flowing water binding to my negative energy and removing it from my body until my mind became empty.

Once I'd cleansed and grounded myself, I went back to the changing room and changed into a fresh white robe before making my way up the stairs. My heart rate sped up, and I struggled to keep an empty mind as the thoughts of which element I would have kept intruding.

The High Priestess stood at the top of the stairs in a long modest purple dress, her blond hair tied neatly behind her back. She greeted me with a polite smile as I reached the entrance. 'Sky, are you of clear mind and soul?'

I nodded. 'Yes, ma'am.'

She bowed her head. 'Blessed be.'

'Blessed be,' I said as I returned her bow before entering the temple.

It was a massive empty room with a lingering smell of burnt sage and torches along the stone walls. The marble floor was chilly on my bare feet as I walked past my mother and Night and up to the raised platform where the wooden altar stood, at the far end of the temple.

The altar contained several symbolic tokens, flowers, herbs and candles, all representing the different elements. The grimoire had been placed in the middle and opened to the page displaying the affinity ceremony. Even though we had gone through the ceremony in school, I quickly skimmed through it to remind myself.

Memories of Dawn's affinity ceremony from two years ago entered my head. I had watched in awe as flowers, fire and mist had manifested all around her when she called on the elements in turn, informing us she had an affinity for earth, fire and water. I hoped I would have an affinity for three elements as well. Or better yet, four. Unfortunately, that was uncommon. In fact, the only known witches who had four elements belonged to the High Priestess bloodline.

My mother, Night and the High Priestess watched me from the side. I carefully picked up the salt from the altar and created a circle around myself to focus the elements in one place. Once I'd closed the circle, I took a seat in the middle and faced north. I called upon Earth and let the elemental energy wash over me. The stone floor below turned into soil. I pressed my hands into it, and to my amazement, my fingers became roots, making me aware of every single tree that existed around me.

Once the energy around me had faded, I shifted to the east and called upon Water. I became one with the element. My body turned into mist, and I felt a connection with the clouds in the sky and the river that ran through our village. I was part of the creation of all living things.

I turned to the south and called upon Fire. Heat swept through me, awaking all my senses. There was a fiery burn inside me that burst out, engulfing the whole of me in flames. But I wasn't burning; instead I felt revitalised.

Finally, I turned to the west and called upon Air. My hair swirled in the wind, and I grew lighter as the energy of air washed over me. The feeling of weightlessness became stronger, and I rocked back and forth with the ebbs and flows of life itself, feeling its connection with every breathing being.

A moment later, it was all over. I thanked the elements and opened the circle, eager to know my verdict. We had been told we would probably feel each element, but I hadn't just felt them; I had become them.

My mind raced as I made my way to the High Priestess standing by the entrance.

'Congratulations. You have an affinity for air and water. Blessed be.'

My heart rate sped up and I did a double take. 'What? Are you sure?' I asked with a frown. It had felt so real.

My mother came up behind me and discreetly pinched my arm, reminding me where we were and who I was speaking to.

The High Priestess stared into my eyes, her face stern and devoid of emotion. 'Though it is common to feel all the elements, your affinities are only the ones that cause visual manifestations for the onlookers. Which for you was water and air.'

I bowed my head. 'Blessed be.' I walked towards the exit with a sinking feeling in my chest.

My mother said her blessed be to the High Priestess, and when she caught up with me, she grabbed hold of my arm and dragged me down the stairs. As soon as we had descended, she spun around to me, her jaw clenched. 'I cannot believe you disrespected the High Priestess like that. What were you thinking?'

Tears burned in my eyes, but I held them at bay. 'I'm sorry. I was just making sure—'

'You do not question the High Priestess. Ever. Or would you like to be exiled?' She shook her head and let out a sigh as Night caught up with us. 'I'll see you two at home,' she said and walked away, leaving me and Night on our own.

I went to change back into my normal clothes and joined Night on a nearby bench. 'Are you sure you only saw two elements manifest?'

He nodded. 'I don't understand why you're upset. I would be happy with two affinities.'

Males weren't as in tune with magic, and it was almost unheard of for a male to have more than two affinities. I gave him a forced smile and ruffled his black hair. 'Yeah, you're right. But what if I get chosen to sacrifice my magic?'

He shrugged. 'The chances of you being picked are quite low. A lot of people have had their magic awakened since the last Samhain. Besides, being picked isn't the end of the world. They even give you your own space and a job.'

'Yeah, but they take your magic.'

'True, but you've been without it for sixteen years and you've been managing just fine.'

'But all my studying would have been in vain. And I won't be able to become a scholar.'

'If we stop the sacrifices and the demon destroys our village, none of that will matter anyway. Besides, what's the point of worrying over something you can't change?'

Maybe Night was right, but the emptiness in the pit of my stomach wouldn't go away. If I got chosen, I'd never be able to earn my parents' love and respect.

We sat there in silence for a while before making our way home. When we arrived at the house, Night went over to the stable to see what my father was up to.

I lingered in our garden, debating what to do. I wasn't ready to go inside and face my mother just yet. I started walking towards the fields to check on the horses, but I didn't get very far, as I found a bucket of water and an idea struck me. Water was my affinity, right? So I should be able to make it move.

I took a deep breath, cleared my head and slowed my breathing, recalling what they had taught us at school about controlling an element. At first, nothing happened, but I kept trying. I don't know how long I stared at the bucket, willing the water to move, but my head pounded from concentrating. Why wasn't it working?

'Sky, please come in and set the table.' My mother's voice sounded from the house.

I clenched my fists in anger. Why was it always me that needed to do everything, even on my birthday? I was so sick of it. The water in the bucket exploded, drenching me. I gasped and stared at the now empty bucket in awe and started laughing. I'd done it. I'd wielded magic.

SKY

Samhain

'Mum, leave the bowl on the counter and I'll bring it to the table,' I said as I finished setting the table, excited to show her what I had been learning in my new classes in the last few weeks since the affinity ceremony.

She pursed her lips, her dark eyes piercing mine. 'Please be careful. If you drop it, our dinner's ruined.'

'It's okay, Mum. I can do this,' I said with a smile. I reached inside myself and concentrated on moving the bowl, using my affinity for air. The bowl slowly raised itself from the counter and drifted towards the table.

'Very impressive,' my father said as he walked into the kitchen with Night at his heels.

Dawn shuffled in her chair. 'It's not like it's that hard to move an object. It's one of the first things they teach you.'

I turned to Dawn with a smirk. 'Then show me what you got.' I knew she would be unable to, as she didn't have an affinity for air.

Letting out a sigh, she moved her hand towards her glass and tiny droplets of water rose from it and made their way underneath it, carefully lifting it into the air. 'See – not that hard.' She gave me a smug grin, and I sank back in my chair.

'Let's stop playing and enjoy the food before it goes cold,' my mother said as she took a seat at the table.

'How was everyone's day?' my father asked as he dished up potatoes onto his plate. 'Night finished working on his first pair of shoes today, and they turned out great. Soon he'll be running the show.'

'That's awesome,' I told Night with a smile.

Night's face brightened at the compliment and he looked up at our father. 'I have a great teacher.'

'We've been planning the Samhain ceremony. I may even be a part of the circle,' my sister said.

'That's great news. Sounds like you are making a name for yourself,' my mother said.

Dawn straightened up with a twinkle in her eyes. 'I am. They're letting me conduct my own Esbat next year. Will you be there for it?'

'We wouldn't miss it for the world,' my mother replied.

I bit my tongue. Our family didn't attend Esbats. My mother thought it was a waste of time going to the temple at midnight just to celebrate the full moon. Obviously there was more to the ceremonies than that, but the sabbats were the most important ones, along with the Dark Moon Ritual. I swallowed the sick feeling in my mouth. The names of the sacrifices would be drawn at tomorrow's Samhain ceremony.

'Can I be excused?'

'Is something wrong?' my father asked in a concerned voice.

I shook my head. 'I'm just not hungry.'

'You know you can talk to us if there's anything bothering you,' my mother said with concern.

I doubted the authenticity of her words, as she never seemed to care about my feelings, but there was only one way to find out. I took a deep breath and hesitated. 'What ... what if I get picked tomorrow?'

'It's an honour to be picked and help the village stay safe,' Dawn said. My mother nodded in agreement.

Anger and frustration built up inside. Why had I even bothered saying anything? I pushed my chair away from the table. 'If it's that much of an honour, why don't they pick the people that want to lose their magic?'

I didn't wait for a reply as I stormed out of the kitchen and up to my room, slamming the door behind me. Why didn't any of them understand?

The waning moon glimmered in the sky above us as we stepped out of the horse-drawn carriage. I tugged my jacket tighter; a sense of impending doom stirred within me as we approached the temple.

The stone stairs had been decorated with lanterns, autumn leaves and pumpkins. We stopped at the queue leading to the pool. Because we weren't part of the ceremony, full cleansing wasn't necessary, but to symbolise the cleansing and show our respect, we washed our hands.

When we entered the temple, we had to navigate around several groups of people, a stark contrast from how empty it had been during my birthday ceremony. The torches on the walls helped illuminate the interior, and several rows of chairs had been placed on either side of a candlelit path. We made our way to some empty chairs and sat down.

The altar had been moved into the middle of the raised platform. It was covered in a black cloth and displayed the grimoire along with items symbolising the celebration of life and death, such as feathers, pinecones, pumpkins, candles, crystals and herbs.

The High Priestess, wearing a black robe, walked out and gestured for the doors to the temple to close. Everyone stopped talking.

Thirteen women in white robes entered the platform and walked around, creating a circle. Once done, four people with robes the colour of the elements entered the circle. They moved clockwise, each stopping at the representative cardinal direction. The one wearing a yellow robe, representing air, stopped at the east; the one in a red robe for fire stopped at the south; the one in a blue robe, representing water, stopped at the west; and the one wearing a green robe for earth stopped at the north.

Last, the High Priestess joined; she walked around the outside of the circle, and when she was back where she'd started, she stepped inside and rendered the circle closed.

I searched for Dawn but could not see her. Maybe she hadn't been picked after all. The High Priestess called upon the elements. Each representative repeated the High Priestess's words, calling the element into the circle. After all four elements had been called, the High Priestess invited the element of Spirit to join.

She spoke about the spirits and the afterlife, how everything goes in cycles and how we look forward to new beginnings. I was too preoccupied thinking about the name drawing that came afterwards to pay much attention, but it wasn't like I hadn't heard it all before, as the High Priestess delivered a similar speech each year.

Once she'd finished speaking, she thanked and bid all the elements farewell, then opened the circle.

She walked to the front and faced the crowd. 'Our village has much to be thankful for, especially for the Goddess Hecate. Without her protection, our village and everyone in it would have perished under the wrath of a demon. However, we must pay our penance. As with all magic, there needs to be balance. For Hecate to keep us hidden, to keep us safe, magic needs to be sacrificed for the greater good during the Dark Moon Ritual. As is traditional, Hecate herself will draw three names at random from the cauldron of fire. Please remember it is an honour to be chosen.'

Hecate herself appeared in a cloud of smoke. The room fell silent, and everyone bowed their head. A powerful aura surrounded Hecate, and the shadows themselves appeared to obey her command. She looked in her thirties, with dark features and a long black dress that covered her completely but highlighted her curves. The High Priestess bowed her head at Hecate and said 'Blessed be' before backing away and stepping out of sight.

The shadows around Hecate turned into a cauldron in front of her, and when she moved her hand over it, a raging blue fire appeared from nowhere.

My insides twisted, and I prayed to the Fates I wouldn't be picked. The probability of being picked out of the fifty others who'd had their magic awakened this year was low, but I still couldn't shake the knot in my stomach.

Hecate reached into the cauldron and collected a small flame that faded and turned into a piece of paper. 'The witches blessed with continuing to protect this village are: Aurora Woodward.'

I let out a breath of relief. Only to hold my breath again as she collected another blue flame. 'Heath Allaway.'

As she picked up the last name, I clasped my hands together and held them to my head as I closed my eyes, begging that she hadn't picked my name.

'Sky Farrier,' Hecate called out and my heart stopped. My vision became blurry and everything went out of focus. Hecate continued talking, but I couldn't process anything. It was a good thing we were sitting down, as I wasn't sure my knees would hold my weight.

The High Priestess started talking again, but I had zoned out, too preoccupied with how losing my magic would crush my dream of becoming a respected scholar. It wasn't fair!

My mother acted like nothing had changed and gently nudged me to let me know it was our time to go up to the altar and place our blessings for our ancestors that had moved on. My body followed them to the altar, but inside I was screaming. Why me?

Still feeling empty and disconnected from reality, I followed my family out of the temple. The High Priestess stood by the entrance wishing everyone a 'blessed be', to which it was proper manners to respond back, 'Blessed be.' However, I did not feel very blessed, so I passed her without a word.

I walked over to our carriage and sat down. My family tried to talk to me, but I tuned them out. I didn't care how much of an honour they thought it was, nothing they said could change the situation I was in.

'I'm so sorry they didn't let you be part of the ceremony, Dawn. I know how hard you worked for it,' my mother said.

I blinked. Dawn? When did she join us? Anger built up inside me. They were worrying about Dawn, but what about me? I was the one who was going to lose my magic. I swallowed a scream. Why didn't they care about me and what I was going through?

When we returned home, we got down from the horse-drawn carriage and made our way inside.

'Sky, would you mind setting the table?' my mother asked.

I clenched my fists. My whole body vibrated from trying to contain my anger. 'Yes, I would. My whole life has been turned upside down and you don't even care.'

Dawn rolled her eyes. 'It's not the end of the world. So what? Your magic gets sacrificed; it's not like it'll kill you. Actually it's an honour. You're helping the village stay safe. They're even offering you a great-paying job in the temple and you get your own place. I don't see why you're so upset.'

I gave her a blank stare. 'I don't want to work at the temple.'

'Then don't work at the temple. If you're really that bothered, I'm sure Hecate wouldn't mind sending you to the human world, like she has with Sandra and some others.'

'You don't get it. None of you do.' I stepped outside and slammed the door behind me. Silent tears fell down my face as I made my way to the field where we kept the horses, but it was empty, as the horses had already been taken in for the night.

The wind hugged my body, and I shivered from the cold, wishing I had kept my jacket on. I gazed up at the star-filled sky and the waning moon. Soon it would be gone, and the Dark Moon Ritual would be upon us.

I created my own circle in the dirt and called upon the Fates, begging them to help me find a way to keep my magic and offering my cooperation in whatever they had planned for me.

I sat out there until my tears dried up and my body became numb waiting for a sign that the Fates had heard me. A star fell from the sky, and I decided that was it. It had to be.

That night I had a strange dream. I found myself in a field next to the forest. The sun shone brightly and the trees with their colourful leaves swayed in the breeze. The silhouette of the village loomed behind me as I trudged into the forest. My destination remained unclear, but a sense of purpose urged me forward. After I had walked through the woods for a while, I found myself entering another field. The feeling of another presence swept over me. I scanned the area, but I appeared to be alone. A water-filled ditch separated the field I was in from another, I walked along it, seeking a way to cross. Whatever I was looking for was on the other side.

A massive willow tree split in half offered a way over. I crossed and continued my journey. Beyond a broken fence, a distant shape took form. A house, maybe? A sudden feeling that I was running out of time made me rush towards it, but before I could reach it, I awoke in my bed drenched in sweat.

My late outing had made me ill, and for the next few days, I was in and out of feverish dreams. A lot of them didn't make sense, but the dream where I walked along the field trying to get to the house kept recurring, only I never made it there before I woke up.

My mother knocked on my door and entered the room.

'How are you feeling?'

I pushed myself into a sitting position and looked up at her. 'If I told you I felt worse, would you let me skip the Dark Moon Ritual?'

Ignoring my question, she placed her hand on my forehead. 'It feels like the fever has gone. I made some lunch if you feel like eating.'

I shook my head. The thought of having to face my family felt like too much.

'Mum, I don't want to lose my magic,' I said with tears in my eyes.

She stroked my face. 'Don't worry, Sky. You'll be fine. It might seem scary now, but it's an honour to work at the temple. I'm sure Dawn wouldn't mind introducing you to others in your situation.' She gave me a reassuring smile before standing up and heading toward the door. 'Why don't you have a shower? I've warmed it up for you,' she said as she left the room.

SKY

DARK MOON RITUAL

With a feeling of dread in my heart, I approached the temple with heavy steps. When I reached the stairs, I stopped, unable to force myself up them.

A girl walked up to me from behind. 'You're Sky, right?'

I turned around and nodded in response. The girl in front of me was a stark contrast to myself. Her skin was pale with freckles everywhere and she had short ginger hair. Her green eyes stood out. I had seen her around school. We even had a few classes together, but I hadn't paid much attention to her.

'I'm Aurora,' she said with a wide smile, which faded as her eyes met mine. 'Are you okay? You don't seem happy to be here.'

I shook my head. 'I'm not. I don't want to lose my magic.'

She made a face. 'Me neither.' She scanned the area and lowered her voice. 'I know our magic is supposed to keep the village safe, and it's an honour to be chosen, but why are they insisting that we live and work at the temple after?'

I shrugged, already liking her. 'Maybe they're just trying to help. It would be hard to get a job without magic, unless it's a strenuous job.'

She leaned closer to me. 'You think that's the reason? I think they are trying to keep an eye on us.'

'Why would they want to do that?'

'Haven't you heard the rumours about people disappearing?'

'You mean the people Hecate is sending to the human world?'

Aurora frowned. 'You really think she's sending them to the human world?' She shook her head. 'It's a cover-up. Only I'm not sure if it's to cover up the fact that they died or that they ran away.'

I furrowed my brow in confusion. 'Ran away? There's nowhere to run. The whole place is shielded. If you continue through the forest, you'll reach the edge and there's an impenetrable magic barrier.'

'Are you sure? There's talk about a sanctuary. But no one knows where it is. My sister said we could try and find it so I wouldn't have to sacrifice my magic, but I'm worried about

what they'd do to my family if I didn't turn up. So here I am.'
She grimaced.

'At least your family seems to understand. Mine keep telling me what an honour it is to be chosen and that I'm just being silly.'

Aurora shook her head. 'You're not silly. If you were, there wouldn't be whispers.'

I'd just opened my mouth to say something when a guy our age with brown hair and blue eyes joined us. 'Are you the other two chosen ones?' he asked.

Aurora smirked. 'What do you think? Would we just hang around the stairs to the temple for the sake of it?'

The boy's jaw dropped slightly before he plastered a smile on his face. 'I'm Heath. Isn't it such an honour to be chosen? I've been looking forward to it all week. I can't wait to get a place of my own.'

Aurora rolled her eyes, and I stifled a laugh. Somehow I had connected with Aurora and she felt like an old friend. I wondered why we'd never spoken in school before.

Heath cleared his throat. 'Do you think we should cleanse ourselves before we go inside?'

'You can if you want to, but there's a couple hours until the ceremony. Besides, I'd like to see what's expected of us first,' Aurora said. 'Come on, Sky, let's get inside and see what they will make us do.' She hooked her arm around mine and pulled us up the stairs. Heath followed.

A couple of hours later, we had cleansed ourselves in the pool and changed into black robes. I tried to remain calm as we waited in the holding room behind the raised platform. But my nerves were all over the place, making it hard to be still. My heart pounded in my chest and I struggled to breathe, and the smell of burnt sage wasn't making it easier.

Looking out from the doorway, I tried to spot my family as people filled the chairs in the temple. It was a big event that only happened once a year, and almost everyone in the village was there.

The main door closed, and the audience fell silent and bowed their heads as Hecate appeared in a cloud of smoke. She faced the crowed and started talking. 'Two centuries ago, the High Priestess and the Elders summoned me, pleading for me to become the guardian of their cherished village. As a deity of protection, I could not deny them. However, magic always comes with a price. To protect the village from the demon, a covenant was forged. Year by year, through the sacred offerings of magic, I have shielded this village not only from the demon's clutches but also from external perils. It is this very purpose that brings us here today to witness these three young souls relinquish their magic in devotion to the preservation of the village. Please show them your gratitude.'

We walked out and positioned ourselves in the middle of the platform as the crowd called out 'Blessed be' in unison.

Hecate moved her hand and a circle of blue fire appeared, enclosing us within the ring of flames. She spoke in a language I didn't understand, and the blue flames ascended around us. My insides twisted as the fire moved closer. I closed my eyes, waiting for my skin to burn, but it never did. Instead, the flames swept over us, leaving us cold as they licked our skin and syphoned our magic from deep within. Dizziness washed over me and I fought the urge to be sick as I tried to hold on to my magic, but as the fire died down, the only thing left was an empty feeling in my chest and I knew without a doubt that my magic was gone.

Hecate thanked us for our sacrifice, and I glanced over at Aurora. Her eyes were glossy from unshed tears. I couldn't blame her. I felt the same way. She took my hand as we stepped off the platform. Maybe we should have run away when we had the chance. I knew we couldn't escape the village, but surely no one would come looking for us by the edge?

An identical version of Aurora but with long hair neared us. 'That's my twin sister, Star,' Aurora said and waved at her. 'I'll see you around.' She gave me a smile and ran and embraced her sister. Jealousy stabbed my heart. Why couldn't I have someone as supportive in my life? I scanned the room for my family and slowly made my way towards them.

'Here's our saviour,' Dawn said with a smirk as I approached my family with heavy steps.

Night put his arms around me, and I could feel my wall breaking. I took a deep breath. I would not let them see me cry.

When he pulled away, my mother looked over at me. 'I know you're hurting right now, but it's because of you that the village is still safe.'

Later that night I had the same dream as before, only this time it started at my home. The need to get to the house in my dream overwhelmed me. Was this the sanctuary Aurora had mentioned? Something or someone was telling me to find it. Maybe it was the Fates themselves? I woke up in the morning with my mind made up. I needed to find this place.

The sky showed signs of light, but the sun hadn't risen yet and frost coated the ground as I snuck out before anyone was awake. I debated whether to leave Night a note but decided against it. The longer it took me to leave, the more likely someone was to stop me.

I walked over to the stable and made my way over to Lightning, my favourite horse. I'd been seven or eight when she arrived. My father had let me name her, and due to a lightning bolt mark on her head, I named her Lightning. I learned later that it was a scar, but no one knew what had caused it.

I stroked Lightning's head. 'I wish I could take you with me. You're the only real friend I have, but I'm not sure where I'm going or if I'll be back. Besides, my family needs you. So you be a good horse.' I kissed her muzzle, and she pushed me away, almost like she was telling me to go.

Leaving the stable behind, I scanned our pastures and the forest by the horizon as I recalled the dream. It was time to figure out what the Fates wanted to show me. Maybe there was a way for me to get my magic back after all.

I walked along the edge of one of our horse pastures and followed the path my dream had shown me as best I could. Was I really brave enough to walk away from the only place I had ever known? Though it didn't really matter, because even if I stayed, I'd have to leave and live in the temple.

The path led me further away from the village and into the forest. I continued walking through the forest, and eventually I entered a field. The afternoon sun had started its descent behind the trees. Where was I? All the fields looked the same, harvested and left for the winter to come. I was tired and hungry and my feet hurt from all the walking. I'd easily walked further than I would have if I'd gone into the village and back, but the path had kept me on the outskirts. It surprised me that I hadn't encountered the magical barrier. I slumped down in defeat. Why had I thought it was a good idea to follow a dream?

I was contemplating what to do and whether to turn back when an enormous grey cat appeared from the undergrowth and started towards me. I reached out and moved my hands along his smooth coat as he passed. The cat headbutted me before continuing on his way. I followed him with my gaze. 'At least you know where you're going.'

He turned around. His bright yellow eyes bored into mine, and he let out a loud meow.

'What are you trying to tell me?' I asked.

He returned to me, scratched at my leg, meowed and ran off again. When he was a few metres ahead of me, he stopped and looked back. The cat was acting so strangely.

'Do you want me to follow?' He replied with another meow.

I got up from the grass. Following a cat wouldn't be any stranger than following a dream. What did I have to lose? Then I remembered. My dream. Someone had been with me in my dream, walking alongside me. Could it have been the cat?

With renewed energy, I marched over to the cat. 'I'm ready. Where are we going?'

He let out a chirp and stroked his body along my legs before moving in front of me, leading the way. We reached a small ditch at the edge of the field separating it from another and continued along it until a broken willow tree came into view – the same one I'd seen in my dreams. I rushed towards it as the memory of the dream floated back to me. I knew how to get to the house. All I had to do was turn left by the grove of trees and follow the next field to a broken fence. With a smile, I turned back to my companion, but he was gone.

I followed the path to the left, and when I reached the broken-down fence, a white cottage next to a wooden barn appeared in the distance. Just like in my dream, I ran towards it, my heart racing, terrified I would wake up in my bed before I reached it. Except this time it was real.

SKY

HOUSE OF THE HIDDEN

I slowed down and scanned the area. There were two buildings, a spacious cottage and a barn on either side of a courtyard. The cottage was in a fair condition with white stone walls, whereas the barn looked like it would collapse at any moment. The paint was peeling from the wooden walls, displaying the rotten wood underneath, and the roof sagged in places. It was a miracle it still stood. Was this really the sanctuary Aurora had been talking about? If so, where was everyone?

The sky above had darkened, and the sun was about to go down. What should I do? After wanting to reach the place in every dream, I'd never thought about what I'd do once I got here, but there must have been a reason the Fates had led me to this place.

Even though the area appeared abandoned, I crept closer and knocked on the door of the cottage. I waited, but when no one answered, I gently pushed it open. The smell of cooked meat filled my nose as I stepped inside, and my stomach grumbled. 'Hello?' I called out, but no one answered and the house remained quiet.

The hallway had a homely feel to it. A carpet covered the polished stone floor, and the white walls seemed to have been recently painted. There was a staircase in front of me and a closed door to my left. I followed my nose, turning right, and walked into the kitchen. There was an old metal stove with firewood burning underneath. A middle-aged woman with curly blond hair stood by the kitchen counter, chopping vegetables and placing them in a large pot on the stove. She had her back to me. Had she heard me come in, or should I call out? I jumped as the woman spoke without turning around.

'Hello, my dear.'

Was she talking to me? I turned to see if anyone else was around, but this woman was the only person I'd seen since I arrived. My heart raced as I thought of the books I'd read about people being abducted or about evil witches living in the woods, kidnapping children to eat. I shook my head to brush off the thought. Those things only happened in books.

'Hi,' I said with a nervous voice, giving her a small wave even though she couldn't see it. I kept my distance, trying to gauge whether she was friend or foe.

She turned and looked at me with warm hazel eyes. 'I'm Leaf, and you must be Sky.'

I took a deep breath as my eyes darted around the room. How did she know my name?

'Don't worry, I mean you no harm. The Fates told me you were coming.'

A calming sensation washed over me, and my body relaxed.

She untied her apron and hung it on a hook next to a kitchen cupboard. 'Let me show you around while the stew is cooking.' She waved her hand in the air, and the energy in the room shifted. When I looked around again, the kitchen had become cluttered with toys and books, and there were noises coming from the other rooms.

My mouth opened in awe. I knew we were witches, but magic like this wasn't normal. I'd never met someone who could create a cloaking spell like this. As far as I knew, not even the High Priestess had that power.

I followed Leaf as she walked out of the kitchen, across the hallway and into a room that looked like a massive sleeping area. There were several beds against the walls on both sides and a few wardrobes and cupboards.

A guy with blond hair and blue eyes was sitting on a bed talking with two girls. One of the girls had long blond hair in a braid, and the other had shoulder-length auburn hair and a darker complexion. They looked about my age, maybe slightly older.

'This is Sky,' Leaf said.

They turned to look at me. My cheeks flushed, and I lowered my gaze to the floor as I awkwardly waved at them.

The girl with the auburn hair spoke up. 'I'm Eva.' She gestured towards the others. 'And this is Astrid and Clay. It's nice to meet you.'

Leaf walked to the end of the room, where a bed stood empty. A duvet and pillow, along with its cover, were folded neatly at its end. 'This will be your bed if you choose to stay. It's not much, but we make do with what we have.'

I took a seat on the bed, overwhelmed. I wasn't sure what I had expected, but it wasn't this. However, my gut told me this was where I was supposed to be.

Leaf placed a hand on my shoulder. 'I know it's a lot to take in. You may rest if you like, and when you're up for it, I can show you the rest of the house and introduce you to the others.'

I took a deep breath. 'It's okay. I'm happy to continue.' Maybe seeing the rest of the house would give me some clarity on why the Fates had led me here.

I followed her as she walked past the stairwell and through the door at the end of the hallway. A massive bookcase took up the entire wall to my left. My eyes wandered over the books. Leaf cleared her throat. Behind her were two long tables with chairs taking up most of the room. A few teenagers were scattered around with books open in front of them.

'This is our dining room, but we also use it as a study and

common room in between meals,' Leaf continued.

'What is this place and what are all the people doing here?' I asked, looking around the room.

'This is the house of the hidden. It's a sanctuary. Everyone here has had their magic sacrificed, and the Fates gave me the responsibility of looking after them.'

I nodded as she confirmed my suspicions that this was indeed the sanctuary.

We walked through the kitchen and back out into the hallway again. Leaf gestured with her hands while explaining the layout. 'Upstairs to the right is the library, and opposite is my room. If you ever need anything, please come and find me.'

My excitement was piqued. 'There're more books?'

'The books in the library are about magic. We keep them separate so as not to upset anyone,' she answered.

I placed my hand on the banister and had just begun to walk up the stairs, eager to check out the library, when Leaf opened the front door. I turned to face her. 'We're going outside?'

Leaf nodded. 'There is one more thing I need to show you.'

Several lanterns had been lit around the courtyard, and I realised there were people out here too. How had I not noticed them before?

Leaf strolled towards the barn, and I followed her with hesitant steps. Surely we weren't going inside? It appeared like it'd collapse at any moment.

'It's sturdier than it looks,' she told me before pushing the wooden door open.

I was speechless when I stepped inside. The interior of the barn had been converted and consisted of a long corridor branching off to several repurposed stalls. It looked and smelled clean and fresh, with no sign of the decay that was seen on the outside. As we walked down the corridor, a girl came up to us. She seemed familiar.

'Are you Dawn's sister?'

I sighed. Even here I could not escape my sister. I opened my mouth to answer but nodded instead.

'I'm Sandra. I was a friend of Dawn's.'

Of course I remembered Sandra. She used to come around the house all the time to play with Dawn when we were younger, but after Dawn started studying under Hecate and the High Priestess, Sandra came around less and less.

'Dawn said you had gone to the human world after the sacrifice,' I said.

Sandra gave me a grimace. 'Of course she would think that.'

'So how did you end up here?' I asked.

'After they took my magic, I felt lost and confused. In a way, I had been lucky, because I'd had my magic for almost a year before it was sacrificed, but it just made it all much worse. I trained with my auntie to become a neonatal nurse, but once my magic was gone, I couldn't seem to soothe the crying babies. My parents told me to ask the Fates for guidance. And that's how I found this place. Because of my medical knowledge, Leaf thought I could be of help here.'

I looked around, trying to decipher what this place was for. 'Be of help for what? What is this place?'

'This is our version of a healing centre. We currently have four patients.' Sandra opened a door that stood ajar. Inside, a guy in his mid-twenties with a pale face was lying on a bed.

'What's wrong with him?' I asked.

Leaf answered with sadness in her voice. 'This is the destiny of all those who Hecate stole from. This is what happens after the magic has been sacrificed. Sooner or later, the body gives up and they wither and die. Unfortunately, there is nothing I can do to save him. We are only capable of easing their passing. Without magic flowing around the body, it slowly shuts down. Over the years, I have tried several things. I even attempted to infuse some of my own magic into them, but their bodies rejected it.'

A knot appeared in my stomach, and bile rose in my throat. Was this what the High Priestess was trying to cover up by insisting that everyone who had their magic sacrificed should work at the temple? It wasn't right. Even if the sacrifices were needed to protect the village, this was too steep a price. There had to be a way to stop it.

'What if we found a way to reverse the spell?' I asked.

Leaf sighed. 'Unfortunately, I don't think it's elemental magic. And even if there was a way, we don't know the specifics of the magic – the spell's composition, preparations or intentions.'

I stared at her in disbelief. 'So you're saying it's

impossible? I thought all spells could be reversed.'

She tilted her head and placed her hand on the chin. 'I'm not saying it's impossible, but different magics follow different rules. It's why I have put my efforts into figuring out a way to stop the withering instead.'

'If there's nothing I can do to get my magic back, why did the Fates lead me here? To show me that I'm going to die?'

Leaf shook her head. 'I don't know. The Fates work in mysterious ways. They may have guided you here, but in the end, we make our own path.'

I tapped my chin with my finger. There had to be another reason. 'I'm going to reverse the spell. It's the only thing that makes sense.'

'Don't set yourself up for disappointment.'

'I won't. But I'm not just going to give up either. I asked the Fates for my magic back and they sent me here. This has to be the reason. Maybe I can start by asking everyone what they remember.'

Leaf hesitated. 'Most of them don't remember anything of value, and asking them to recall that day again may be too much for them. Everyone here has worked hard to put it behind them and move forward. I would hate for them to relive such painful memories.'

'But—'

Leaf cut me off. 'Let's return to the house. I believe dinner should be ready.'

When we got back to the house, Leaf sorted us both out with bowls of stew. She sat down at one of the tables in the common room and gestured for me to sit next to her. Sandra, Astrid and Eva joined us at the table, but they remained quiet.

'How did you end up here?' I asked Leaf.

She placed her hand on her chin and gazed out of the window. 'I ended up here by accident. Hecate and the High Priestess at the time placed me in a ceremony, much like the one you went through. Only I was much younger. As the flames closed in, I was terrified and somehow teleported myself here. I met a lovely old man who took me in. I thought about going back, but something inside me knew that if I did, they would only try to take my magic again. So I stayed.'

'How come you had magic when you were young? I thought we could only access it when we turned sixteen.'

She turned her gaze towards me. 'I didn't get my elemental magic until my sixteenth birthday, but I could do other things, like creating objects from thin air and teleporting. It took a while to piece it together. The old man, Edmond, who lived here looked after me and showed me how to survive. He encouraged me to use my magic and tried to help me. He said it reminded him of his friend Jax's magic, who had left without a goodbye after the funeral of his wife, Katie Whitelake.'

My jaw dropped. 'Katie Whitelake? But that's ...'

Leaf nodded. 'That's right. Jax was the demon that fell in love with the High Priestess in training. I believe he is my father. It's the only way to explain my magic or the fact that I'm almost two hundred years old.'

'That's crazy. We got told that you died during labour.'

'Well, as you can see, I am very much alive.'

If Hecate and the High Priestess had lied about that, what else had they lied about? I leaned forward. 'So was he really as evil as Hecate makes him out to be?'

Leaf shook her head. 'I think that's another lie. Edmond said he had the most caring soul he'd ever known. But my father is the reason for your magic being sacrificed. Only Edmond believed it was to keep Jax a prisoner, as he said Jax would never have abandoned his daughter if he'd had a choice.'

'Is that why you look after everyone who turns up here?'

She glanced around the table at the other people sitting with us. 'Partly. After Edmond passed away, I felt lost, but the Goddess in my dreams told me to stay. I wasn't sure why until others stumbled upon this place. They were traumatised from losing their magic and needed time and space to come to terms with it. At that time Hecate used to sacrifice the magic of thirteen witches, but nowadays she seems to only need three.'

I continued to eat my stew while I thought about what Leaf had said.

After a while, Leaf got up from the table. 'Please, if you'll excuse me, I need to make the rounds before retiring to my room. Sandra and Eva will help you get settled and answer any questions you may have about this place. For now, make yourself at home.' She walked towards the kitchen and disappeared from view.

Astrid turned to me. 'Did you have a dream that showed you this place too?' I nodded. Astrid's eyes sparkled. 'Leaf says dreams are a powerful tool used by the Fates to show us what they want us to do. And all of us were shown this place in a dream.'

'How many of you live here?' I asked.

'There are fourteen of us now, if you include the ones in the barn,' Sandra said.

But we usually get one, sometimes two people joining us each year,' Eva said.

'And some people last longer than others. Females seem to feel the withering quicker. But most of us don't get sick until we're around twenty,' Sandra added.

We all sat around in silence for a while until Astrid got up and collected our dishes.

'Come, let's get you settled in,' Eva said as she got up from her chair.

SKY

A REUNION

I opened my eyes and stretched my arms, hitting the wall behind me. Where was I?

'Are you okay?' Eva asked as she sat down next to me.

I nodded as the memories of where I was flooded back to me. 'I'm okay. Just took me a while to realise I wasn't in my own bed.'

She gave me a reassuring smile. 'It takes a bit to adjust, but once you do, you'll be happy you came here.'

I looked around at all the empty beds. 'Where is everyone?'

'They've started their chores for the day.'

'We have chores?'

Eva nodded. 'Yes. Leaf may be powerful, but she can't run a house with all of us on her own. So we help her out. Some of us help with the sick, others help with the cleaning and maintenance of the house, some will take care of the animals and others of the vegetables, so we have something to eat.'

Of course we needed to help out. It would have been unfair to ask Leaf to do all the chores herself. 'What can I do to help?'

'Depends. What do you like doing?'

My eyes went wide. 'You mean I can choose?'

Eva chuckled. 'We all have our strengths and weaknesses. Let's get you dressed and I'll show you around a bit more. It was too dark to show you the outside parts yesterday.' She placed a pair of trousers and a top on my bed. 'I think these should fit you. There's a bit of slim pickings around here.'

After I got dressed, we grabbed a sandwich from the kitchen and stepped outside. I wrapped my jacket tighter around me as the wind picked up.

'Should we start with the barn?' Eva asked.

I shook my head. 'I'd rather not. Leaf showed it to me yesterday. That place makes me depressed.'

'No worries. Being a healer isn't for everyone. Come on, let me show you the back of the house,' she said as she started walking.

I followed her as we turned the corner and were met by a few enclosures. They had a large chicken run, some rabbit huts and a couple of fenced-in pastures. 'What animals are in the fields?'

Eva pointed towards the different pastures. 'We have a few cows and sheep and a horse. Did you have animals at home?'

I nodded, a smile appearing on my face. 'My father's a farrier, so we had several horses.'

'That's great. You will probably feel at home helping with the animals.'

My heart sped up at the thought of home. Would they have realised I'd run away by now? 'Does anyone here have contact with their families?'

'Not really. Only the ones where the family encouraged them to go. They help us get resources, as we can't risk going into the village and being forced to reveal this place.'

'Wouldn't it be just as risky having them come here?'

Eva nodded. 'Because of that, they don't. There's a bench near where the road leading into the temple starts. They leave resources there once a week. Someone from here will collect them. If we have any special requests or want to inform them about something, we usually leave a letter behind. Though we have a few other ways to contact them in an emergency.'

We passed a large greenhouse as we continued the tour. 'We grow our own herbs and vegetables there. Astrid is amazing with the plants. Her whole family has been horticulturists for several generations.'

A few drops of rain started to fall. Eva looked up at the sky. 'There's not much else to see – just a few fruit trees behind the greenhouse. Let's get inside before the sky opens up.'

We got back into the house and entered the common area. 'This is where most of us hang out. We try to spend a few hours a day studying, so during the day this is a quiet place.'

I scanned the area for a curriculum or any sign of what they might study. When I couldn't find anything, I turned to Eva. 'What do you study?'

She gave me an open gesture. 'Anything you want.'

A spark ignited inside me, and a grin crept over my face. 'Can I continue to study magic?'

She scratched the back of her neck. 'Umm ... sure, but you would need to do that in the library upstairs.' She held out her hand to me. 'Let me show you.'

We exited the common area and walked up the stairs.

She opened the door on the right and gestured for me to step inside. 'This is the library.'

The room smelled of old paper and leather. Bookcases covered one wall, though there were fewer books than I had expected, considering the overfilled bookcase downstairs.

Several books were spread out over a large table in the middle of the room, along with notes and scripts. Next to the table was a cork board covered in drawings of fire, runes and Celtic symbols for protection and healing, along with other symbols I hadn't seen before. It must be Leaf's research on trying to stop us withering away without magic.

I was taking it all in when Leaf walked past us. She gave me a smile. 'Oh great, you're here. I have thought over what you said, and if you think the Fates led you here to reverse the spell, I would be happy to help.'

I smiled. 'Thank you.'

Leaf clasped my hands and looked into my eyes. 'What do you remember?'

I thought back to the ceremony, trying to remember all the details, but the raw anxiety from that day crept up from within and slithered around me, making it hard to breathe. 'I don't remember much, but Hecate didn't call the elements before the blue fire appeared. And she spoke in a language I had never heard before.'

Leaf tilted her head and placed her hand on her chin. 'She's a Greek entity, so it's reasonable to assume she was speaking in Greek. Is there anything else you can remember?'

I shook my head. Why couldn't I remember? I attended the ritual every year, but somehow the more I tried to remember, the less clear it became. Had the spell itself been enchanted?

Annoyed with myself, I walked over to the cork board and let my fingers move over the notes and drawings. 'Even if it doesn't follow elemental magic, she would still need a conduit to be able to take the magic. I think the blue fire may have absorbed our power, but something would have had to convert and contain it.'

Leaf gave me a smile. 'It sounds like you know your theory. Unfortunately, that isn't the only thing we need to consider. A witch's magic is innate, and though it can be temporarily dissipated, it will always regenerate. Only for you, it doesn't.'

Eva gave us a confused look. 'I think I'm going to leave you to it. Spells were never my strong suit. I always struggled to understand how our elemental magic could transform into the magic used in spells. I'll see you later.'

A couple of days passed, and I got into a routine of helping Clay with the animals in the mornings and spending my afternoons in the library. I was in the library with Leaf debating different ways the spell might be reversed when she became quiet and stood up. 'Someone with magic is here,' she said as she made her way down the stairs.

I followed her. 'Do you normally get visitors? I thought only people without magic could find this place.'

Leaf ignored my questions. 'Wait here.' She cast me a stern look and waved her hand. An energy went through me and the house, making all our belongings disappear from view. And probably me too. I remembered how everything had seemed abandoned when I'd first arrived.

Curiosity got the better of me, and despite Leaf's warning, I followed her outside. She shook her head in disapproval but remained silent.

We stood there for a while before two people appeared in the distance. I couldn't make out any features, but they looked like teenagers. As they got closer, I recognised the ginger hair. 'It's Aurora and Star,' I said to Leaf as I started running towards them. Leaf said something in a hushed voice, but I didn't listen; I was too excited to see Aurora again.

As I ran towards them, I pushed myself through an invisible force that was probably caused by the cloaking spell.

'Sky?' Aurora's voice rang out, and she quickened her steps. 'I can't believe you're here,' she said as we embraced each other.

'I can't believe you found this place,' I replied, excited to see her again. Even though I hadn't known her for a long time, I had felt an instant connection with her when we'd met on the stairs at the temple. It seemed like such a long time ago, but less than a week had passed since then.

Star, Aurora's twin sister, caught up with us. 'What is this place?'

'It's the sanctuary, isn't it?' Aurora asked.

I nodded.

'But it's abandoned,' Star said, gesturing to the house behind me.

I shook my head. 'No, it isn't.'

Leaf walked up to us with a polite smile on her face. 'It's only an illusion to keep unwanted guests away.'

I looked over at Leaf. 'This is Aurora and Star, her twin sister. Aurora lost her magic at the same time I did.'

Leaf studied them for a while. 'So, Star, you still have your magic, is that correct?'

Star gazed around uncomfortably before answering. 'Yes. I wasn't chosen. But my magic isn't as strong as it used to be. Something happened to it when Aurora lost hers.'

Leaf gestured towards the cottage. 'Let's go inside and

talk. I'm sure you can do with some food and some rest.'

I hooked my arm in Aurora's and followed Leaf into the house.

SKY

Aurora and Star

After we returned inside, Leaf handed us a hot drink and we sat down at the table. Aurora stifled a cough, and I studied her more carefully. Her already pale skin looked almost translucent and her green eyes seemed lifeless, with dark bags under them. Star seemed in better shape, but even her eyes were losing their brightness. Was this related to the lack of magic? Eva had said most didn't get ill until they were around twenty ... but it had only been a few days.

Star caught me looking. 'It's been like this since the ceremony. At first we thought maybe she'd caught a cold, but it seems to be worse when I'm not around. I don't know what to do. I can't lose her. She's my second half.' Star reached for

Aurora's hand, and tears fell from her eyes.

Leaf had been silent, but she finally spoke up. 'I think I understand why both of you were shown the dream. It's mentioned briefly in one of the books I have. Twin magic is one of the strongest forms of magic, because between you, you will have an affinity for all four elements.'

Aurora and Star nodded in agreement.

'But because of the twin bond, your magic is connected, working as one unit. I think when one part loses its magic, the other part tries to compensate. Which means Aurora is slowly draining Star's magic. If we break the twin bond, we can ensure that Star won't succumb to the same sickness that plagues the ones without magic; however, I'm not sure if it will slow down or speed up Aurora's disease.'

I rubbed my arm and my eyes settled on Star and Aurora, who were holding on to each other as if life itself depended on it. 'Why don't you know what will happen to Aurora if they break the bond?' I asked Leaf.

'Because of how the withering seems to work. The more powerful the magic within, the quicker the illness progresses.'

Was that why they didn't pick anyone with three affinities? I shook my head to get back to the problem at hand. 'So where does this leave Star and Aurora?'

Leaf shrugged. 'I don't know.'

Aurora and Star looked at each other with wide eyes. Aurora put her other hand on top of Star's. 'It's okay, Star. I'm willing to take the chance. I want you to live.'

'I can't lose you,' Star answered.

'What if I find a way to reverse the spell that took our magic?' I asked.

Leaf gave me a sad smile. 'I know you're optimistic about reversing the spell, but don't get their hopes up. You've only been working on it for a few days. I've spent the last hundred years trying to stop the withering without success.'

'Well, it's worth a try,' I said. I knew in my heart that Leaf was right, but I didn't want to admit it. I turned to Aurora. 'What do you remember from the ritual?'

'I remember staring at my feet, willing myself to run away as the fire swept over us. Something was drawn on the ground, but it wasn't a normal circle, and I don't think it was a pentagram either. It was something else. Like two concentric circles with a maze between them.'

Leaf raised her finger like she had just thought of something and got up from the table. 'Wait here,' she said as she exited the room.

'Where's she off to?' Star asked.

I shook my head. 'I'm not sure. Something Aurora said must have given her an idea. I'm sure she'll be back.' I cleared my throat. 'So what have you been up to since the ceremony?'

'Not much. I've been feeling poorly and sleeping a lot. I kept dreaming of this place, and when Star realised we'd had the same dream, she thought we should check it out, but I wasn't sure I had the energy. Your mother came over one night asking us if we knew where you were. She seemed worried, and by the sounds of it she was grasping at straws trying to find you. It got me thinking maybe you had been shown this place too.'

I sucked in a breath. I'd never considered the possibility of my mother being worried about me. Maybe I should have let them know I was leaving. Guilt tugged on my conscience. I hadn't meant to just abandon my family without a goodbye, but when I'd got here, something had told me I had to stay. In all honesty, part of me thought my family wouldn't realise I was missing. But maybe I was wrong. Maybe my family did love me after all.

Aurora continued. 'Anyway, Star and my parents convinced me to follow the dream. That's how we ended up here. Only it took longer than we expected, as we got lost along the way.'

'Did the cat guide you here when you got lost?' I asked.

'The cat?' Star asked with a frown.

I was about to explain what had happened on my journey when Leaf walked back into the room. She placed a piece of paper with an image drawn upon it on the table in front of Aurora. 'Is this the symbol you saw on the ground?'

Aurora picked it up and examined it. 'I think so.'

'It's called Hecate's wheel. But I'm unsure what significance it holds.'

'But at least it's something new to look into,' I said with a smile.

'I'm going to go and have a think about this,' Leaf said as she picked up the image. She placed a hand on Star's shoulder. 'Please consider what I've told you. If you have any questions, we can talk about it more tomorrow. But the longer you stay connected, the more it will affect you.'

Sandra came and sat down next to us. She gave Aurora a sympathetic smile. 'I can help you feel a bit better if you want. We have some herbs to help with your energy and cough, but it will only treat your symptoms. When you're ready, I can show you to the barn. You're more than welcome to stay here with the rest of us, but I think you may be more comfortable having your own room.'

Aurora reached her hand out to her sister.

'Don't worry. We can fit another bed in there so you can be together,' Sandra added.

The travelling had taken a lot out of Aurora, and though I would have liked to catch up a bit more, she fell asleep almost immediately as soon as she lay down.

Knowing her days were numbered if we didn't find a way to reverse the spell, I headed to the library. There had to be something I could do to help. I took a seat and continued my research, determined to make some headway.

Someone shook my shoulder to wake me and I realised I'd fallen asleep on top of the book I was reading. 'Are you okay, sweetie?' Leaf asked.

I shook my head, tears falling from my eyes. Despite poring over the books for hours, I hadn't found anything useful. My voice cracked as I spoke. 'No. Aurora's dying and I can't find anything that helps with the spell.'

Leaf wiped a tear from my face. 'The Fates work in

mysterious ways. You just need to have faith that everything will work out the way it's supposed to. Come on, let's see how Aurora and Star are doing and what they have decided.'

Despite everything, Star refused to let Leaf break the twin bond. Aurora had good days and bad days, and as the weeks progressed, it became my routine to bring Aurora and Star their dinner and have it with them. We talked about everything from school to childhood memories. Aurora even told me the reason she'd cut her hair was because Star was seeing someone who kept coming on to her, thinking she was Star. It quickly became one of my favourite parts of the day.

'Do you regret not letting Leaf break the twin bond?' I asked one evening while we were having dinner together in their room.

Star hesitated. 'I'm nothing without Aurora. We're connected. It's like I'm a part of her just as much as she's a part of me. I don't want to lose that connection.'

Aurora nodded. 'I feel the same way. Besides, you said you're working on reversing the spell.'

'True, but I'm not sure I can reverse it in time. There's still so much to figure out. We've concluded that Hecate's wheel is used as a conduit, but we still don't know how or why the regeneration of magic inside our bodies stopped working.'

Aurora placed her hand on my arm and looked me in the eyes. 'I believe in you. If anyone can break the spell, it's you and Leaf. Even in school you were more interested in your studies than anything or anyone else.'

My face heated up at the compliment. 'I hope you're right. But I've already been through all the books here. And most of them are very generalised and don't contain the information I need. Maybe the university would have better books.'

Aurora shook her head. 'I know that look and no, you can't sneak into the university. They will catch you, and then you'll need to explain why you've been missing for several weeks. It's not worth it. You said it yourself, the Fates led you here so you can reverse the spell. They didn't lead you to the university.'

I sunk down in my seat. 'Maybe you're right, but they have all the latest research.'

'True, but I'm sure Hecate has made sure nothing can be traced back to her,' Star said.

'What she's doing isn't right. The demon she's protecting us against isn't even evil, according to Leaf. And no offence, but I'm much more likely to believe Leaf over Hecate.'

Aurora let out a yawn. 'I'm really sorry, Sky, but I think I'm going to take a nap. Can we talk about this more tomorrow?'

I nodded and said goodnight. I hated seeing her like this. Even Star had struggled to keep up with her chores. Though everyone kept telling her not to exhaust herself, she still got on with them, but I could see the toll it was taking on her during dinner times.

As the months progressed, so did the withering, and I still hadn't made any breakthrough with the spell. It became more and more common for Aurora to be asleep when I went to visit them, and lately even Star had become bed bound. I hated to see my friends wither away, but I couldn't give up on them.

One evening when I went over to visit them, I had expected them both to be asleep, but to my surprise, Aurora was awake.

'Hi, Sky.' She tried to smile, but it didn't reach her eyes.

'Hi,' I said as I placed a hand on her arm. 'How are you feeling?'

She looked over to the bed on the other side where Star was sleeping soundly. 'Guilty.'

I tilted my head. 'Why?'

'If it wasn't for me, Star wouldn't be sick.'

'If it wasn't for the sacrifices of magic, none of us would be sick.'

She nodded in agreement. 'True, but I can't help wondering what would have happened if I had insisted on Leaf breaking our bond. Having a twin is wonderful. We're so in sync, we can practically read each other's minds, but I hate seeing her like this. I wish there was something I could do.'

'Don't blame yourself. It's not your fault.'

'But it is.' Her face lit up. 'But I can fix it. Please get Leaf. I know Star won't agree, but I know I'm dying. I don't want her to die too. I'm ready for Leaf to break the bond.'

I cocked an eyebrow. 'Are you sure?'

Aurora nodded. 'As sure as I've been about anything in my life. I need Star to live.'

I left Aurora and went to get Leaf, telling her Aurora's wishes. We gathered some tools and returned to the barn. Star and Aurora were having an argument, but they stopped as we walked through the door.

'Are you sure you want to do this?' Leaf asked.

Aurora answered yes, while Star answered no. Aurora turned to Star. 'This is my choice. You don't have a say in it. I know I'm dying, and I can see how the withering is affecting you. I want you to live. I want you to experience the world for both of us. You can't do that if you're dying too.'

Tears appeared in Star's eyes, but all she did was nod.

'If you are sure, then please come join me,' Leaf said as she gestured to the spot where she wanted them to be.

When they'd joined her, she tied their hands together with a rope. 'This represents your bond,' she declared. 'I'm going to call the elements and ask them to break it.' She turned to me. 'I know you want to help, but you will not be able to be part of the spell.' I had already guessed as much, so I took a seat on Aurora's bed.

Leaf picked up a piece of chalk and started drawing a circle on the floor. 'Why aren't you using salt?' Aurora asked.

'It isn't needed. In theory I don't even need to physically make the circle, but by creating a visual reminder, it helps visualise the inner circle that I need to create.'

Once the circle was created, she turned to the north. 'I call upon Earth for your prosperity in aid of breaking this bond.'

She turned to the east. 'I call upon Air for your knowledge in aid of breaking this bond.'

She turned to the south. 'I call upon Fire for your strength in aid of breaking this bond.'

Finally she turned to the west. 'I call upon Water for your compassion in aid of breaking this bond.'

She walked back to the middle and placed her hands on the rope tied between Aurora and Star. 'I call upon Spirit, the creator of the universe, and ask the Fates to allow me to break this holy bond. As is your wish, so mote it be.'

I watched in awe as the elements manifested around the rope and slowly severed it into two, cutting off the connection between Aurora and Star.

'Thank you for your aid. You may leave,' Leaf said before opening the circle.

I rushed over to Aurora and Star as soon as I could. 'How are you feeling?'

'Empty,' Star replied.

'Better. Like some of my energy is back,' Aurora said with a smile. 'Maybe it will even slow my withering.'

I was in the library going over my latest hypothesis on how Hecate had got the magic out of our systems when Sandra burst into the room.

'It's Aurora. She's not doing well. Star told me to get you.' I got up from the table and rushed over to the barn.

I calmed my breathing and stepped into their room with my heart in my throat. Aurora was in bed, her breathing shallow. 'Sky,' she whispered, her voice hardly audible.

I sat down next to her. A numbness spread through me. Aurora looked so weak and pale. 'How are you doing?' I asked, though it was a silly question, as I could see she was struggling.

She mustered a smile. 'The Fates showed me a dream where everyone here was using their magic. And you were there too. It was beautiful. I wish I could see it for real.' My eyes blurred with tears as I held her hand.

She let out a cough, and blood appeared at the corners of her mouth. 'I'm happy you're my friend.'

I looked back at her with tears streaming down my face. 'I'm happy you're my friend too.'

She turned toward Star and reached for her hand. 'The white light is waiting,' she said as she closed her eyes. A moment later her breathing stopped.

A strangled sob erupted from Star as she scooped her sister into her arms. 'Don't go. Don't leave me,' she repeated over and over, her body shaking with grief.

I couldn't believe my friend was gone. With a numb feeling in my heart and tears falling down my face, I stared at Star. I didn't know how to console her. Rising slowly, I turned, walked out of the barn and ran to the fields. I let out a scream. I had failed them. I fell down in a heap. Sobs erupted from me, and I put my hands over my face as I mourned the fact that I would never see my friend again.

Star kept to herself and spent most of her time in the fields. On the day of Aurora's funeral, their parents came to the farm. Leaf had made an exception so they could say goodbye to their daughter.

It was a simple ceremony. I watched Aurora's body burn, and as her soul became one with the universe to be reborn at a later point, I recalled what she'd told me. She'd seen us with magic. Which meant the Fates still had something up their sleeves, and I couldn't help feeling like I was a part of it.

The next morning Star sought me and Leaf out. Her eyes were sad, but she had a determined look on her face. 'Leaf, thank you for everything you have done for me and Aurora.'

Leaf gave her a hug. 'You're always welcome here.' She handed Star a calling stone. 'Take this so you can get in contact with me again.'

'For Aurora's sake, I will make this right. The village needs to know the truth about the sacrifices. We need to stop them. No one should have to go through watching their sister or brother die.'

'Please be careful,' Leaf said solemnly. 'The village must not learn of this place. I'm not opposed to overthrowing the High Priestess, but not until I know we can stop the sacrifices for good. Everyone here is my responsibility, and without magic we are unlikely to succeed.'

'I know several people who don't agree with the High Priestess, even before all of this. Let me find them and spread the word. Together, we can change it. I'm ready to fight,' Star said.

Hearing Star's determination gave me new strength. Even if we did find a way to stop the sacrifices, the ones who had already lost their magic still had their days numbered. It was up to me to find a way to reverse the spell. Nobody else should have to die because of what the High Priestess and Hecate had done to us.

SKY

The Strangers

I slammed the book shut. 'This is useless. We've been through these books several times and there's nothing in them that can tell us anything about the spell. Even if Hecate's magic followed elemental rules, we still don't know how she stopped our bodies from regenerating magic. It shouldn't be possible.' It felt like we were going around in circles. We had been at it for almost a year, but we weren't any closer to figuring out how to get the magic back.

Leaf pointed towards a note on the cork board. 'I still think the fire is the key.'

I reeled in my frustration. 'Maybe. We know it wasn't a normal fire, because it was cold. Once it engulfed us, it consumed our magic and transformed it with the help of Hecate's wheel. But it still doesn't answer why we can't regenerate new magic.'

'What if—' Leaf stopped talking mid-sentence and got a distant look on her face. She waved her hand and everything disappeared, making the house look abandoned once more.

'Is it another witch who lost their magic?' I asked, knowing the Dark Moon Ritual would have been less than a week ago.

Leaf shook her head. 'No. Whoever they are, they aren't from around here.' My ears pricked up. Leaf shook her head. 'I know you're curious, but please stay here until I know it's safe. I'm not sure why they are here or what their intentions are.'

'But—'

'No buts. It's my responsibility to keep you all safe.'

A knock sounded from the front door downstairs. Leaf gave me a warning stare before walking out of the library, closing the door behind her.

I crept over to the door. Maybe I could eavesdrop from the top of the stairs. I put my hand on the doorknob and twisted, but the door was locked. Had she really locked me in? Did she not trust me? With a sigh, I went back to our research. Hecate was the only one to perform the spell, but would she have written it down somewhere?

After a while, Leaf came back into the room.

'You locked me in?' I asked in a flat tone without looking up from my book.

'I took precautions. Besides, you wouldn't have known I locked you in unless you were disobeying,' Leaf said.

I rolled my eyes. 'It was a year ago. I can't believe you haven't got over it already.' I looked up at Leaf and realised her eyes were red, as if she'd been crying. 'Is everything okay?'

She nodded, giving me a reassuring smile. 'I'm more than fine. The Fates brought my daughter and my father to me.'

'What? I didn't know you had a daughter. And I thought Hecate made sure your father couldn't come back. Isn't that the reason for the sacrifices?' I put the book down and looked straight at her.

She brushed some hair away from my face. 'My dear, the Fates' powers are infinite. If we were meant to meet, Hecate's magic would not be able to prevent it. As for my daughter, I sent her and her father to live in the human realm many years ago. I didn't want the High Priestess to know about her and take her from me. After all, we are a threat to the High Priestess's regime.'

'Because of your father?'

'No, because we carry Whitelake blood.' Leaf started looking around the room. 'Where are the tools for creating a connection circle?'

I cocked an eyebrow. 'They're not staying?'

Leaf shook her head. 'No. They came here looking for answers on how to help their friend get his abilities back, but I'm afraid I could only offer them more questions.'

'How did he lose them?' I asked. A deep tug in my gut told me I needed to meet this person.

Leaf shrugged. 'I'm not sure, but I believe it's somehow connected to the sacrifices. Why else would the Fates have led them here?'

I frowned. 'Then why are they leaving?'

'They need to go back to the human realm. The longer they are here, the more likely it is that Hecate can feel their presence and find this place, but perhaps you should go with them. We haven't made much progress with the spell, and if it's connected, like I believe, they may hold the key to figuring it out. What do you think? After all, you believe the Fates sent you here to find a way to reverse the spell and get the magic back.'

'I don't know. My gut is telling me I should go. I've been through all our books several times. I need more information, and if the sacrifices are happening somewhere else, maybe I can pick up on something that I've missed, but I know nothing about them. Except for the horror stories, which you told me aren't true.'

Leaf picked up a box of crystals and other magical artefacts. 'I need to go back. Listen to your heart. If you want to go with them, just come downstairs.'

I lingered as my body fought for a decision. Should I stay here or should I listen to my intuition that was telling me to go – that this was the way to get the magic back? I thought of Aurora. She believed in me. If I was going to save myself and all the others who had had their magic sacrificed and get their magic back like in Aurora's vision, I couldn't let fear hold me back. I walked downstairs with determined steps but hovered by the door.

I swallowed and carefully pushed the door open.

Leaf cast me a look as if to ask if I had decided to go with them, and I nodded in response.

'Sky, why don't you come inside? This is my father Jax and my daughter Leah.'

I stepped into the room. My cheeks heated up as they stared at me. Both of them looked around my age. I studied them for any resemblance to Leaf. The guy appeared to be a teenager. He had the same caring eyes as Leaf, but instead of her blond hair, his was dark brown. This was the demon I'd been taught to fear, but standing next to him, all I could feel was sympathy. He'd lost everything because of what he was. According to the books, a demon couldn't love; they could only feel hate. But here he stood in front of his daughter with tears in his eyes after he'd travelled to another realm to help his friend. I quietly cursed Hecate. It was clear we didn't need the sacrifices to protect us from this demon, so what was she using the magic for?

My eyes shifted to the girl. She had long blond hair and looked almost like I would have expected Leaf to look like in her younger years, but paler and with green eyes instead of hazel.

Leaf gestured towards me. 'Sky can help you get in contact with me again, but it's safer for everyone if you don't come back. The Goddess is more than likely already aware you are here, and the High Priestess does not take kindly to outsiders, especially the kind that carry demon blood.'

I looked over at Leaf, wanting confirmation. The feeling in my stomach told me I needed to go with them, but I wasn't sure if I was ready to leave this place that had become a home to me. 'Are you sure you'll be okay?'

Leaf gave me a reassuring smile and nodded. 'Don't worry, my child. The Fates have plans for me yet.'

I took a deep breath and ignored my tense muscles and dry mouth and approached. 'Hi, I'm Sky. Leaf told me about your problem and how it seems to be connected to ours. I've been researching how to reverse the spell for a long time, so she asked me to go with you to see if I can help.'

Jax gave me a smile. 'Thank you. Hopefully we can help each other.'

I nodded as Leaf's voice rang out. 'It's all ready.'

I looked over and saw that she had set up a connection circle. They were usually used to connect people in the village when they wanted to see each other but couldn't meet up. I had my doubts that it would support teleportation, but Leaf seemed certain.

Jax approached Leaf and gave her a hug. It looked like she was saying goodbye to her son, not the other way around. But I guess being immortal kept him looking young.

After Leaf had said goodbye to Jax and Leah, I walked up to her. I opened my mouth to tell her I appreciated everything she had done for me, but I couldn't find the words.

'May the Fates guide you,' she said as she gave me a hug.

I nodded and hugged her tighter. 'Thank you.'

She reached into the pocket of her tunic and handed me a broken quartz crystal. 'Here, take this calling stone. I've placed the other part by the mirror in my room so you can stay in touch and let me know you're safe.' She nudged me towards Jax and Leah. 'Blessed be.'

Jax stood in the circle, with Leah holding on to his hand. He held out his free one to me. 'Come on, let's go home.'

I hesitated before slowly placing my hand on top of Jax's.

He gave me a reassuring smile. 'It will only take a second, but if you haven't teleported before, closing your eyes will help with the disorientation. Ready?'

I nodded and closed my eyes. Gravity disappeared and everything started spinning, making me dizzy. It felt like I had been thrown into a vortex, but a moment later, everything went still and I could feel solid ground under my feet.

'I'll be back in a bit,' Jax said and disappeared.

I opened my eyes and took a breath, trying to fight the nausea. We were inside a room, and the air was stuffy. Bile rose in my throat and I covered my mouth with my hand. My eyes darted back and forth, looking for somewhere to go. Luckily, Leah caught on and rushed me to the bathroom.

She held my hair as I was sick in the toilet. When I was done, I slumped down on the floor.

'Are you okay?' she asked with a caring voice.

I nodded. 'Just a bit travel sick.'

'Let me get you some water.' She left but came back shortly after with a glass of water. 'Regretting coming with us yet?' she asked with a wry smile.

I shook my head. 'No. But I would have preferred another means of travel.'

Leah became thoughtful. 'You think you're okay to go back to the living room?'

I nodded and she helped me up from the floor. The living room was spacious and open. Two sofas were to my right, and to the left was a dining table and doors leading towards a garden. At first glance it could have been a house in my village, only I didn't know anyone who would frame a large piece of black glass and display it on a wall.

We sat down on one of the sofas. 'Tell me about your friend,' I said after a moment of silence.

Leah lifted her head from the headrest and tilted her head. 'You mean Mark?'

'I mean the one who lost their magic.'

Leah muffled a yawn. 'He's a werewolf.'

My eyes went wide. 'A werewolf?' I hadn't realised they were real. The only things I knew about them were what I had read in books. 'Are they common in the human world?'

'Not really, but a pack lives on the reserve not far from here.'

'Does he live with them?'

She shook her head. 'No. Mark, his brother Seth, me and Cassie were all adopted by a lady called Abigail. We've grown up with her since we were young. And everything was fine until one night when Cassie disappeared and Mark lost his ability to shift.'

I tilted my head. 'Do you know what happened?'

Leah shrugged. 'Not really. We think Abigail might be involved but we aren't sure how. We thought she was human, but now we're second guessing it. She works at a place called Whitelock Unlimited. It's how we stumbled upon your village.'

I tapped my finger on my chin. 'If this is connected to the sacrifices in my realm, then this Abigail person is probably a witch that works under Hecate. Maybe Whitelock is related to Whitelake somehow? That's the name of our village and the family name of the High Priestess lineage.' I straightened up and turned back to Leah. 'Wait – you said someone named Cassie disappeared. Where is she now?'

'She's fine. We rescued her. Jax has gone to get her from the cabin she was staying in with the wolves while we were away.' It looked like she was about to say something more when the back door opened. Leah got up from the sofa and rushed over to Jax and another girl with brown hair and blue eyes. I followed behind. She gave the girl a hug before turning back to me.

'Cassie, this is Sky. Sky, meet Cassie, the reincarnation of Leaf's mother.'

I took a step towards the girl called Cassie in awe, unsure about the greeting rituals. She gave me a warm smile, which I returned. 'Everyone was always talking about the powerful Whitelake witch that fell in love with a demon while I was growing up. Do you still have your powers?'

A frown appeared on Cassie's face before she shook her head, sadness shining in her eyes. 'I'm not the same person now. I'm not a witch anymore.'

I nodded, feeling bad for having brought it up. I knew how it felt to lose your magic, so I decided not to ask her any more questions about it. Instead, I turned to Jax. 'Leah filled me in on what's been going on. No doubt Abigail's a witch that's part of the movement that brings sacrifices to Hecate in exchange for protection. Let me see this wolf that can't change. The quicker I know all the facts, the sooner I can try and fix them.' I wondered if this was the reason they had sacrificed fewer witches in the village for the last hundred years – but why would they sacrifice non-witches? None of this made sense anymore.

Leah gave me a grimace. 'I don't think it's wise for you to go to the house right now. We're still trying to keep up appearances. Let me bring him here later.' She pulled an item from her pocket. 'I should head back before Abigail realises I'm not home.'

Why was Leah going back to Abigail when they knew she was involved somehow?

Leah started towards the door but stumbled. Before I realised what had happened or had a chance to react, Jax was by her side and grabbed her before she hit the floor. 'Leah, you're in no condition to go home. Maybe you should stay here?' he said as he led her to the sofa.

She refused to sit down, holding on to the armrest. 'I have to go home. Mark and Seth are there. Besides, it's our best shot at figuring out what part Abigail is playing in all of this. I'll be fine. I'm just a bit tired from being up all night.'

Looking her over, she looked tired. Maybe her paleness wasn't her natural complexion but because of exhaustion. A memory of when Dawn had just got her powers entered my mind. She'd been so excited about working under the High Priestess but worried she would be behind everyone that she'd spent a whole day practising her magic until it ran out. She'd cried for hours, worried she'd lost it. Even when I'd explained that her magic just needed recharging, she hadn't listened to me. I was just a stupid thirteen-year-old who didn't understand anything. It wasn't until our mother had come up to our room and told her magic had its limits but would be back after some rest that she had finally stopped crying.

Jax let out a sigh, which brought me back to reality. 'Okay, but let me at least drive you home.'

Leah nodded at him, and he led her out of the house.

I was left with Cassie. Unsure what to do with myself, I sat down on the sofa. I wanted to ask her more about being the High Priestess in training, but the look of sadness on her face from before made me keep my mouth shut.

'Are you tired? I can show you to my bedroom if you want to lie down for a bit,' Cassie said.

'I'm fine,' I replied. 'I wasn't up all night like them two.' I took a deep breath, trying to understand the dynamic. 'If you're trying to keep up appearances, why didn't you go back with Leah? I thought both of you lived together.'

'We did, but after I was kidnapped, we thought it was better that I stayed here. If Abigail had something to do with it, like we think she did, she'd likely try to do something to me again and also realise that it was Jax and Leah who rescued me.'

An awkward silence developed between us.

'Would you like something to eat?' Cassie asked.

'No, thank you. I'm still feeling queasy from the teleportation,' I answered.

She offered me her hand. 'Come on, let me show you the shower and get you some new clothes. It'll make you feel better.'

Cassie led me upstairs and showed me her room before guiding me to the bathroom. 'There're some towels in there and I'll leave some clothes out on my bed that you can try. If you need anything else, I'll be downstairs.'

I thanked her and got into the shower, similar to what we had at home except the heat could be regulated by turning a dial. I probably spent longer in there than I should have. It was nice to have a hot shower and know no one was waiting to get in. Back home, the water had been room temperature unless it had been magically warmed, but even then my mother would complain about using up all the water and having to replenish the cistern. And during my stay with Leaf, we'd only had one bathroom in the house, so we'd tried to wash ourselves as quickly as possible.

I walked back to Cassie's room with a mix of emotions. While I was with Leaf, there was always the possibility of going home to see my family. But now I wouldn't be able to even if I wanted to. I picked up a baggy T-shirt and a pair of stretchy black trousers before heading downstairs. The shower had made me feel better, and the nausea was a distant memory.

When I got downstairs, Jax and Cassie were talking but stopped as I entered the room. 'Do you feel better?' Cassie asked.

I nodded in response. 'Thank you.'

She picked up a small device that looked similar to what Leah had pulled from her pocket earlier. 'We have another fifteen minutes until we're meeting up with Mark and the other wolves.'

'He's coming over?' I asked. My stomach twisted in excitement.

'No. We're meeting him by the cabin to discuss what to do about Abigail. I had an altercation with her when I dropped Leah off. She's definitely not human. So we need a way to get them all out of there safely,' Jax answered.

I hesitated. I did not want to teleport again. 'The cabin? How far is it? Can we walk it?'

Cassie laughed. 'Don't worry. We don't need to teleport. We have time to walk there.'

SKY

Meeting the Wolves

We walked out to the back garden and passed several trees that had lost most of their leaves, but one little tree stood out. It still had green leaves and apples hanging on it, despite being past its harvesting time. 'Why does it still have apples?' I asked Cassie.

She looked at the tree, a small smile appearing on her lips. 'Leah created that tree a while back when she was learning what she could do with her magic.'

I glanced at it with admiration. Leah must be very powerful to create a tree that wasn't affected by the seasons.

We continued along the path and entered the woods at the far end of the garden. Despite the trees being mostly bare, their branches blocked the light from the sun, making it look like twilight. The thought of getting lost made me take Cassie's hand as Jax guided us along the path. After we'd been walking for a while, the trees opened up into a meadow surrounding a dark wooden cabin. I tightened my grip on Cassie's hand as I spotted a few massive wolves. I had never seen a normal wolf before, let alone a werewolf. Their backs were the same height as my chest. But the humans and children around us didn't seem fazed by it. Were they werewolves too?

A guy with ginger hair and broad shoulders broke away from the middle-aged man he had been talking to and walked up to Jax. 'I heard everything Abigail said to you. I may not like you, but you have my respect and alliance along with the pack's.'

Was this the Alpha? If I remembered correctly from my readings, only the Alpha was allowed to speak for the pack, but he looked our age. And why didn't he like Jax?

He continued to speak. 'We need to come up with a plan to get Leah and Seth out of the house, but she's watching us like hawks now. I'm not sure if she knows we know. Leah's in no state to do anything, so I couldn't get her out, and Seth didn't want to leave her alone.'

A light went on in my head. This must be Mark, their friend, the werewolf that couldn't shift. And he was probably talking about what had happened when Jax dropped Leah off. I took a few steps closer to him to get a better look.

He sniffed the air and glanced around until his eyes met

mine, and I froze. My heart rate sped up and became louder, and my body was flooded with warmth.

'Hello. Who are you?' he asked without taking his eyes off me.

All my thoughts disintegrated as I stared back at him, getting lost in his mesmerising green eyes. Butterflies fluttered in my stomach, causing a whirlwind of nervousness. I had never had any interest in guys, but this was different. I couldn't quite explain it, but I was drawn to him somehow. 'I'm here to get your wolf back,' I blurted out. His lips pulled up at the corners. I cringed inwardly at my awkwardness. Why did I say that? Why couldn't I just act like a normal person? It would have been better to just ask for his name, but no, obviously I had to say something stupid.

Jax cleared his throat and broke the enchantment. I quickly shifted my gaze to the ground. My cheeks burned, and the warmth spread like wildfire as Mark's eyes remained on me.

'Mark, this is Sky from the witch village,' Jax said before turning to me. 'And as you already seem to know, this is Mark, who lost his ability to shift due to something Abigail did to him.'

Jax's words seemed to snap Mark back to reality, and he looked over at Jax. 'I need to go. Abigail thinks I went to the shop. She'll be expecting me back soon. I'll let you know if anything changes.'

I lifted my eyes from the ground and followed Mark with my gaze as he walked away from us. The wind swept through me, making me shiver. It was almost like Mark had taken all the warmth away with him.

'Come on, let me show you to your room,' Jax said as we got back to the house. He led me upstairs and into an empty room. 'What would you like?' he said and gestured around the room with his hand.

I shifted my weight as I looked around the bare room, unsure what he was asking me.

'This will be your bedroom. I can conjure anything you want. What would you like to have in the room?'

Before I had a chance to answer, a bed materialised out of thin air, making me jump. My gaze wandered around the room, trying to discern where the bed had come from. The realisation dawned on me that he could make things appear from nothing just like Leaf. 'A desk and a wardrobe would be great,' I said with a smile.

I watched with amazement as a simple wooden desk and a matching wardrobe appeared in the room. It was a handy ability to have. It made me think back to my own magic. Or lack thereof. Despite my extensive knowledge and understanding of magic, I'd never got a chance to see what I'd be capable of. Not to mention how I would slowly wither away until there was nothing left of me unless I found a way to reverse the spell.

'Do you want anything else?'

Jax's voice brought me back to the moment. I looked at

him with hopeful eyes. 'Can you conjure books?'

He shook his head, a hint of sympathy in his eyes. 'Sorry. I have to picture every detail of what I want to conjure, and I don't tend to memorise every single word in a book.'

'How about a pen and a notebook?'

He grinned. 'Now that I can do.' A basic black pen and notebook materialised on the desk.

I lifted an eyebrow. 'You can make anything you want appear and you choose the most basic things. Where's your imagination?'

Jax shrugged. 'You didn't specify what you wanted, and that gets the job done, but fine.' A playful spark gleamed in his eyes as a small notebook with black feathers appeared next to a black feather quill and an inkwell. 'Better?'

I nodded with a smile.

'Great. If you need anything else, just let me know. I'll be in the opposite room.'

I thanked him and he left. A mixture of emotions swirled in my mind. It was strange having this much space to myself again after sharing a room with the others for such a long time.

I let out a yawn. It'd been a long morning, and though I was tired, I didn't think I would be tired enough to sleep. I went over to the desk and picked up the quill. I needed to figure out how to get Mark's ability to shift back, and hopefully my own in the process, but where to start?

I wrote down everything I remembered from the research I'd done with Leaf. Had they used the same spell on Mark?

I'd have to ask him later.

As I was scribbling away, a knock sounded on the door. 'Come in,' I called out.

Cassie walked into the room carrying a bunch of clothes. 'Hopefully some of these will fit you.' She placed the pile of clothes on the bed.

'You didn't need to. What I'm wearing now is fine.'

Cassie smiled. 'A girl can never have too many clothes. At least that's what Leah always says.' She walked over to me at the desk and looked down at my notes. 'What are you doing?'

'It's what we have been able to piece together from the ritual that took our magic,' I replied, meeting her gaze.

'Are you going to do the same ritual on Hecate to get the magic back?'

I shook my head. 'A spell can't be neutralised by repeating it. Besides, I don't think Hecate would allow us to cast a spell on her. But by figuring out the spell's structure and its intent, it's possible to pick up the key elements and reverse engineer it and allow the magic to go back to its origin. We have most of it figured out, but I still don't know how she managed to completely drain us and stop the magic inside from regenerating.'

Cassie pursed her lips. 'It sounds complicated. Would they have used the same spell on Mark?'

'I'm not sure. Maybe. I thought I'd ask him what he remembered next time I see him.'

'I don't think he remembers anything. He was asleep.' A shadow of concern flickered over her face. 'The chanting woke me up, and when I went to investigate, I saw several people in black robes standing around Mark's bed. But someone knocked me out and imprisoned me. I was lucky Jax and Leah found me and came to my rescue or I might have been stuck in that awful place ...'

A moment of silence engulfed us. I wasn't sure what to say.

Cassie gave me an apologetic smile. 'Sorry. That definitely killed the vibe. How about we go downstairs and get some food?'

While we were in the middle of cooking, Jax came into the kitchen. We finished up and brought a large stack of pancakes to the table. We ate in silence, but it didn't feel awkward. I thought about how similar yet different this realm was to mine.

'Do you have a scrying bowl?' I asked when we'd finished eating.

Jax looked at me with a raised eyebrow. 'I thought you didn't have any magic.'

'I don't, but I promised Leaf I would let her know we had arrived safely.'

'I'm sorry I won't be able to help you. I don't have the ability to scry,' Jax said apologetically.

'But I do,' Cassie said with a smile. 'It's very new, so I don't know if I'll be able to get it to work, but I'm willing to give it a go.'

She looked very pleased with herself, so I didn't have the heart to tell her it wasn't necessary and that the stone would work on its own. 'Don't worry, I'll guide you through it,' I told her as I returned her smile.

Jax handed over the scrying bowl to me. 'I'm going to patrol,' he said and gave Cassie a kiss before walking out of the house.

I picked up the calling stone Leaf had given me, placed it in the scrying bowl and poured some water into it. Since it contained magic and was connected to the other half of the stone, traditional scrying wasn't necessary. Instead, it could be activated by directing thought energy to it. But I wanted to boost Cassie's confidence, so I told her what she needed to do as if she was scrying. 'Clear your mind and look into the water and visualise talking to Leaf.'

Cassie bit her lip and gave me a confused look. 'I'm not sure I can do that. I've never met Leaf. The only memories I have of her are holding her in my arms when she was born, but it's not even my memory.'

'You're connected. Even if you haven't met Leaf in this life. She's still a part of you. Use that connection to reach her.'

Cassie nodded and stared into the water in the scrying bowl. At first nothing happened, but eventually the water started vibrating. A moment later Leaf's face appeared in the water.

Cassie froze, staring at Leaf's reflection. I opened my mouth. 'Hi, Leaf. This is Cassie, Katie's reincarnation.'

'Hi,' Cassie said and waved at her.

Leaf's eyes lit up. 'It's an honour to meet the soul that belonged to my mother.' Leaf shifted her gaze to me. 'I take it you got there okay. How are you doing?'

'I'm okay. I thought this world might have been primitive without magic, but it isn't. It may even be more advanced than ours, and all without magic. Instead of using vibrations to activate the orbs of light, they have a switch on the wall.'

Leaf chuckled. 'I'm glad you're settling in. Have you got any further with the research?'

I shook my head. 'Not really. But apparently there was a group of people in robes chanting before their friend lost his ability to shift. So I wonder if elemental magic was used. If so, there should definitely be a way to use elemental magic to reverse it.'

'That's great news.' She looked behind her before facing us again. 'I'd love to talk a bit longer, but unfortunately I have matters to attend to. Please let me know if there's anything I can do to help on my end. Take care of each other.' A second later, the water rippled again and the image of Leaf disappeared.

'Is this what you use to talk to each other in the village?' Cassie asked.

I nodded. 'Yeah. It's one way, but the village isn't that big, so we don't use it very often.'

'What about phones?'

I wrinkled my nose, confused as to what she was talking about. 'Phones? I've never heard of phones before.'

Cassie pulled something from her pocket and handed it to me. It was a thin piece of plastic framing a bit of glass. She pressed a button and the whole screen lit up. I stared at the object in my hand in awe. 'How do you use this to connect with people?'

She showed me a few different things on the phone and then started talking about computers and the internet. It was all new to me and I struggled to wrap my head around it.

Feeling overwhelmed, I sat down on one of the sofas. I pointed towards the framed black glass on the wall in front of me. 'Is this a phone too?'

Cassie laughed and reached for a rectangular object with buttons on. 'This is called a TV.'

The reflective surface sprung to life. People appeared inside the box. I walked up to it, astonished at how images of people could appear on a piece of glass at the press of a button. Was this an electric scrying object? 'Who are these people?'

Cassie shrugged. 'I don't know. It's a TV show.'

'A TV show?'

'Yeah. People watch them for entertainment.'

'You're spying on other people?'

Cassie chuckled. 'No. It's scripted. Like a story in a book, but instead of reading, you watch the story unfold. Would you like to watch it for a while?'

I nodded and went back to the sofa. I used the rectangular object and pressed a button. Every time I did so, the screen blinked and a new scene appeared.

Jax walked into the room and kissed Cassie before taking a seat next to her. She let out a worried sigh. 'Mark texted.

Leah's still asleep. She hasn't woken up yet.'

Jax took her hands in his. 'Leah used a lot of magic, and moving through different dimensions takes a lot out of you, especially if you're not used to it.' Cassie didn't look convinced.

I shifted on the sofa. 'He's right, you know. Magic is a wonderful thing, but it drains you, especially if you haven't learned how to control it.'

Jax gave me a grateful look. 'As soon as Leah wakes up, Mark will let us know, and we can proceed with getting them out of the house.'

'Surely Abigail will come after you when she realises they aren't coming back,' I said, wondering if they had thought this through. Jax shrugged. I wasn't sure how to interpret that, so I went back to watching TV.

An hour or so later I jolted awake at the sound of a howling gospel outside. It sent a surge of adrenaline through my veins and put me on edge. Why were the wolves howling?

Jax stood up from the sofa and looked around. His face remained neutral, but the worry in his eyes shone through. 'Stay here,' he said and disappeared from the living room.

I turned to Cassie. 'Do you know what's going on?'

She shook her head. 'I think Jax is checking it out. Maybe we should go upstairs until he comes back? Just in case.'

I got up from the sofa and took Cassie's hand. She turned the lights off as we exited the living room and made our way to the second floor.

We hid in Cassie's bedroom. I wasn't sure it would

actually help if we were truly under attack, but it made me feel safer, as did the fact that I wasn't on my own.

After what felt like a long time, Jax shouted from downstairs. 'Cassie? Sky?' His voice was laced with panic. This couldn't be good.

'We're here,' Cassie shouted back and rushed towards the door.

Jax must not have heard her, as the panic in his voice became more evident with every shout. We hurried downstairs, and the moment Jax laid his eyes on Cassie, his body relaxed. He rushed over to us and gave Cassie a hug.

Cassie looked up at him with a furrowed brow. 'What's going on?'

'Leah's missing. I need to talk to Freya so she can tell me where she is. I'll teleport you and Sky to the wolves. Mark can fill you in on what's happening.'

Who's Freya? I wanted to ask, but I knew it wasn't the right time. Instead I followed Cassie's lead and took Jax's hand. I swallowed the bile in my throat and prepared myself for the weird sensation that accompanied the teleportation. The thought of seeing Mark kept me grounded, and I tried to focus on that as the dizziness overcame me once more.

SKY

Special Connections

When we arrived in the woods outside the cabin, I let go of Jax's hand and made my way to the cabin to see Mark. Butterflies played in my stomach, but maybe it was just the nausea. I wasn't sure.

Mark was sitting on an L-shaped sofa with another guy. He was younger, probably a similar age to my brother, with a skinny build but with the same ginger hair.

Mark looked up at me, and our eyes locked for a moment before he spoke. 'Sky, this is Seth, my little brother.'

'Hi, Seth,'' I said as I waved my hand awkwardly.

Seth looked my way but avoided eye contact. 'Hi, Sky.'

I was about to say something more when Cassie entered

behind me. Seth got up from the sofa and went to give her a hug. She returned the hug before looking over at Mark with worried eyes. 'What's going on with Leah?'

Mark took a deep breath. 'Abigail took Leah to the hospital. Or at least that's her story. She said Leah's magic was making her ill.' He shook his head. 'I shouldn't have gone out. But we thought it was best to keep up appearances. Though I'm pretty sure Abigail's onto us now, so Seth and I bolted from the house as soon as we could.'

Cassie embraced him in a hug. 'It's okay. We'll get her back. Jax will come back with a plan.'

Seeing the love and care they had for each other stirred something inside me. Was it jealousy? I struggled to understand where it had come from. Of course Mark would care about the people he grew up with.

Mark caught my gaze, almost like he could sense the turmoil inside me. 'Guys, I need to talk to Sky. Would you mind giving us some privacy?'

'It's cold outside. Why don't you just go into the bedroom?' Cassie suggested, making herself comfortable on the sofa.

Mark eyed her for a moment before he spoke up, irritation clear in his voice. 'Well, I didn't want Sky to get the wrong idea, closed bedroom and all.'

Cassie rolled her eyes before glancing over at me with a smile. 'Sky, yell if you need rescuing.'

My cheeks heated up, and I glanced down at the floor, feeling a bit flustered by the attention. 'Thanks. I'm sure I'll be fine.'

A small smile played on Mark's lips as he got up from the sofa. He led me into the bedroom. His hand rested on the door handle. 'Is this okay?' he asked. His gaze darted back and forth over my face as if seeking confirmation. I nodded and he closed the door behind us.

I sat down on the bed, suddenly nervous. My palms were sweaty, and I wasn't sure where to look. I wiped my hands discreetly on the bedcover, hoping Mark hadn't noticed. What was going on with me? I jumped as he sat down next to me, startled by the unexpected closeness. Heat radiated from his body, and I got an urge to touch him, but I refrained. He obviously had something important to tell me.

Mark's gaze wandered around the room as he cleared his throat. 'Umm, I'm not sure how to say this. Umm ...' He let out a deep breath and changed the subject. 'What do you know about wolves?'

It caught me off guard, and I blinked. Taking a moment to find my voice, I replied, 'Only what I've read in books.'

Mark fell into a brief silence, his eyes fixed on something in the distance. 'Do you know about mates?'

I shifted my position and looked at him, a bit puzzled. His green eyes met my gaze for a brief second before he glanced away and continued talking. 'As a wolf, who we end up with is, to a point, predetermined. We call them mates. They are someone who we cherish and share a special bond with. A wolf won't always find their mate, and we don't know who they are until we meet them. But once we do, there's an immediate connection, and they become the most important thing in our life.'

Was that what was happening to us? It would explain why my body reacted every time I was near him. But I wasn't a werewolf, so how was that possible?

He turned to face me, taking my hands in his before gazing straight into my eyes, his face serious. 'You're my mate.'

'How do you know that?'

'Because my heart became yours the moment I laid my eyes on you, and the wolf inside me created a connection with your soul.'

My heart stopped. I took a deep breath while I processed the implications of his words. 'How is this possible? I'm not a werewolf.'

'You don't need to be a werewolf. You just need to be a being with a soul. As I said before, who becomes our mate is predetermined. We have no say in it. I wish I didn't have to spring this on you and that we would have more time to get to know each other before you have to make a decision, but in about three weeks, before the next full moon, you have to either accept or reject me. If you choose to accept me, we'll share part of ourselves with each other and solidify our connection, meaning we'll be able to fully feel each other's emotions. Because you're human, if you choose to reject me, you'll forget we ever met and can go back to living a normal life.'

'What will happen if I don't decide before then?'

Mark opened his mouth to answer but then closed it again and looked around the room. He sighed. 'I'm not completely sure. I've never seen it happen, but I've heard horror stories about the wolf inside going rabid. So if you're unsure, it's better to just reject me.'

My heart ached at the sorrow in his voice. All I wanted to do was cheer him up, to tell him I trusted the Fates, but doubt and surprise clogged my throat and kept the words tucked inside me.

Nothing I did seemed to usher them forth. And a whirlwind of uncertainty raged within me. I'd never been with anyone before, not even kissed someone, so how could I decide in less than three weeks whether I wanted to spend the rest of my life with him?

Mark got up from the bed and glanced back at me when I still hadn't said a word. 'It's confusing for me, so I can only imagine what you must be going through. But you've been on my mind constantly since I first saw you, and when you're around it's almost like I can feel your mood. But when you're not around I feel restless, like a part of me is missing. I know all of this can be a bit overwhelming. Would you like me to give you some time alone to process it all?'

I nodded, still unable to get any words out.

'I'll be in the living room if you need me.' He gave me a smile and walked out of the door.

I dropped my head into my hands. What should I do? Confusion swirled in my mind. I couldn't deny there was something about Mark that made me feel like I belonged, that I was safe. Every time I thought of him my heart beat faster. Having him as my mate wouldn't be a bad thing, but there were so many uncertainties, and it didn't help that I had very little knowledge about wolves. Besides, was I really ready to commit myself to someone I'd just met?

Getting nowhere with my thoughts, I walked out to join Seth, Mark and Cassie as they sat silently on the sofa. I wasn't sure if they were asleep or not, but it was the middle of the night.

Mark opened his eyes and met my gaze. His presence drew me in, calming the storm of thoughts swirling around in my head. I took a seat beside him. 'There's still time, so I think I would like to get to know you better before I make my decision.'

'Of course. I wish I could give you more than three weeks, but unfortunately it's not up to me,' Mark said.

Without thinking, I leaned into him and placed my head on his shoulder. Once I realised what I had done, I started to move away.

'Don't move on my account,' he said, a smile tugging at the corner of his lips. He carefully wrapped his arm around me in a protective hold. A sense of belonging washed over me, and instead of pulling away, I nestled further into his embrace, finding solace and reassurance in his presence. This was where I belonged. I drifted off to sleep, the bond between us growing deeper with each breath.

A hushed conversation woke me from my sleep. It took me a while to realise it was Jax and Cassie talking.

'Freya said to follow our hearts and use our connection to Leah to find her.'

'That doesn't make sense.' Cassie answered in a confused voice.

Before I even registered what I was doing, I spoke up. 'But you're related.' I stifled a yawn. Jax and Cassie looked over at me, and heat flushed over my cheeks. Had I joined a private conversation? Maybe I should have stayed quiet.

'Does that make a difference?' Jax asked.

His answer surprised me. He was supposed to be a powerful demon. Why didn't he act like one? 'Of course it does. You should be able to sense her with a bit of magic.'

Jax let out a sigh. Frustration laced his voice. 'Magic we don't have. You forget that none of us are actually witches.'

What was up with him? Why was he so frustrated? I'd just been trying to help. It wasn't my fault Jax wasn't thinking outside the box. Just because they didn't have their own elemental magic didn't mean they couldn't use objects that had them. 'Magic is all around us. What about the tree Leah created?'

Jax gave me a surprised look. 'What about the tree?'

'It's infused with Leah's magic, so you should be able to use it to locate her. Especially as she's from your bloodline.'

Jax took a deep breath. It seemed like he was trying to reel in his emotions. When he answered, all the hostility in his voice was gone. 'Okay. How do we do that?'

'You could try to eat the apple and visualise finding her.' I stared at my feet. Without a witch with magic, location spells were out of the question, so this was their best option. 'Depending on your connection, it may work.'

In reality, I didn't know if it would be enough. A witch who still had their magic could locate someone by touching something belonging to the person they were looking for, but without magic it wouldn't work. I hoped the apple would have enough of Leah's magic inside it and, along with the bond Jax and Cassie shared with her, they would be able to find her.

'Okay. Let's try it,' Jax said as he pushed the sleeves of his jumper up.

I slowly got up from the sofa, taking care not to wake Mark. How he hadn't woken up from all the talking was beyond me. I walked over to Jax and Cassie. Bile rose in my stomach as Jax took my hand and got ready to teleport. 'Can't we just walk instead?' I asked, even though I knew the answer would be no.

'It's dark. Besides, it's quicker this way,' Jax answered.

I took a deep breath as he teleported us to the living room of the house. A sense of déjà vu came over me as I rushed to the bathroom to be sick. Cassie followed, holding my hair out of the way.

Once I'd sorted myself out, we walked back to the living room. Jax was standing there with an apple in his hand. 'What do we need to do?'

I shuffled my feet. 'Umm ... take a seat on the floor. Get

into a comfortable position where you can face each other and visualise finding her.'

Jax gave me an amused smile. 'I meant with the apple.'

I took a breath, hitting myself internally. Of course he meant the apple. 'Just eat it and take each other's hands. Being physically connected will help intensify the magic, and both of you have a connection to Leah.'

They nodded in unison and got into position. Jax cut up the apple and offered one half to Cassie. They ate it and took each other's hands, closing their eyes. Their slow breathing calmed my racing heart as I waited patiently for any sign that it had worked.

After what felt like an eternity, Jax spoke up. 'She's in the basement of Cassie's house, but on the other side of the portal.'

Cassie's house? He must mean the house Cassie had lived in with the others before she was kidnapped. Abigail's house. But why would she have a portal in the house? Did it lead to Whitelake village?

Cassie opened her eyes and wrapped her arms around herself. 'I couldn't locate her, but she's feeling scared and worried.'

Was Cassie some sort of empath? I had read about them. Empaths had an easier time picking up feelings and emotions from others. Maybe she'd connected with Leah's mind instead of her physical location.

Jax got up from his sitting position and started towards the door. 'Let's go get her.'

'Wait. Running into the house without a plan would be foolish,' I said, feeling like a hypocrite. But at least I hadn't been running into danger headfirst.

Jax stopped in his tracks and turned around. 'You're right. We need a plan.'

Cassie walked up to Jax and put her arm around him. 'Let's go back to the cabin and talk to Mark and Seth. Maybe the wolves will be able to help too.'

We teleported back to the cabin and woke Mark and Seth up. Jax told them everything they had discovered.

'So how are we getting Leah out?' Mark asked.

There was a moment of silence before Cassie spoke up. 'Abigail thinks I'm dead. Maybe we can use that to our advantage?'

Mark shook his head. 'She knows you're not dead. You may catch her by surprise, but what are you going to do?'

Cassie crossed her arms and opened her mouth to speak when Jax cut her off. 'Mark's right. Besides, I'd rather have you here, where I know you're safe.'

If looks could kill ... She pressed her lips together and stared at Jax. 'That's not going to happen. She's my family, so I'm going to help get her back whether you want me to or not.'

Jax's mouth dropped open and he stared for several seconds before shutting his mouth with a grimace and a sigh. 'Cassie and I will go to the house.' He glanced over at Mark. 'I think you, Sky and Seth should stay here where it's safe.'

Mark let out a grunt but didn't argue.

A moment later, Cassie turned to Jax. 'Ready to go?'

Jax nodded while I shook my head. 'You still don't have a plan.'

Jax shrugged. 'If we go now, we'll have the protection of the darkness and maybe Abigail will be asleep.'

Would they have a chance if they ran into Abigail? I didn't know her, but I had a feeling they were underestimating her – but maybe I was underestimating Jax. 'Wouldn't it be better to wait until she leaves?'

Jax nodded in agreement. 'Probably.'

Cassie took his hand. 'We can wait her out by the house.'

In the next moment they were gone, without any indication they'd even been here.

'I hope they're going to be okay. It seems dangerous going there without a plan,' I said.

Mark placed a comforting hand on my leg. 'I'm sure they'll be fine. Jax wouldn't risk Cassie's safety if he didn't think he could handle the situation.' He got up from the sofa. 'I know it's still early in the morning and dark outside, but how about we go for a walk?'

I gave him a nod and followed him out of the door and into the fresh night air.

SKY

GETTING TO KNOW MARK

Outside, I hooked my arm in Mark's as he led me into the forest in the opposite direction from Jax's house. It was hard to see clearly because of the darkness, but the stars shone brightly along with a waning crescent moon. The carpet of leaves dampened the sound of our footsteps, and apart from the occasional hooting of owls, the night remained silent.

'What's your world like? Do you have seasons like here?' Mark asked in a gentle voice.

I nodded. 'It's very similar. We used to be part of this world before everything happened and Hecate hid our village away.'

'How was it growing up there?'

I shrugged. 'I was the black sheep of the family, which sucked. I dreamed about becoming a scholar of spell magic, but everything changed when I was picked to sacrifice my magic. My family couldn't understand why I was so upset about it. It's one of the reasons why I left and ended up with Leaf, where Jax and Leah found me.'

'I'm sorry.' Sadness laced his words. 'Do you regret leaving?'

I shook my head. 'No. But I guess I could have handled it better. I wasn't sure how my family would react if I told them, and I didn't want to risk being stopped, so I just left without telling them anything.'

'Families are tricky. Just look at our situation. Abigail took us in and cared for us when we were young. And until recently I thought she loved and cared about us, but it's clear now that she never did.'

We continued walking along the path in silence until it split. Mark halted and looked between the two. 'Come on, I want to show you something,' he said, pulling me to the right.

'What are you showing me?' I asked.

'You'll see when we get there.'

We continued walking through the forest until we came to a clearing with a gigantic oak tree in the middle. It was huge and very old, with black paw prints carved into the trunk. 'What is this tree?'

'This tree is sacred to the wolf pack. This is where they buried the first Alpha and Luna, and from their ashes the tree emerged. The engraved paws are those of the pack.'

'Is Luna what you call the Alpha's mate?'

Mark nodded. 'I'm sorry – these titles are so common to me now, I forget not everyone knows what they are.'

I walked up to the tree and traced my fingers over the engraved paw prints. 'Is your paw print on the tree?'

Mark shook his head. 'Not yet. Our paw print doesn't become engraved until we reach maturity and become one with the pack, but I'm not officially part of the pack yet. And can't be until I get my ability to shift back.'

I turned to face him and lifted my hand to cup his face, but stopped myself and let it drop to my side. 'Don't worry, Mark. We'll find a way to get your shifting abilities back.' I gazed into his eyes, hoping he could hear the sincerity in my voice. Whether I decided to accept him or not, I would do anything in my power to get his and the witches' magic back.

Mark smiled, and I could feel my knees go weak. Were all my feelings towards him because of the mate bond or was there more to it?

Mark turned back to the tree and ran his hand over an engraving on the trunk. 'This is my dad's engraving,' he said with a hint of sorrow.

I looked at the paw print he'd run his hand over. It had faded into an auburn colour instead of the black colour the others had. 'Why is it faded?'

'Because when he died, he didn't find his way back to the pack. When a wolf dies within the pack, they bury them here, and as they descend and become one with the first wolves, their engraving disappears from the tree. But because there was nothing left of my dad to bury, he never descended.'

Mark's eyes had gone glossy, and I could feel the weight of his emotions. I wrapped my arm around him, hoping my touch would provide him with comfort. 'I'm sorry. Is that why you ended up living with Abigail and the others instead of in the pack?'

Mark moved away from the tree and grabbed my hand. 'How about we have a seat?' He led me to a bench built from branches. After we sat down, he faced me and placed my hands in his, intertwining our fingers. 'It happened thirteen years ago when I was five and Seth was two. I woke up coughing, only to realise that there was smoke everywhere. My dad stormed into the room yelling our names. He picked Seth up and grabbed my arm, pulling me along, until we were outside.'

Mark fidgeted with my hands as he continued. 'Our dad left us on the pavement and told us to stay put before running into the house again to get our mum. I kept staring at the door, waiting for them to walk out. But ... but they never did.' His voice was laced with pain and loss.

A tear fell on his cheek, and I reached over to wipe it away. It was hard to see him this vulnerable. I couldn't imagine what he must be feeling. Even though I loved my parents, I'd never had a good relationship with them, and it had been my choice to run away.

He gave me a wistful smile. 'For the next couple of days, we stayed in a house with other children. They told us it was only temporary until they could locate any relatives. Eventually, Abigail came for us. We got told she was a distant relative of our mum, and it took a long time before she told us the truth. But at the time, we didn't care, as she was the closest thing we had to a family. She also adopted Leah and Cassie, who had become orphans at a young age too. We grew up as siblings, and I'm as protective of them as I am of Seth.'

'How did you find out about your ability and magic?'

Mark chuckled. 'It's actually quite funny. It was Leah's sixteenth birthday, and me and Leah were having a row. I can't recall why, but one moment she was shouting at me and the next, all the lights exploded around us. We all panicked, but Abigail remained calm. I guess that should have been our first tell something was up. Anyway, we ended up ordering pizza, as the food Cassie and Abigail had prepared had been contaminated with glass. While we waited for it to arrive, Abigail explained that Leah seemed to have developed magical abilities. It was a shock to us all, as none of us knew magic actually existed.'

'That's crazy.'

'Not as crazy as my seventeenth birthday. That's when everything changed for me. It was one of the most terrifying days of my life.'

I gazed into Mark's eyes, eager to know more. 'Was that when you first shifted?'

He nodded. 'I had always thought of myself as human, but when the moon appeared, my body started to change. It wasn't really painful – more distressing. I didn't know what was going on. The next second, I was a wolf, and instinct took over. I remember feeling trapped inside the house. While I was trying to escape, Abigail found me. Again, she didn't seem scared – instead she talked soothingly to me, calmly explaining what I needed to do to turn back into a human. At that point, I still trusted Abigail, and when she told me it was better for me to avoid shifting, I believed her.'

'That must have been so scary.'

'That's not even half of it. As the months went by, my senses changed. I could see better, smell more. It scared me, but I knew it had to do with me being a werewolf. I felt like I had no one. Sure, I could talk to Seth or even Cassie and Leah, but no one knew what I was actually going through. It made me wonder if there were any other werewolves around, maybe a pack I could belong to – one that could be there and help Seth when he changed. After a bit of searching, I heard rumours about wolves being seen in the nature reserve we're in now and that it was something strange about the old settlers that lived here. It raised my suspicion. I wasn't sure what I would find, but I knew I had to check it out. I went to see them one evening, and they invited me and Seth over to spend a weekend with them.'

'So these settlers were werewolves?'

Mark nodded. 'It took a while for them to open up, but as me and Seth kept coming back, they told us about the legends – about how we were created to keep vampires and demons in check. I'd never believed in vampires, but then again, I had never believed in werewolves or witches, for that matter. They told us it was wrong to deprive ourselves of our wolf, and that I and the wolf inside me are one. That we can't function without each other. And if I stayed in my human form for too long without allowing myself to shift, I would become ill. I learned how to shift on demand and how to control my wolf and its instinct. The pack felt like a second family to me, and I hoped Seth felt the same.'

Mark paused for a second. 'If it's too much, just let me know. I don't want to bore you with my life story.'

I smiled at him. 'You're not boring me. It's fascinating hearing about your life, and I'm happy you found them so you didn't have to be alone. How did you learn your dad was part of this pack?'

'One weekend, the Alpha sat us down and told us a story about one wolf finding a human mate. It didn't happen often, but sometimes the Fates work in mysterious ways. This wolf had been powerful, and the Alpha had been sad to see him leave the pack, but he'd accepted it, knowing the importance of a mate bond. The wolves had kept an eye on him, as after all, they were pack brothers. They had watched over his two children until one night the house they lived in had gone up in smoke. The wolves spent days trying to determine if anyone had survived, but after losing their scents, they'd given up.'

I could already see where this was going, but I remained quiet, waiting for Mark to continue.

'My memories of the night we lost our parents came back in full force, and I realised my dad was the wolf they were talking about. He'd been part of this pack. The Alpha knew we were descendants as soon as he saw us, but he hadn't wanted to scare us. Apparently, by having a human mother, there's a possibility we wouldn't have carried on the wolf gene.'

Mark stopped talking and gazed into my eyes. 'That's pretty much how I ended up here.' He took my hands in his and glanced back at the tree. 'There is something else that you need to know,' he said with a bit of caution in his voice. 'Because my parents were mated, my dad would have died a few days after losing my mother. That's why he went back inside. Bonded mates can't survive losing their other half, so even if he hadn't gone back into the burning house, we still would have ended up orphans.'

An awkward silence developed between us as I thought of everything he'd said and how it would affect us.

Mark's eyes searched mine. 'Are you okay?'

I nodded.

'I'm sorry if it's too much. I just wanted you to have all the facts before you make your decision.'

'It's okay. I'm glad you told me.' This complicated things. Even if I decided that I wanted to accept Mark as my mate, I couldn't. My years were numbered if I didn't get my magic back, and his would be too if we bonded. I couldn't do that to Mark. If I couldn't find a way to get my magic back before the next full moon, I'd have to reject him whether I wanted to or not.

'Come on, let's get back,' Mark said, breaking me out of

my thoughts. He got up from the bench and offered his hand.

We walked back through the forest in an awkward silence. The sky had brightened, making it easier to follow the path back, but my heart and head were all over the place.

When we entered the cabin, Seth was building a tower from wooden blocks. 'Bored of playing Jenga with yourself?' Mark said jokingly. I didn't really follow what they were talking about.

Seth shrugged. 'Well, it's not like watching TV is an option until we get a generator, and I'm too worried to sleep.'

Mark sat down on the sofa and removed a block from the bottom of the tower and placed it on the top. 'Do you want to join us?' he asked as Seth repeated the procedure.

I shook my head and sat down next to them as they continued to take turns removing the wooden blocks without saying a word.

I yawned, my body and mind tired from everything I'd experienced since I'd got here. Mark turned to face me. 'You can go to the bedroom and have a nap if you're tired.'

'I'm not tired,' I said, muffling another yawn.

He placed a hand on my arm, and my body relaxed from his touch. 'It's okay. I'll wake you up when we have some news.'

'Are you sure?'

Mark nodded. 'There's nothing we can do but wait.'

I leaned into Mark and he kissed my forehead. The stack of wooden blocks tumbled onto the table with a crash, startling me. My cheeks flushed with embarrassment.

Seth looked over at me with a mischievous grin. 'Sorry. We'll try playing something less loud next.'

I went into the bedroom and pulled the curtains before lying down on the bed. A thousand thoughts and scenarios went through in my head, and despite feeling tired, I didn't think I could sleep.

Someone shook me gently, and when I opened my eyes, Mark was next to me. 'Sky. Are you awake? They're back, and they got Leah.'

'They're okay?' I asked sleepily, rubbing my tired eyes.

Mark nodded. 'They're back at the house. Seth's already there. I said we'd come over too.'

Knowing Mark was eager to see them and make sure they were alright, I got out of the bed and we left the cabin. It was still early. I couldn't have been asleep more than a couple of hours. The dew lay heavily on the ground as we sped through the woods towards Jax's house. Despite all the thinking, I was no closer at figuring out the right thing to do. Maybe I should tell Mark about my situation and have him decide?

Mark placed his hand in mine, and warmth coursed through me. His touch made me feel safe and wanted, and the selfish part of me wanted to just accept him as my mate, consequences be damned. But the thought of losing him or knowing I'd be responsible for his death tormented me and got me to reconsider.

As we stepped inside, Cassie and Leah got up from the sofa and hugged Mark. I felt a stab of jealousy, as their care and worry for each other shone through in the simplest of actions. Why couldn't my family have been like that?

'I'm so glad you're okay,' Mark said to them.

Leah smiled. 'Yeah, me too. If it hadn't been for Cassie and her abilities, we would have been toast.'

Mark frowned. 'How come?'

'As soon as they had got me out from the portal in the basement, Abigail threw an energy bolt towards us, but before it hit, Cassie teleported us to the wood where I used to practise my magic.'

'Teleported? Like what Jax can do?' Mark asked as we walked towards the sofas.

Cassie nodded. 'Yeah. Jax always—' She stopped talking and looked at the ceiling with a worried expression and pursed lips. 'I'll be right back.' She ran towards the stairs leading to the floor above.

Mark gave Leah a questioning look. 'What's going on?'

She shrugged and rolled her eyes. 'I don't know. Maybe Jax needed something. They can talk to each other's minds,' she said as she sat down on the sofa.

'Soon we'll be able to do that too,' Seth said excitedly.

I glanced over at Mark. 'Can you talk to the other wolves?'

He shook his head. 'It only works once you've been initiated into the pack. Once that happens, it creates a mind link to everyone in the pack so we can communicate with each other even when in wolf form.'

'That's really cool. Is there a reason why you didn't initiate when you first joined the pack?'

'It's a commitment for life. And I didn't want to commit until I could get guardianship over Seth so he could be a part of the pack too. Besides, because we aren't part of the pack at the moment, we are free to move and live like any other human and we don't need to worry about territories and pack laws. Once we are initiated, we have to follow the pack laws and the only way we can leave the pack is by becoming a rogue.'

I furrowed my brow. 'What's a rogue?'

'It's someone who has been cast out by their pack.'

'That doesn't sound good. Was that what happened to your father?'

Mark shook his head. 'No. There's different rules regarding mates.'

Leah cleared her throat as Cassie and Jax walked into the living room. There was something about Jax I hadn't noticed before. His eyes looked tired, like something was weighing him down. Cassie guided him to the opposite end of the sofa and sat down next to him.

Jax remained silent while the others talked about how crazy the last couple of weeks had been. I leaned my head on Mark's shoulder and listened quietly. The rhythm of his heartbeat lulled me into a half-asleep state. They seemed happy to be back together. It made me wonder whether they'd even realised Mark was still missing his ability to shift.

Were they even thinking of ways to get it back? Would Abigail know how to reverse the spell? Maybe she was the key to getting our magic back.

Suddenly I was wide awake. 'What happened to Abigail? Is she alive? We need her. She knows about the spell that took Mark's magic.'

Everyone's eyes landed on me, and my cheeks burned.

'We fought, but she's still alive. I left her with my friend Nick. She'll be there until we need her,' Jax answered quietly.

Cassie looked over at me, her voice full of authority. 'Maybe we can worry about that another day. We all need rest after everything that has happened.'

I opened my mouth to argue, but Jax stood up. 'Speaking of rest, I'm going to retire to bed, but please stay as long as you like.'

Cassie looked up at him with a worried expression. He gave her a reassuring smile before walking out of the room.

JAX

Next Step

The door to my bedroom opened, and my senses were immediately on high alert even though nothing could get through my protective spells without my knowledge. The bed dipped down and I got a whiff of Cassie's flowery shampoo. I lifted my arm and waited for her to cuddle up against me. Our relationship had finally started to go the right way, and though I didn't want to rush her, I loved having her next to me in bed. I pulled my arm around her and fell back to sleep.

I woke in the early hours of the morning. Needing to clear my head, I carefully slid out of bed so as not to wake Cassie up. I opened the window and transformed into a crow.

I kept to the sky, enjoying the chilly breeze through my feathers. Some stars were still out, but the sky showed signs of light. This time of year, the sun was slow to rise and fast to go away. I didn't really mind. My eyes easily adjusted to the darkness.

My senses picked up on a few wolves making their patrols as I flew over the forest. I hadn't wanted to involve the wolves, knowing our species' shared history and them being created to hunt down and kill demons, but they seemed happy to help despite what I was. The change in the wolves after their Alpha had accepted me warmed my heart. Even Mark seemed to have got over, or at least suppressed, his grudge against me. But after what had happened yesterday, I wasn't so sure I deserved it. I had lost control. After Abigail had tried to kill Cassie and Leah with a bolt of electricity, I had let anger and fear take over, feeding the demon inside me until he broke free. Luckily I had regained control before I killed Abigail, and she was now safely imprisoned in Nick's dimension. I knew we needed to talk to her. Sky seemed to think she held the key to undoing whatever spell had taken Mark's shifting abilities. But I wasn't ready to face Abigail, or rather deal with what I became around her, knowing she was the reason for Cassie's suffering.

Just thinking about it made my blood boil, and I could feel the demon inside me stir. It scared me. It had never happened when I'd been in my crow form before. It was one of the reasons why I preferred being a crow.

I flew over to the window and watched Cassie sleeping

peacefully. It surprised me how much faith she had in me. She might think she had got over the fact I was a demon, but if she ever saw the demon inside me, she would run. I was sure of it. I still thought it would be safer if I stayed far away from them, but I had promised Cassie I would stick around. That only left one option. I needed to push the demon so far down that there was no chance of it ever surfacing again. Or maybe Freya could bind the demon part.

I left Cassie a note so she wouldn't worry and teleported to Freya's realm and started the journey to her house. I never understood why she had made it so I couldn't teleport directly to her house, but I suspected it was a safety precaution.

The sun shone brightly in the middle of the sky. To blow off some steam, I swiftly soared through the trees close to the ground, competing with myself to see how fast I could fly while still avoiding crashing into the trees. Before I knew it, the forest opened up to a wooden cottage surrounded by birch trees. It had been about a day in the human world since I had last seen Freya. She had left abruptly, and I wondered if she would even be home, as in this realm it'd probably only been a few hours. Maybe I shouldn't have bothered.

I shook my head. It didn't matter; I was here now, so I may as well check if she was home. I descended onto the veranda and transformed into my human form.

Freya wasn't sitting in the chair outside. I walked towards the front door. Maybe she was inside, though it wasn't very likely. As I entered the living room, one of her cats strolled up to me with a meow.

I stared at him for a moment. 'What are you trying to tell me?'

He meowed again and looked towards the kitchen. 'Is there something for me in the kitchen?' I asked. He nodded.

I let out a sigh. Why couldn't Freya have got familiars I could actually talk to?

As I stepped into the small kitchen, I saw there was a teapot on the hob, along with a cup and a note on the counter. 'Have some tea and relax. I will be back shortly.' I stared at the note again. When did she have time to write this? And how did she know I'd be back so soon?

I put the hob on, hoping Freya wouldn't be too long. I needed to talk to her, but I also knew Cassie would worry about me if I was away for too long. While I waited for the teapot to heat up, I did a quick sweep upstairs. My childhood room was exactly how I had left it. I hadn't stayed here long enough to need it for a very long time, and I had told Freya I didn't need it, but she had insisted, saying she wanted me to know I always had a home here.

The teapot whistled downstairs, notifying me that the tea was ready. I poured the water into the cup and added some herbs. Freya was always trying out new combinations. With the cup in my hand, I walked outside to take a seat in one of the chairs overlooking the surrounding nature. Things would have been so much easier if I had just stayed a crow.

'Escaping reality will get you nowhere. And if you had not decided to help Nick, you never would have met Cassie,'

Freya said as she materialised in front of me. She gave me a warm smile. 'Lovely. You made some tea.' The next moment, a cup appeared in her hand. 'Tell me what is bothering you.'

I turned to face her. 'I lost control. The demon took over and I almost killed Abigail.'

'You speak like the demon is an entity of its own. It is not. The demon is a part of you, but by suppressing it, you are giving it its own life.'

'But what if it takes over? What if it kills Cassie and everyone I love?'

Freya let out a sigh. 'I have told you before. It will not. You need to accept that it is a part of you. Nourish it and it will not feel like you are losing control. Instead you could harness the power.'

'But I hurt Nick.'

'That was different. You were tortured, and your body had forgotten who you were and was acting in self-preservation. Besides, it would not have happened if you had accepted the demon as a part of you.'

I remained silent.

'If you are worried, you can always use the necklace I gave you. I am sure Cassie would not mind giving it back,' Freya said.

I shook my head. 'No. It was a gift. Besides, she needs it.'

'Cassie is much stronger than you give her credit for. Her light will shine through.'

I looked out at the birch trees. Maybe Freya was right. Cassie saw the best in people, and she had much more faith in me than I had in myself.

'You should listen to her more often. Believing in yourself is half the battle. You have quite the journey ahead of you.'

I raised an eyebrow and looked her in the eyes. 'Care to share?'

'We all have our secrets,' she said with a smile before taking another sip of her tea. 'Now, let us talk about the issue at hand. Do you have any idea how to return the magic?'

I shook my head. 'Not really. Sky thinks Abigail holds the key.'

Freya nodded. 'She is a clever girl. It is always easier to reverse something when you know how it is created.'

'But I dropped Abigail off at Nick's. His dungeons were the only place I could think of that would strip her of her magic. It's too dangerous to bring Sky there. The demon realm would kill her.'

Freya was about to say something when one of her big grey cats jumped onto her lap and meowed loudly. She glanced into the cat's eyes, like she was having a conversation with him. When he jumped off, she turned to me. 'If there is a will, there is a way. You will see. Now, if you will excuse me, I am needed elsewhere.'

I was about to ask her how when she disappeared again. Letting out a sigh, I glanced at the cat. 'You always seem to know more than me. Care to tell me how?' The cat stroked its tail around my leg before letting out a meow and running into the house. I guessed I was on my own.

Cassie and Leah were in the kitchen cooking when I got back to the house. 'Are you okay? We were worried about you,' Cassie said as I walked up to give her a kiss.

I nodded. 'I'm fine. I went to see Freya. How are you two feeling?'

'No rest for the wicked,' Leah replied sarcastically. 'No, but seriously ... we're home and we're safe. It's all I could ask for. Besides, we still need to figure out how to get Mark and Sky's magic back.'

I picked up a piece of bacon from the plate on the counter. 'Where's Sky?' I hadn't expected her to be anywhere but here, but Cassie and Leah didn't seem worried. I looked around the kitchen and living room and noticed Seth watching TV.

'She's with Mark,' Cassie answered.

'Why?' I asked with a frown. What had I missed?

A smile appeared on her face. 'He's showing her around. I guess I forgot to tell you. Sky is Mark's mate.'

'What!' I almost spat out the bacon I had been eating.

Seth's laugh blasted into the kitchen from the living room. I wasn't sure if it was in response to my outburst or if he was just watching something funny on the TV.

I glanced back at Cassie. 'When did that happen?'

'The day they first met.'

In a way, it was a positive sign. It meant Abigail hadn't been able to take all of Mark's shapeshifting magic. 'That must have been confusing for Sky.'

'Maybe, but she hasn't tried to run away or avoid him,' Leah said, giving me and Cassie a smirk.

'That's good,' I said absentmindedly, my thoughts wandering to how shaky my and Cassie's relationship had been in the beginning.

'I meant to ask you. What do you think we should do about college?' Leah asked.

'It's probably not a good idea to go back while we're still trying to figure out how to get Mark and Sky's magic back. Besides, if you need the certificates, I can conjure them for you.'

Leah shook her head. 'It's not so much about getting good grades, it's more about getting back to routine. So much has happened in a short amount of time that it would be nice to feel normal again for a change. But you're right. Getting their magic back is more important.'

SKY

Why Doesn't Anyone Care?

Mark guided me through the forest towards Jax's house. I was smiling from ear to ear. Despite the less than perfect weather, the day had been amazing, and I already felt like I belonged here.

Mark opened the door to Jax's house and gestured for me to step inside. The smell of burgers hit my nose and my stomach growled.

'Great. You're here,' Leah said as she made her way over to say hello. Cassie followed behind. Jax remained by the kitchen counter, but I could feel his eyes on me as we said our hellos.

'Thanks for cooking,' I said as I took a seat at the table.

'Seth, turn off the TV and join us for dinner,' Cassie said.

A moment later, we were all gathered by the kitchen table. 'How was your day? Did you get up to much?' Cassie asked me.

'Mark showed me around the pack grounds. It was amazing. I wouldn't have seen the cabins if he hadn't pointed them out. They blended in perfectly with the surroundings. And the pack house is massive.' I grabbed Mark's hand under the table to show my appreciation.

'It's pretty cool,' Seth agreed. 'I can't wait until I'm seventeen so I can finally shift and be initiated into the pack.'

'Speaking of shifting, what are we going to do about Mark and Sky?' Leah asked. 'I had a look in my book, but there's nothing.'

I looked over at Jax. 'I need to talk to Abigail. I think she's responsible for the spell that was placed on Mark. From what Cassie told me, it seems different from the spell Hecate placed on us, but if the outcome is the same, there might be a way to use it not just to get Mark's ability to shift restored but to return the magic to me and the other people at Leaf's too.'

'She's in a demon realm. I'll talk to her for you,' Jax said.

I crossed my arms. 'You wouldn't know what questions to ask.'

'Then tell me,' Jax replied.

Frustration was building up inside me. 'It's not that simple. I've been studying how to reverse this spell for a year, and even before that, I was researching spell magic. How much do you know about elemental magic?'

Jax ran his hand through his hair. 'Not much. I never saw the point in learning about magic I can't use. There's so many different kinds, and they all have their own set of rules.'

'And this is the reason why it has to be me. No offence, but I doubt Abigail would just give you the answer.'

'Maybe, but it's not safe for you. Only demons can enter a demon realm.'

'Then make it safe,' I said in a huff and stood up from the table. 'This is our best shot at getting our magic back. Why can't you understand that?'

'How about we all just calm down? We're not getting anywhere by arguing,' Cassie said.

My heart sped up, and it felt like the walls were closing in on me. I needed air. I quickly walked out of the back door. Mark followed me and grabbed my arm. 'Are you okay?'

The warmth of his hand made my body relax, and I took a few deep breaths. 'Can you believe them? It's like they don't even care.'

'You're overreacting.'

I stared at him. 'Overreacting? Why aren't you bothered about this?'

He caringly placed his hands on my shoulders and looked me in the eyes. 'I am, but anger will get you nowhere. I'm sure they will come up with something. Besides, Jax said he would talk to Abigail.'

I shook my head. 'He won't know the right questions to ask, and we only have a couple of weeks to get our magic back.'

A crease appeared on Mark's forehead. 'If you're worried about the mating, we can still be mated without me having my ability to shift.'

I shook my head. 'It's not that.'

'Then what is it?'

I opened my mouth, the words on the tip of my tongue, but closed it and shook my head. 'It's nothing.'

Mark met my gaze. 'I can tell something's bothering you. What is it?'

I sighed. 'Can I stay with you and Seth at the cabin? I don't feel like going back inside after my outburst.'

Mark smiled. 'Of course. You're always welcome in the cabin.'

I let out a yawn as we got into the cabin. Mark looked at me with a bit of uncertainty. 'I'll take the sofa. You make yourself comfortable in the bedroom.'

'I don't mind. The bed's big enough for both of us,' I said. My senses told me I needed to be close to him.

When I walked into the bedroom after getting ready, Mark was already lying down. He looked up at me. 'Are you sure you don't mind?'

'I'm sure,' I said happily as I crawled into the bed and cuddled up to Mark. He tensed up at first but relaxed after a while and put his arm around me. His embrace calmed my busy head and made me feel safe, and a moment later I was asleep.

The next morning, Leah and Cassie came by the cabin.

'We're sorry about the dinner last night. We know you came here hoping to find new information that can help you reverse the spell, but Jax is just looking out for you,' Leah said.

'It's my responsibility to figure out how to get the magic back. The people at Leaf's are counting on me, and my friend Aurora had a dream where everyone had their magic back. She told me about it just before she died. So there has to be a way for me to talk to Abigail.'

Cassie bit her lip. 'Maybe there's another way. Jax told you it's too dangerous for a non-demon to enter a demon realm.'

I crossed my arms. 'But I can't just sit around doing nothing. Time is ticking.'

'I know what would make you feel better. Let's go shopping,' Leah said with a wide grin.

'Shopping?' I asked, with confusion in my voice.

Leah nodded. 'Yeah. You didn't exactly bring much when you got here. Besides, it's the best type of therapy for when you're stressed.'

'But I wouldn't be able to pay for anything.'

'Don't worry. Usually I'd say that's what credit cards are for, but with Jax around, things are even better.' Leah gave me a wink. 'And it's a good thing too, because I haven't been able to work because of everything that's been going on.'

I hesitated. My priority was to get the magic back, and I didn't see how shopping was going to help with that.

Cassie gave me a small smile. 'I know you're concerned about reversing the spell, but sometimes it helps to step away from the problem and do something else. Besides, I would really like it if you could come along.'

I let out a sigh and nodded. Maybe Cassie was right.

Mark came up and gave me a hug. 'Have fun,' he said with a cheeky grin.

We walked through the woods as Leah mumbled random names to herself. I had no idea what she was talking about or what a River Island or H&M was.

We reached the front of Jax's house, where a small black vehicle was stationed. Leah opened the door and pushed a seat forward, ushering me to get in behind it. She pushed it back and Cassie got into the seat in front of me. The vehicle sprung to life, and we reversed out to the road. The landscape blurred outside the window, and the trees and fields were replaced by buildings. This was much faster than cycling. We drove into a large concrete house. I was in awe of all the vehicles parked in rows. Leah manoeuvred into a free spot.

'Do you not have any cars in the village?' Cassie asked.

I shook my head. 'No. We don't have anything that would move this fast. Most people use bikes or horse-drawn carriages.'

We got out of the car, and I followed the others into a small room. I inspected the room with a confused look on my face.

'It's a lift. It moves between different floors,' Cassie explained.

I was about to ask how when the floor shifted, causing my knees to jerk with the vertical motion along with a sinking feeling in my stomach. When the floor stopped moving, the doors opened again and we were greeted by white floors, high ceilings and a bright atmosphere filled with shop fronts and people. Cassie and Leah stepped out, and I followed, trying to take everything in. It was overwhelming. The people, the noises, the smells ... I wasn't sure what to make of it all.

'Where do you want to go first?' Leah asked, eager to get going.

Cassie looked at me. 'Maybe we should start small – go to Starbucks or something so Sky can get used to it first.'

Leah nodded and started walking. Cassie and I followed. The shops were massive and they were everywhere, showcasing whatever they were selling in gigantic windows. This was far from the small market back at Whitelake village I was used to.

'Why is there a decorated tree in the middle?' I asked Cassie as I pointed at the gigantic pine tree covered with lights and colourful balls.

'The shops are getting ready for Christmas, but it's not until the end of the month.'

'Is Christmas what you call Yule?'

Leah turned around. 'Not exactly. Christmas is a Christian holiday. Yule is a few days before, but no one really celebrates it here.'

We walked into an area with tables and chairs that had been fenced off next to a sales counter, which was displaying different cakes and drinks. 'Try and find us a spot and I'll get the drinks,' Leah said before walking to the counter.

Cassie and I navigated through people sitting down until we found an empty table. I looked around, amazed at the size of this place. The whole place was much bigger than the temple, which was the largest building in the village.

Leah came back to the table and handed me a cup with a red liquid in it. 'It's a smoothie. I thought it was the safer option in case you didn't like coffee.'

'Thank you.' I took a sip. It tasted like strawberries. Leah and Cassie were talking, but I'd zoned them out, trying to make sense of this place.

After we'd finished our drinks, Leah dragged us around to different shops. After a couple of hours, as she was about to enter another shop, I pulled on her arm. 'I think I'm going to sit this one out,' I said as I took a seat on the bench outside.

Cassie came to sit beside me. 'Are you okay?'

'Yeah. I'm just a bit overwhelmed and exhausted by all the people and noises. We only have a small market in the village, and since I went to live with Leaf, it was too risky for us to leave the farm.' I looked around the shopping centre. Beside us was a big walk-in box with a sign next to it calling it a teleportation box. 'Is teleportation common amongst humans?'

Cassie frowned and I pointed at the box. 'Oh, you mean the VR. It's not really teleportation. You put on some goggles and you can walk around and play in a computer game. The box is there to act as a sensor for your movements but also to stop you from walking into people while you're playing.'

'So they're not really at another place?'

She shook her head.

I was lost in thought when Leah came to join us. 'Ready to go home?'

'Yes, please,' Cassie and I said in unison.

When we finally got back to the house, I sat down on the sofa and let out a sigh. Who knew shopping would be this exhausting? However, I'd been thinking about the VR box all the way home. Maybe there was a way that I could astral project to Abigail. That way I wouldn't physically have to enter the demon realm. 'What do you think about astral projection?'

Leah cocked her head. 'For what?'

'To talk to Abigail.'

She shrugged. 'I don't know. I don't know much about it.'

'Me neither. But if I could astral project to Abigail, I wouldn't have to actually be in the demon realm.'

'If you're that set on talking to Abigail, we need to find a way to make it safe. Only I wouldn't have a clue where to look. And I doubt there's much about it in my book.'

'You think Jax would let me go if we found a way?'

Cassie fidgeted with her necklace. 'Maybe. If you're desperate to talk to Abigail, it's worth a go. Jax is stubborn, but it doesn't mean he doesn't see reason.'

I remained quiet, thinking things over. How could I make it safe? Maybe Leaf would know something.

I looked around the living room. 'Where's the scrying bowl?'

'It's in the bookcase. What are you thinking?' Leah asked.

'I'm going to talk to Leaf. Maybe she will have some suggestions, or at least know where we can start. I'll see you later.'

'Do you want us to come with you?' Cassie asked.

I shook my head. 'No. I know the way.' I walked over to the bookcase and picked up the scrying bowl before leaving.

On the way to the cabin, I went over what Cassie and Leah had said. I was feeling hopeful. Maybe with the help of Leaf, I could pull it off and Jax would have no choice but to let me go.

I stepped inside and put the bowl down. Mark was sitting on the sofa reading a comic, but he stood up when he saw me and opened his arms. I marched up to him with a smile and he put his arms around me. His breath tickled my neck, and my tense muscles relaxed with his embrace and I let out a tired breath.

He laughed. 'Looks like Leah went all out with the shopping.'

I looked up at him and met his gaze. 'Yeah. I'm exhausted. We went into so many different shops, it all became a blur.'

'Did you get anything nice?'

I nodded. 'The bags are at the house.'

He released me from his embrace and gestured for me to sit down on the sofa. 'Actually, there's something I wanted to talk to you about.' He scratched his face. 'I know you technically have a room at Jax's house, but how would you feel about living here with me and Seth?'

Part of me wanted to scream yes, but I contained myself. 'One bedroom between the three of us? How would that work?'

'I've spoken to the Alpha while you were out. He's happy to help us extend the cabin and add one more bedroom for Seth. And fit a generator so we can get electricity. So what do you say? Would you like to share a room with me?'

'Yes, I would love to,' I said, giving him a kiss without thinking. I pulled back, my cheeks burning, but he just gave me a cheeky grin.

JAX

Memory Lane

Cassie and Leah were sitting in the living room when I got back from my flight. I'd been out flexing my wings and thinking about what Freya had said. I knew Sky wanted to talk to Abigail. I just wasn't sure how it would be possible, and bringing Abigail back here, where her powers weren't bound, would be too dangerous.

'How did the shopping go?' I asked as I made my way over to give Cassie a kiss.

'It went well,' Leah answered as she gestured to the bags on the floor.

I sat down between them on the sofa. 'What are you two up to?'

Cassie smiled. 'We were waiting for you.'

I looked over at Leah, feeling like they were planning something they knew I wouldn't agree with.

'We want to go back to our old house to pick up some things. Cassie thought you'd prefer to come with us.'

I nodded. Sometimes it was like Cassie could read my mind. To be fair, if it wasn't for the fact I had been gone for several hours, I may have been more worried she'd finally broken through the mental wall I had put in place for that specific reason. Cassie's powers were growing, especially her mental abilities of empathy and mind reading. 'Thank you for waiting for me. I would feel better if I could accompany you there.'

'Great. Let's teleport over,' Leah said. 'It would save us some time.'

I took their hands and teleported to the neighbourhood of the house they used to live in.

Leah sighed. 'Wouldn't it have been quicker to teleport into the house? Or at least next to it?'

'Just because we took care of Abigail doesn't mean someone else isn't watching. The spell around the house is still there, so why take any risks?' I answered.

'Because it would involve less walking,' Leah said as she made her way towards the house. 'And I doubt anyone would be watching.'

'I don't know. The spell was created by ancient magic. Either someone else made it and is potentially still monitoring the situation, or Abigail is much more powerful than we first thought.'

Leah put her arms around me and Cassie as we walked. 'You worry too much. If someone else was monitoring, don't you think we would have known something about it by now? After all, you were fighting Abigail in the house.'

I gave her a stare. 'Well, it never hurts to be careful.'

She rolled her eyes. 'Whatever.' She stepped away and took the key out of her pocket. 'Right, I have a few things I need to collect from my room, and Mark and Seth wanted me to get some things from their room too,' she said as she walked through the door.

I accompanied Cassie to her room. My eyes fell on the window, where the red blanket she had once laid down for me remained.

She caught me looking. 'Yeah, we better bring that with us. Too many memories to leave it behind.'

She walked up to me, and I put my arms around her, happy with how everything had turned out. I had been so close to losing her, but instead we had gained our memories from the past, realising we were in fact soulmates.

I gave her a kiss before releasing her. 'I love you,' I whispered.

I wasn't sure if she had heard me, as she didn't say anything back. Maybe she wasn't ready. Maybe I had moved too fast?

I met her gaze and she smiled. 'I'd better get started with the packing or we'll still be here by nighttime,' she said as she pulled out a suitcase.

I lay down on the bed, confused. Had she not heard me or had she ignored it? I brushed it aside. She was still by my side; that was enough for now. 'Do you need me to help you pack?' I asked even though I knew I wouldn't be much help. I had no clue what Cassie needed from her room – probably a lot of girly stuff.

She shook her head. 'I'm good,' she said as she started getting things from the shelves and cupboards.

After half an hour, Cassie zipped up the suitcase. Leah knocked on the door. 'You guys decent?' she asked with a laugh before stepping in.

I kept my mouth shut, knowing Cassie probably wouldn't agree with what had been on my mind and knowing Leah most likely did.

'Very funny, Leah,' Cassie said sarcastically, though the blush on her cheeks made me wonder.

Leah handed Cassie some clothes. 'Can you fit these into your suitcase?'

Cassie nodded and unzipped her suitcase to put them inside.

I got up from the bed and clapped my hands together. 'Ready to go?'

Leah looked over at me. 'Yeah. I just need to get the boxes from downstairs and get it all into your car. Have you made it appear yet?' A playful smile appeared on her lips and her eyes went wide. 'Or maybe we can just teleport everything over to your house.'

'No. I'll get the car.'

'Can't you just make it appear on the drive?' Leah looked over at me with puppy eyes.

'I prefer not to, for the same reason I won't teleport in the house. We still don't know if someone's watching.'

'Fine. Get the car and we'll meet you in the driveway,' Leah said.

'I'll see you in a bit,' I said and kissed Cassie before leaving the room. As I walked downstairs, I could hear them laughing.

I walked until I couldn't see the house anymore before conjuring my car. Would there be enough space for everything Leah had packed? Maybe I should have conjured a van. I had never understood why humans needed so many things.

When I parked in the driveway, there were already two big boxes there, and Leah and Cassie walked out the door with a suitcase and several bags in their hands.

'How do you have this much stuff? And why do you need to bring it all back to the house?'

Leah smirked. 'We might need it.'

We packed the car full. There was no way all three of us would fit in the car, as we had used the back seat for the suitcases.

'I'll meet you at the house. Please drive carefully,' I said and gave Leah my car keys.

Cassie kissed me and got into the car. I walked away from the house and watched them drive past. When I had got a fair distance away, I turned into a crow and caught up with the car, observing them from the sky. My senses continued to search for any threats that may be about, but fortunately, I detected none.

SKY

I Have To Go

I placed the calling stone in the scrying bowl and waited for Leaf's face to appear.

'Hi.'

'Hello, my darling. How are you doing?'

'I'm good. But the being that took their friend Mark's magic is being held in a hell dimension. They seem to have used a different spell from the one Hecate used on us, but Jax won't let me talk to her because I'm not a demon and therefore can't enter the realm, as it wouldn't be safe for me.'

Leaf nodded. 'I have heard about that.'

'Well, I need to find a way to talk to her. I know she holds the key to reversing the spell. Anyway, we were out shopping yesterday and they have these weird boxes where you are teleported into a game, and it got me thinking of astral projection. Do you think that would work? Because technically then I wouldn't be in the realm.'

Leaf tapped her finger on her chin. 'I don't know. There is a reason why both parties create a connection circle. Without the connection circle, the astral projection is volatile. If it's in the same realm, it may be possible to go where you want and come back without it, but to travel between realms ... Someone would need to anchor you to that place, and it's just too risky, as there would be a high chance of getting lost in between dimensions, especially if you're inexperienced and don't know where you're going.'

I let out a defeated breath. 'So there's no way of me getting there?'

'I didn't say that. But astral projection isn't the answer. Let me have a look around and see if I can think of anything that might help you.'

'Thank you.'

'Take care of yourself,' Leaf said before her image disappeared.

I sighed. I was back where I'd started with no way of talking to Abigail.

A couple of days after I'd spoken to Leaf, a box with my name on appeared in Jax's living room. Mark helped me bring it back to the cabin before leaving to help the wolves with the expansion of the house.

I rushed over to the box and opened it. All the research I'd been working on was in there, including a note from Leaf: 'I thought you might need this.' The note was attached to a book made of black leather, with the inscription 'Demonic entities and realms.'

I wondered how she'd transported it to the human world and where she'd got the book from, but I was too eager to figure out a way to talk to Abigail to ponder it. After all, Leaf did have abilities normal witches didn't.

The notebook contained my most recent notes and my attempts to discern all the components of the spell they had used to take the magic away, but it was mainly bits and pieces, and nothing explained why the magic could not be replenished. I needed more information on why our magic had stopped regenerating itself. And I was positive I could get that information by talking to Abigail.

I put the notebook aside and scribbled down questions that would help me understand how the magic had been taken from us. When I was done, I opened the book about demonic entities and realms.

The first part went through different demons the witches had come across at some point or another. The pages were thick and yellowed from age, and I wondered how old this book was. Some demons had images next to their description, and I questioned whether I really wanted to go to a demonic realm. But then again, Jax would be by my side. If he could take down Abigail, then hopefully he could protect me from demons as well. Besides he seemed to think going into the demonic realm was the part that wasn't safe, not the actual demons themselves.

I continued reading about the realms. It mentioned that the frequency of particles was smaller and could invade a being all the way to the soul, causing a reaction that would make the flesh melt and cause a horrendous death. If the text was correct, it meant I would have to come up with a spell or potion that would work as an extra skin, coating me from head to toe. And if the text was wrong and that wasn't the danger, going to the realm would kill me.

I shook my head at the graphic image that appeared in my head. Maybe it was too risky after all.

Mark walked through the door, and I looked up from my research. 'Ready to go to the wolves' for dinner?' Mark asked.

I nodded and put the books and notes away. 'Where's Seth? I thought he was having dinner with us.'

'He's there already. He made some friends, and as they are wolves like us, I've encouraged him to spend time with them so he has someone to talk about the transformation with. They may have more knowledge, but they haven't turned yet either and probably have similar fears.'

'That's very thoughtful of you,' I said as I put my coat on and linked my arm with his.

We walked over to the pack house in silence. It was drizzling and the clouds covered the moon, so I couldn't tell how close it was to being full, but I knew time was not in our favour.

After a while, small wooden houses appeared between the trees. We walked past several of them before we came to the pack house, which consisted of a massive wooden cabin. The door was open and Mark led me inside. A table of tracksuit trousers and shirts of several different sizes stood by the entrance, along with a few robes hanging on a rack by the wall.

As we continued down the hallway, there were some stairs leading up to another floor, but they were blocked off, with a sign saying it was off limits. Mark had explained they reserved it for pack business and meeting rooms. But it was also where the families of the Alpha and the Beta lived. We walked past the sign and entered a massive communal area. Several people were sitting around eating food and chatting. Young, old, males, females, all gathered together. Some had injuries or scarred faces, but despite all of this, no one seemed to pay any more attention to them than they did the others.

After we had passed a few tables, I spotted Seth. He was sitting with some other kids about his age. They chatted and laughed as if they had been friends for a long time. It made me think of Night, and I wondered what he was up to.

The Alpha walked up to us. 'Mark. Sky,' he said as Mark bowed his head. I followed his lead, as I wasn't sure of the correct way to greet the leader.

'Any news on your shifting?' the Alpha asked.

Mark shook his head. 'Not yet, but hopefully we'll have some answers soon.'

'Very well. I have a proposition for you, Mark.' The

Alpha looked over at me. 'Sky, would you mind if I steal him away for a moment?'

'Of course.' I nodded towards the serving area. 'I'll get us some food while you talk.'

Mark kissed my forehead and told me he would join me soon. I went over to the serving area and picked up two plates. I was curious about the proposition. It was easy to see that the Alpha was keen on Mark and treated him almost like his own son. Mark had told me his father had been the Beta until he'd left the pack for his mate, and the Alpha only had daughters. From what I'd read, the Alpha position gets given to the Alpha's heir, but I'd never read about a female Alpha. So who was going to take over the Alpha position? I shook my head. It wouldn't make sense for the proposition to be about that.

A lady behind me cleared her throat, and I quickly took the plates, which were now filled with potatoes, meat and vegetables, embarrassed I'd been too caught up in my own thoughts. I found an empty table and sat down, looking around to see if I could spot Mark. When I didn't have any luck, I started eating.

Mark came over shortly afterwards. He gave me a playful kiss and sat down next to me. He seemed thrilled. 'The Alpha is considering me for Beta training. He said because of my dad being the Beta before he left, I'm an heir and have the right to the position once I officially become a part of the pack. Obviously I don't want to step on anyone's toes, but I'm very excited.'

'That's great news. I'm so happy for you,' I said as I squeezed his hand.

We ate in silence. My determination to get our magic back had come back with a vengeance after hearing Mark's news. Maybe it was worth the risk. After everything he has been through, he deserved to be a part of the pack and a Beta like his father, but that could only happen if he got his wolf back.

Seth walked up to our table. 'Mark, do you mind if I stay with Jake and Dexter tonight?'

'That's fine. Just text me in the morning.'

Seth smiled and patted Mark's back before joining up with two other boys he had been sitting with.

After we'd finished eating, Mark turned to me. 'We should probably head back too.'

On the way home, he talked about the extension and how excited he was about it. Seth would finally get a separate bedroom and wouldn't have to sleep on the sofa anymore, and they would fit a generator so we could have electricity. I tried my best to seem interested, but my attention was elsewhere.

When we got back to the cabin, I excused myself and got back to my research. I needed to come up with a safe way to enter a demon realm. There had to be something in the books Leaf had sent over.

'Sky, are you coming to bed or do you want me to walk you over to Jax? You've been at it for hours,' Mark asked.

'I'm just going to figure this out first. I'll join you soon,'

I answered.

He kissed my cheek. 'Don't stay up too late.'

I nodded and went back to my research. By the time I'd figured out a spell I thought would work, the sun had come up. Excited to be one step closer, I grabbed my coat and rushed over to Jax's house. There was no way he could deny me from talking to Abigail now.

I stopped at the back door. Should I knock? Everyone always just walked in. I reached for the door handle. The door was unlocked as usual, so I stepped inside. The living room was empty. I shouted hello but didn't get an answer.

I took a seat on the sofa, unfolded the paper with the notes of the spell that would get me into the hell realm unharmed, and was reading it again when Cassie and Jax walked into the living room.

'Hey, Sky. Are you okay? Do you need anything?' Cassie asked.

I nodded and turned to Jax. 'Yes. I need to speak to Abigail.'

Jax sighed. 'We've been over this. She's in a demon realm. It's not safe for you.'

I stood up and crossed my arms. 'But what if I figured out a way—'

Jax interrupted me. 'It's too dangerous.'

The frustration built up inside me, and I tapped my foot in anger. 'It's like you don't even care about getting our magic back.'

'You know that's not true. When you left with us, you

became my responsibility, and my priority is to keep you safe.'

I huffed. 'Safe? If I don't figure out a way to reverse the spell that took our magic, I won't be safe. Why do you think I came with you? To see the human world?' I shook my head. 'No, Jax, I came with you because time is ticking. I've spent my entire life studying spells, and the sooner I can figure out a way to reverse the spell, the less people will die. So it's a risk I'm willing to take. The least you can do is hear me out.'

Jax let out a defeated breath. 'I'm sorry. I never heard of a non-demon ever wandering into a demon realm unharmed.'

'What about Abigail? Isn't she a non-demon?'

Jax went still. His eyes widened. He ran his hand through his hair. 'I guess not.'

I shook my head in disbelief. 'You honestly took her to a demon realm without knowing if she would survive?'

'She wasn't really my main priority at the time.'

'Well, speaking to Abigail is my priority, and there's a spell that can protect me in the demon realm that Leah can do.'

'What can I do?' Leah asked as she joined us in the living room.

I turned to her. 'I need you to place a protective spell on me so I can talk to Abigail.'

A crease appeared on Leah's forehead. 'I'm happy to help, but are you sure about this? It seems risky.'

'I'm sure. Being without magic is horrible, like part of my

soul is missing. You won't possibly understand, but think about Mark. They have taken his entire identity from him. Surely it's worth a bit of risk to get that back?'

Leah glanced over at Jax, who shrugged. She turned back to me with an unsure smile. 'Okay. Let's do it.'

'Any sign of it not working and we're leaving,' Jax said in a serious voice.

I bowed my head. 'Thank you, Jax.' I handed Leah the paper I'd written the spell on. 'It's quite a powerful spell, so it may be better to do it tomorrow once you've familiarised yourself with it.'

Excited that I'd finally found a way to talk to Abigail, I strolled over to the cabin to tell Mark the good news. He opened the door as I approached it. 'Where have you been?' he said with a hint of anger in his voice as he looked me over.

I gave him a questioning look before I stepped inside and hung up my coat. Mark followed me as I made my way to the sofa.

'I don't mean to pry, and you are by no means a prisoner. I'm just worried. You never came to bed last night and then when I wake up, you're not here. You could at least have left me a note or something, letting me know where you've gone. I worried something had happened to you.'

'Well, nothing happened.'

'What were you doing?'

'I came up with a way to enter the demon realm.'

Mark started pacing. 'I don't like this. It sounds dangerous.'

I let out a frustrated sigh and swung my hand in the air. 'Why don't any of you get it? It's not just about you and me. Every year several people sacrifice their magic, their identity, so the village can stay hidden and be protected against the evil demon. Only we know this demon, and we know he won't do anything to destroy the village despite what they did to him. So there is no need for it. It doesn't serve a greater good. All it does is ruin people's lives.'

Mark put his arms around me. 'I'm sorry. I know what it's like. I'm just not willing to risk your life to get my wolf back. You mean more to me.'

Butterflies fluttered in my stomach at the thought that he was happy to give up his wolf for me, but I knew he would change his mind eventually. 'You say that now, but a magic being without magic is weak. Our bodies are supposed to contain magic. You may think not being able to shift is a sacrifice you're willing to make, but you told me yourself, you have to shift to remain healthy. And us witches, well, I've seen firsthand what a life without magic does to us. They wither away. I don't want that for us or for the others of my people.'

Mark's eyes went wide. 'Why didn't you tell me this sooner? I could have helped.'

'Helped how? You have no powers.' The moment the words left my mouth I regretted them.

Mark sunk back into himself and gave me a hurt look. Pain erupted in my heart, and I could tell I had upset him.

'I'm more than capable of looking after my woman,' he

said with anger.

'Your woman? Last time I checked, I was still a free woman. And whether or not I accept you as my mate, that isn't going to change.' I put my hand over my mouth, regretting the words immediately. It wasn't Mark I was angry with, it was the situation.

He let out a grunt. 'You know what I mean.'

Of course I knew what he meant. Our connection had been growing stronger every day. I reached for his hand. 'I'm sorry. I know what you mean, and if it was any normal human being, you would, but this isn't normal. We're not normal. Besides, I'm sure Jax wouldn't allow me anywhere near Abigail if he didn't think he could keep me safe.'

'So he agreed?'

I nodded. 'He did.'

Mark walked towards the door without a word. 'Where are you going?' I called after him, but he was already gone.

JAX

Justifying the Choice

The sound of the back door slamming got my attention. Because of my protective barrier, I knew it wasn't an enemy, but I thought I'd better check who it was. I had my suspicions.

Mark marched towards me as I stepped into the living room. His breathing was shallow, like he had been running, and his muscles tense. His face held a sour expression, and if looks could have killed, I would have been dead several times over by now.

'Why did you agree to it?' he yelled as he invaded my personal space and glared right into my eyes. His pupils were dilated, and I could feel his breath on my face. I could have sworn he was growling. If he'd had his ability to shift, he would have turned into a wolf and tried to make demon soup of me by now. Luckily for me – or him, depending on how you saw it – he couldn't.

The demon stirred inside me, longing for a fight. I pushed the urge down and took a step back. Unsure whether it would work or not, I sent out some calming energy. 'Trust me, I don't want her there any more than you, but that girl of yours is very determined and didn't take no for an answer.'

He looked at me again. 'I'm not happy about it.'

'Neither am I,' I admitted. I met his gaze. 'I will keep her safe, Mark, I promise.'

Mark didn't look convinced. 'Well, she'd better be. I will hold you responsible if she isn't. Wolf or no wolf, I will tear you to pieces if anything happens to her.' He clenched his fists, maybe to stop himself from punching me, or maybe he was just trying to control his anger.

I spoke to him in a calm but sincere voice. 'Nothing will happen. Leah is working on a strong protective spell that will keep her safe.'

He grunted. 'You'd better be right,' he said before disappearing out of the back door.

I was standing there staring at the door when Cassie and Leah walked into the living room. 'Was that Mark? He seemed upset?' Cassie said in a worried voice.

'Yeah. He's worried over Sky.'

Cassie nodded. 'Can you blame him?'

'No.' I looked at Leah. 'Are you sure the spell is powerful

enough to get her safely through the portal?'

Leah nodded. 'Sky seems to know what she's talking about. The spell seems solid. But I've had a look in my book too. And there's a talisman for protection against evil that I will do as well. I figured it wouldn't hurt to have her double protected.'

'Good. If not, Mark may have me for dinner.' I smirked, hoping it would loosen the tension. I could easily take on a wolf, but I wasn't so sure about a wolf that had gone rabid from losing their mate.

'I've never tried demon. I wonder if it's tasty?' Leah said in a mocking voice, giving me an evil smile with a twinkle in her eyes.

Cassie chuckled and turned to me with a hopeful smile. 'If Sky gets back unharmed, does that mean I can meet my father?'

I gave her a serious look. 'No. I am not willing to risk it. Besides, you will be able to go through when you turn eighteen.' She gave me a sour pout. 'I wouldn't know what to do if I lost you,' I said as I took her hand and pulled her close, placing a kiss on her forehead.

Leah made a hurling noise. 'Get a room, guys.'

I let go of Cassie and looked over at Leah with a cheeky grin. 'Technically, it's my house, and if you don't like it, you can leave.'

'Guess I'll go and pack,' she said through laughter.

I released Cassie from my arms and gave Leah a stern look so she knew I was back to being serious. 'Leah, would you mind showing me the spells?' I wanted to make sure Sky had covered the actual demon realm issue and not just the evil that may reside within. After all, we were only going to Nick's, so hopefully we wouldn't encounter any other demons.

'Sure. Let me get it.'

Leah walked out of the room, leaving me and Cassie alone.

Cassie looked up at me with love in her eyes. 'I've been thinking ... I know I have my own room here, but how would you feel if I officially moved into your room?'

My heart sped up. I hadn't wanted to rush things, knowing it may push her away. Especially because I knew we had the rest of eternity together. But hearing her say that created a warm and fluttery feeling in my chest. 'I would love nothing more,' I said with a big smile. I embraced her and gave her a deep kiss.

Leah cleared her throat. 'Jax, these are the spells.'

I let go of Cassie and walked up to Leah to look in the book. I also looked over the paper Sky had given her. This spell did indeed cover the issue of stepping into a demon realm. 'What ingredients do you need? I'll get them for you.'

'I'll make you a list.' Leah picked up a pen and some paper and started scribbling. She looked up at me with a smile. 'Why don't you take Cassie out to celebrate?' I gave her a confused look. 'She told me about moving in with you, and from how you two were acting, I assumed she asked you.'

'Yeah,' I said with a smile.

She handed me the paper. 'Don't worry about me. I can look after myself. However, if you could conjure some fish and chips before you go, that would be great.'

I turned around to face Cassie. 'Let me get this sorted, and then I'll come back and take you out for a date.'

'Where are you taking me?'

'It's a surprise,' I said with a smile. I kissed her before teleporting away to the spiritual shop in the next town over.

I thought about where to take her as I collected the crystals and herbs we needed for the spells. I could take her to a fancy restaurant, but it didn't feel like the right place. No, I wanted something that represented us both – somewhere we could be alone. Suddenly I knew where I wanted to take her. It would be perfect. I paid for the ingredients and walked out of the shop. I had been in luck and they had everything we needed, including black tourmaline dust.

I took a detour to the cliff near the woods. I wanted to make sure it was safe and the weather had not made it unpleasant. I conjured some blankets and a campfire. Cassie would like this place. The sun had started to disappear behind the horizon, so by the time we got here, we could watch the stars.

I returned to the house, handed over the bag of ingredients to Leah and conjured some food for her before I took Cassie's hand and teleported us to the cliff.

When we arrived, Cassie let go of my hand and scanned the area. She strolled further out towards the cliff edge. 'This is beautiful. You can see most of our town from here. How did you find this place?'

I walked up and wrapped my arms around her, resting my head on her shoulder. 'I have my ways,' I said with a cheeky smile. 'I saw it while I was flying around and thought you would appreciate the view.'

Cassie turned to face me, taking my hands in hers. 'I do. Thanks for bringing me here.'

We embraced each other and shared a passionate kiss.

I looked into her eyes. 'I love you.'

Silence met me. It felt like it went on forever. I knew she had heard me this time. I hadn't meant to say it again. It had just slipped out of my mouth.

I reached for her hands. 'It's okay if you're not there yet. I don't want you to feel pressured or that you have to say it back. I just wanted you to know. I know you have Katie's memories, but I also know you're not Katie and all of this is new to you.'

I took a deep breath. I was rambling. 'What I'm trying to say is, we have time, so don't feel like you have to rush anything. As long as I get to spend time with you, I'm the happiest guy in the world.'

A smile broke out on her face. 'I love you too, Jax.'

My smile widened. 'Great. I can't wait to have you in my bedroom.' As I heard myself say the words, the realisation it may have come out with a different meaning from what I'd intended hit me. 'I mean, I'm happy we will officially be sleeping together.' Shit, that came out all wrong too. 'What I meant was—'

Cassie kissed me so I couldn't continue to make a fool of myself. She laughed. 'It's okay. I know what you meant.'

I let out a breath, glad I hadn't offended her. Taking her hand, I led her to the fire. We sat down and I conjured some hotdogs for us to cook over it.

After we'd finished eating, we moved the blankets further out on the cliff and cuddled up. The sky was clear, and the stars shone brightly. It was a night I would cherish forever.

The warm rays of sunlight on my face woke me up. The air was cold and fresh, but the blankets had kept us warm. I teleported Cassie home and carefully placed her on the bed in my bedroom and tucked her in. Just because I couldn't sleep any longer didn't mean she needed to be awake. I placed a note on the pillow next to her, hoping it would be enough not to freak her out when she woke up in a different place from where she had fallen asleep.

I watched her sleep soundly for a few minutes before I opened the window and turned into a crow. I needed to burn some energy, and the best way I knew of doing that was to soar through the sky.

My thoughts caught up with me. I worried about Sky and if the protection spells would be enough. I had never gone to a demon realm with anyone who didn't have demon blood in them. It was risky, but Sky wouldn't seem to take no for an answer. Besides, Freya had said we would find a way.

I'd hoped the demon realm part would have scared her

off. It would have done me, at least if I didn't trust Nick to get me out of there. But it only seemed to have made her more determined. Even Mark seemed to have failed to deter her, judging from his reaction yesterday. However, secretly I was glad she was coming with me. I didn't feel ready to face Abigail on my own.

My eyes caught some movement between the trees and I swooped down for a closer look. Sky was making her way to the house. Yet again, I'd been flying around for longer than intended. I cut my flight short and returned home. I wanted to be around to make sure the spells went to plan before we made our way over to Nick's house.

I entered the bedroom window and transformed into my human form. Cassie looked up at me with sleepy eyes.

'Good morning, beautiful,' I said as I made my way over to give her a kiss. She pulled me into the bed and I ended up on top of her. She started kissing me, and all my thoughts about making sure the spells would go to plan disappeared from my mind. Leah and Sky should be able to handle it.

SKY

PROTECTION SPELL

Mark's snoring woke me up. I tried to get back to sleep, but I was too restless and nervous. Should I wake him up? I'd promised to say goodbye before I left to see Abigail with Jax, but there was still a lot of preparation to be done.

I got out of bed and got myself ready for the day. On my way to the living room, I grabbed the book containing the incantation spell for protection and left the cabin.

The birds were chirping as I walked through the woods to Jax's house. My heart beat faster and adrenaline pumped through my veins. This was it. But what if something went wrong? I shook my head. No, I wasn't going to think about that. The spell was solid. This was going to work.

When I stepped into the house, everything was quiet. Maybe they were still asleep? I looked around and noticed a large leather-bound book on the table. Curiosity got the better of me and I went to see what it was about. I looked through the book, amazed by all the information and spells it contained. It was old, but the pages and writing were well preserved. This must be Leah's spell book. By the way it had the ceremonies and sabbats written down, I could tell it had belonged to a High Priestess at some point, or at least someone in charge of the ceremonies. Part of me wondered whether it may have been Katie's. I shook my head at the thought. It could have come from anywhere. There were more villages of elemental witches than just ours. I'd been told England had been full of them once upon a time, but one by one the villages had been destroyed.

I flipped through the pages of the book, hoping it would contain some useful information about sacrificial magic.

'Good morning. Have you been here long? You should have texted me. I would have come down quicker.'

I jumped at Leah's voice, too engrossed in the book to even know she was next to me. 'I don't understand how to use the phone you gave me. It doesn't make sense.'

Leah's gaze went to the book. I hesitated, worried she was going to tell me off, like my sister used to do. Instead she just smiled. 'Did you find anything useful?'

'Umm. Not really.'

'That's a shame. There's so much information and spells in that book, I don't even know what half of it is for. Maybe you can help me with it when you get back.'

I smiled. 'Sure. Where did you get the book from?'

'Jax gave it to me. I'm not sure where he got it from, though.' She took the book from me and flicked through to a certain page before giving it back. 'This is the protective talisman I created last night. I know we are making another protective spell, but I thought it wouldn't hurt to be extra cautious.'

I looked at the page she showed me. The talisman was to protect against evil. I doubted it would do much against the actual portal hopping, but it touched my heart that Leah had been thinking about me.

She walked over to the bookcase by the wall and came back with a necklace in her hand. 'What do you think? It took me forever to weave all the different herbs together into a bag to hold the crystals.'

The necklace was a small woven bag containing an obsidian and a jasper stone. 'It looks great,' I said and put it around my neck. 'Do we have everything we need for the main spell?'

Leah nodded and walked over to the kitchen island. She opened a bag and pulled out a black rose, elderflower, rue, St John's wort, fluorite crystal, black tourmaline dust and salt. 'We got everything that was on the note you gave me.'

'Great.' I pulled up the book I had brought over and showed her the spell. 'Place the thorns of the black rose together with the other herbs, add the salt and water and let it simmer with the crystals for a while. At the end, sprinkle the tourmaline dust on top. Once done, this spell needs to be cast on me.' I pointed at the spell in the book.

Leah examined it with a confused expression. 'You sure this will work?'

I nodded. 'I know it isn't a proper protection spell, but I'll enter a realm where I don't belong, so it makes sense to protect from foreign energy, as I'm guessing that's the danger.'

Leah raised an eyebrow. 'Are you sure you want to do this? I have never done anything like this before. I don't even know if it will work.'

I gave her a reassuring smile. 'I'm willing to risk it. This is the best way to get answers. Besides, if I don't do this, I'll be dead in a couple of years anyway.'

'At least that's a few more years you would have if this doesn't work. Think about Mark.'

'I am. This is what's best for both of us. Being mated to him would tie us together. And I can't possibly do that knowing I would give him a death sentence.'

Leah's eyes went wide. 'So this is why you're in such a rush to get the magic back! Have you talked to Mark about this?'

I shook my head. 'Not really.'

A while later, the potion had been sorted and I took a seat on the floor. Leah handed me the glass with the potion and started creating a circle around us with salt. Once done, she called all the elements, asking them to join our circle. When they were all present, I downed the potion and visualised it engulfing me in a protective layer. Leah started an incantation, and I could feel the surrounding energy respond. I smiled to myself. It'd been a long time since I'd felt any magic at all. Tiny glowing particles moved towards me. As they connected, they bonded with each other, creating a glowing layer on top of my skin. After it had covered the whole of me, the glow disappeared.

Leah completed the spell and thanked the elements for their presence before opening the circle again.

'I think it will work,' I said as Leah made her way over to the sofa.

She sat down, exhausted. 'I hope you're right. At one point your whole body glowed.'

I nodded. 'I know. I saw it too.' I smiled at her. 'Thank you. I couldn't have done this spell without you.'

I'd just started tidying up, leaving Leah on the sofa to rest, when Jax strolled into the room. His face beaming with happiness. 'Anyone want any breakfast?' he asked cheerfully.

'Please get me some pancakes,' Leah said from the sofa. A moment later, a plate of pancakes arrived in his hands from nowhere and he walked over to her.

'That's so amazing. I bet you'll never get tired of that ability,' I said. Jax shrugged but remained quiet.

I eyed them with jealousy. Leah had her magic, Cassie was learning and exploring hers, and Jax – well, I wasn't really sure what he could do. He didn't talk about it much, but I hadn't asked him about it either. So far I'd gathered he could turn into a bird, conjure things and teleport. Which was more than enough if you asked me, but every now and again I could sense that was only a small portion of what he could actually do.

Besides, Leaf was very skilful in her own right, and abilities and magic moved down from generations, but it was hard to tell how much of her power came from Jax, considering her mother had been a powerful witch.

'How did the spell go?' Jax asked.

'It went well. I'm all set and ready to go,' I answered.

He looked around. 'Where's Mark? Aren't you going to say goodbye before we leave?'

'I didn't know how long the spell was going to take, and I didn't want to wake him up.'

Leah got her phone. 'Let me text him to come over.'

Mark walked through the back door and engulfed me in a hug. 'I'd rather you stay,' he whispered in my ear.

I looked into his eyes with determination. 'I have to do this.'

'I know,' he said as he gave me a kiss. 'Please be careful.' He looked over at Jax. 'I'm holding you responsible if anything happens to her.'

Jax gave him a nod and went to say bye to Cassie while I mentally prepared myself for the teleportation. Even though I knew it was coming, I still hated it. Just thinking about it made me nauseous.

Jax walked up to me. 'Last chance to back out.'

'I'm ready,' I said confidently.

'Okay, Sky, just hold on to me and I'll get us there.'

I grabbed hold of his arm and closed my eyes. When I opened them again, we were somewhere else. I swallowed the sick feeling in my stomach, grateful I hadn't had anything to eat this morning.

It was still early, and the air felt the same as before, informing me that we were still in the human realm. There were several brick houses in a row, all identical to each other with bay windows; the only difference was the colours of the doors. I looked around in confusion. 'I thought we were going to a demon realm?'

'We are, but I can't just teleport into Nick's house. That would be rude and probably dangerous, since he's not expecting us.'

'Who's Nick?'

'My best friend and Cassie's father,' Jax said.

'And he's a demon that lives in the demon realm?'

Jax smirked and walked up to one of the front doors. He rang the doorbell as I went to stand next to him, not really sure what to expect.

The door opened and a muscular guy in his mid-twenties with long brown hair and the same blue eyes as Cassie looked us over with a frown. 'Oh. It's you.'

'Hello to you too,' Jax answered, but Nick had already walked back into the house without saying another word, leaving the door open for us to enter.

'Are you sure you're best friends?' I asked Jax. 'He

doesn't seem to like you very much.'

'I think we just caught him at a bad time.'

I was about to step over the threshold when Jax grabbed my arm, a concerned expression on his face. 'As you step over the threshold, you may feel strange. If at any time it becomes uncomfortable or painful, let me know. It means the spell didn't work.'

I stared at him for a moment. That meant on the other side of this door, even though I could look straight into it, was another realm. It excited me, but at the same time, my head told me to be cautious.

'What will we do if the spell doesn't work?' I asked with a knot in my stomach.

He tilted his head and gave me a serious look. 'Then we'll have to get you back to the outside as soon as possible and pray to the Fates they won't give Mark a reason to have me for breakfast.' He ran his hand through his hair. 'Are you sure the spell is enough? Because there's still time to change your mind.'

I nodded. 'I'm willing to risk my life on it.'

I took a few deep breaths before slowly stepping over the threshold. As I did, a weird energy bounced over me like hail. It wasn't painful, but it definitely wasn't pleasant. When I got to the other side, I could feel the difference in the surrounding air. It was heavier, harder to breathe, and with a hint of something rotten in the air.

Jax studied me carefully. 'How are you feeling? Are you okay?'

JAX

Visiting Nick

Relief hit me when Sky told me she felt fine. Though I had faith in Leah and her abilities, a small part of me had worried it wouldn't be enough and that I'd have to rush Sky to Freya to be healed.

As we made our way into the living room, I racked my brain as to why we had received such a rude reception. Had we interrupted Nick in the middle of something?

'Who is this?' Nick's detached voice brought me back to reality. He inspected Sky closely. I'd seen that look before. It was almost like he was trying to decide if she was a threat or not.

'This is Sky, from the witch village.'

He stepped up to Sky. Her body trembled slightly as he loomed over her. She swallowed and looked up at him with wide eyes.

I moved between them. His eyes were black, and for the first time ever, I was unsure whether he was going to hurt her. There was something about him, something different, but I couldn't put my finger on what it was.

'Why is she here?' Nick asked.

'We've come to question Abigail. Sky is one of the children that had their magic sacrificed because of me.'

Nick slapped my shoulder. 'Why didn't you just say so instead of wasting my time?'

I rolled my eyes. 'What got your knickers in a twist?' He mumbled something inaudible back. 'Would you mind taking us to her?' I asked.

'Give me a second.' He walked over to a door and opened it. Someone who didn't know any better would think it was just an empty cupboard, but really it was the entrance to Nick's prison. 'She's in the room at the end, behind the giant doors,' he said.

I gave him a nod before Sky and I walked through the portal leading to his prison. We ended up in a dark passage made up of stone.

'Are you okay?' I asked Sky again as I conjured a torch to allow us to see where we were heading.

Sky nodded and looked around. 'Where did Nick go?'

'He's still at home, doing whatever it was he was doing before we interrupted him. Judging by his mood, it seemed to be something important, as he wasn't too pleased to see us.'

'He's one scary guy.'

'He's changed a lot since Lily died.'

'You mean Cassie's mother?'

'Yeah.'

'How did she die?'

'She was protecting Cassie from a demon attack.'

'Is that why she's in the human realm instead of with her dad?'

I shrugged. 'I believe so. Though Nick's house didn't used to be in a demon realm. He and Lily used to live in the human world, but after she died, he moved it so demons wouldn't sense him, but at the cost of his daughter.'

'What do you mean?'

'Because Cassie isn't a full demon, she faces the same dangers as you when entering a demon realm, at least until her powers have matured.'

There was a brief silence as Sky followed me along the damp corridor.

'Why couldn't you just teleport us here?' she asked as she moved her hands over the stone wall.

'Because it's Nick's pocket dimension. He created it, so only he knows the frequency needed to teleport into it.'

'What's a pocket dimension?'

'It's a bit hard to explain, but in a sense, it's a place that can be created between different dimensions or realms. This place is technically under his house but neither in the human world nor in the demon realm.'

'So it's similar to Whitelake village?'

'I think so. At least in theory.'

'So why did he create this place?'

'This is where he takes beings he can't or won't kill for whatever reason.'

Sky's eyes went wide. 'Has he killed a lot of people?'

I shook my head. 'Not people, but some creatures – demons. We all have. It's the sacrifice you have to make to survive in this world.' Guilt tore at my insides when I thought about all the lives I had taken. I remembered every single one of them. Unfortunately they had not given me a choice.

'I can't imagine you killing anyone.'

'I only defended myself and the beings I had sworn to protect. Not one single death from me was offensive. It was all in self-defence, but their blood is still on my hands.'

Sky frowned. 'That doesn't make you a bad guy.'

'I try hard not to be. It's different when it's about survival or if you're fighting in a war. The world is far from black and white. You may believe killing someone is justified and that it would save many people, but you never know what their intentions are. Maybe they believe they are saving people too. So who would then be correct? A war is never as simple as right or wrong, because both sides believe they're right. When you're fighting in a war, it's about not compromising what you believe in. Because if you lose sight of who you are and what you believe in, even though you are victorious, you would have lost the war.'

'And what do you believe in?'

'I believe everyone has a choice. There is a difference between killing and killing in self-defence because they attacked me. If they're not attacking me, how do I know what their intentions are? Are they following orders? Are they forced? Or are they trying to be better?'

'It sounds very complicated. I know you said you only killed in self-defence, but have you ever wanted to kill anyone?'

'Your actions are what defines you, not your thoughts.'

Sky sighed. 'That doesn't answer the question. Did you ever consider killing the witches for what they did to you?'

I stopped walking and turned towards her. I wanted to make sure she knew I was speaking from the heart. 'Due to what I am, I cannot allow myself to give in to temptation, which is why I would never go back and destroy the witch village for what they did to me. Even if I had the chance, I don't know if I could bring myself to kill the old High Priestess. She did what she did because she thought it was the right thing to do. She was wrong to do it, but she acted out of fear. Was the High Priestess wrong to fear me? Yes, and I will never forget the injustice they put me through by separating me from my daughter. But the High Priestess was not wrong to fear demons, so how do you distinguish the difference?'

'I can't believe you're defending the High Priestess. What she did was wrong.'

I started walking again. 'I'm not defending her. I'm just

saying that there are always two sides to a story. Any war will change you, whether it is one you are fighting on the outside or one that is fought inside you. After it's finished, you will never go back to the same person you were before. Even if you win, everything you saw and did to get there will stay with you. It's easy to lose yourself, so before you go into a war willingly, make sure you know where you stand and where your morals lie, and don't ever cross them, even for the greater good.'

When we reached the big wooden doors, I put the torch in the attachment on the wall. 'We're here. Abigail is on the other side of this door. Are you sure you're ready for this?' I asked and opened the doors.

Sky hesitated for a moment before giving me a determined nod. She stepped over the threshold and into the darkness. I followed and closed the door behind us.

SKY

One Scary-Looking Demon

The door slammed shut behind me and I jumped at the sound. The darkness felt suffocating, but Jax's presence was a comfort. I knew he wouldn't let anything bad happen to me.

The torches on the wall lit up, casting an amber light over the room. Instead of the wall of pebbly stones in the corridor, the walls in this room were smooth, and the ceiling was lower.

A dome-shaped enclosure in the middle of the room exuded a dim white light. A skinny middle-aged woman lay on a small bed inside it. I studied her from a distance. She appeared human, but she wasn't hurt when Jax brought her to the demon realm, so she had to be something else –

something demonic.

She sat up as we approached. Her dark brown hair was all tangled and she had dark circles beneath her eyes, which were highlighted by the light from the fire.

'You finally came to see me?' Abigail said in a raspy voice as she spotted us. 'And you brought a girl. Interesting.' She glanced over at me. 'One of the girls from Whitelake village, no less. How did you manage that?'

Her gaze bored into me and I took a step back. Jax placed a hand on my shoulder and stepped in front of me. 'We're not here to answer your questions,' he replied, his voice calm. 'Tell me what you did to Mark.'

Abigail laughed, a crazed cackle that sent shivers down my spine.

'Are we still doing this? It won't help you. Mark can never shift again. It's gone,' she said.

Anger boiled up inside me and I took a step towards her. 'You and I both know that any spell is reversible.'

She got up from the bed and walked up to the energy wall between us, an evil smile plastered on her lips. 'And what is a witch without magic going to do about it?'

I sucked in a breath. 'I'm going to get Mark and everyone else's magic back. What you've done to us is wrong. Don't you feel remorse?'

'You say wrong, I say necessary. We all did what we needed to protect ourselves from him.' She nodded towards Jax. 'If I were you, I'd be running for my life. Demons can't be trusted.'

'Why should I trust anything you say? Aren't you a demon too?'

She pulled back in disgust. 'Do not compare me with those filthy creatures. I'm far above them.'

'So what are you? And what's your connection to Whitelake village?'

'That is none of your business.'

'Well, the way I see it, if you can't even tell me what you are, you can't be trusted either. Besides, you took Mark and the others in and treated them like your children. How could you even bring yourself to do something like that to them – to take away what they are?' I said.

'They would have got themselves killed. I did them a favour. Now Mark can get on with his life as a normal human being.'

I clenched my fists in anger. 'But he's not human. He's a werewolf who, thanks to you, can't shift. Meaning he can't connect with his pack,' I retorted.

Abigail scowled. 'His pack? Don't be ridiculous. He doesn't have a pack. The house got torched because he and Seth didn't have a pack to protect them.'

I took a step towards her. 'You're wrong. His dad was the Beta. They welcomed him and Seth back with open arms.'

'Then he is a fool. Nothing in life gets handed to you. There is always a catch.'

'Yes, the catch is that he ends up being part of a loving pack where he belongs. Not everyone has ulterior motives.'

Abigail let out a chuckle. 'You are so young and naive.'

I shook my head. I hadn't come here to have an argument with her; I'd come to figure out more information about the spell. I cleared my throat, considering what I needed to know. 'So how did you do it? How did you make Mark lose his ability to shift? I know it wasn't the same spell that Hecate used.'

Abigail shrugged, a sly smile on her face. 'I said a few words.'

'What words? How did you stop the innate magic from being accessed and replenished?'

Abigail raised an eyebrow. 'Someone did their homework. But it won't help you. Your magic is gone. And without magic in your veins, you'll die.' She stared into my eyes. 'It's unfortunate, really. Most other beings handle being without magic much better than witches.'

'Is that why you stopped sacrificing thirteen witches each year?'

'We didn't stop. We just branched out. It's easier to go unnoticed without casualties. Less resistance.'

'What do you need the magic for?'

Abigal smirked. 'Wouldn't you like to know?'

My insides shook with anger. Talking to Abigail was like getting water out of a stone. I was on the verge of lashing out when Jax pulled me away from Abigail's view before turning back to her. 'Enough! Are you going to tell us about the spell and how to reverse it or do I need to beat it out of you? Don't think for a moment just because I spared you that I am weak. The only reason you're not dead yet is because of me, and I can easily change that.'

'Oh, you mean you control the demon that put me here? How adorable,' Abigail sneered. 'I thought it was the other way around.'

Jax took a deep breath. I thought he was going to say something, but he stayed quiet. A second later his eyes became red, or maybe it was just the amber light reflected in his eyes. But why hadn't it done that before?

He walked up to the dome and stared at Abigail. 'Tell us about the spell you used.' His voice was filled with authority. If I hadn't known how sweet he could be, seeing him like that would have made me pee my pants.

'I'm not playing around, Abigail,' Jax said, his voice becoming more agitated.

Abigail just glared at him like it didn't faze her at all. 'If I tell you, what's in it for me? Who's to say you won't just kill me?'

'If you don't tell me, I'll make you wish I'd killed you,' Jax threatened.

Abigail laughed. 'You can't get to me. This force field is impenetrable.'

'You would have thought so, but I taught Nick how to make them.' Jax put his hand through the force field. As he did so, the hand turned into a massive black talon with razor-sharp claws. It was a terrifying sight, and I could feel my heart pounding in my chest while I tried to remind myself this was the same Jax I knew wouldn't hurt me.

Abigail backed away from his hand. Her breathing

became shallow and rapid, and she stumbled backwards.

'I'll ask again. Tell us about the spell.' Jax's voice had gone deeper. It didn't sound like him anymore.

'You'll have to beat it out of me,' Abigail answered. It surprised me that her voice was still strong.

'That can be arranged,' Jax said, and a moment later, a dagger appeared in his other hand and he walked into the dome.

I almost passed out as the Jax I knew vanished, replaced by a tall, monstrous black demon with big black wings. His eyes had turned crimson, his face had contorted into a beaked monster with jagged teeth, and both his hands had been replaced by talons with sharp claws. He looked deadly.

Abigail seemed awfully calm, considering. She hadn't moved or tried to get away. If I was in her position, I'd have run the other way as fast as I could. I tried to look away, but my body had frozen in fear and I watched, mesmerised, as Jax put the dagger to Abigail's throat. I wasn't sure why he used it; his claws could have done more damage.

'Spell. Now,' he yelled, his voice bouncing off the walls.

Abigail rolled her eyes. 'Why are you so set on getting the spell? It's not like you can do anything with it. It's not going to help you. You should just accept their fate.'

Jax pressed the blade against Abigail's skin. Blood appeared and trickled down her neck. 'I'm not playing around.'

She let out a breath. 'The spell is in a grimoire, but you need a true High Priestess to jumpstart the magic, and she'll never agree.'

'What grimoire?'

'The sacred one. Though I suppose they're all sacred,' she replied with a smirk.

'Where can I find it?' Jax asked as he pressed the blade deeper into her skin and more blood ran down her neck.

Abigail let out a strained laugh. 'Go on. You know you want to. It's in your nature, after all.'

Just as I thought he might actually kill her, he relaxed his grip and dropped the dagger, allowing Abigail to breathe again. Jax pushed her away and she collapsed on the floor. She was still gasping for air when he strode out of the dome, and as he did so, his whole body turned back into its human form.

I was stunned, staring at him with wide, terrified eyes. I felt a powerful urge to follow Abigail's earlier advice and run. Only I didn't know where to go.

Jax walked towards me, and my knees nearly buckled as I backed away until my back hit the wooden door that led back into the passageway. My heart raced with fear.

JAX

My True Form

Sky's reaction didn't make sense. She was trembling, avoiding eye contact.

The force field. Dammit, why did I bring her here? The force field had stripped me of my glamour and shown her my demon form. No wonder it scared her. Even I feared my demonic form.

I froze on the spot. Worry washed over me. Would she forever see the demon inside me from now on, even though that wasn't who I was?

I took a deep breath, sent out some calming energy towards Sky and ran my hand through my hair. I created a temporary sound barrier so Abigail wouldn't hear us. 'I'm not the monster you saw inside the dome. The dome removes all the magic of anyone inside it. So when I stepped inside, the magic stripped away my human form, which is created by magic in a sense, and showed my demon side. If I had thought about it, I would have warned you, but I'm still me.'

Sky gave me a wary smile. 'You mean that's what you truly look like? No wonder people are scared of you.'

'You're one of a few people that have seen my demon form. It's not something I'm proud of, and I never intentionally turn. I don't enjoy being a demon, but it's what the Fates made me, so it's something I have to live with.'

'It can't be easy to fight your nature.'

'I never let the demon inside me take full control. I'm too worried about hurting someone I love.'

She gave me a sympathetic smile. 'I'm sorry, Jax.'

'What are you sorry for?'

'For not understanding.'

I shrugged. 'It is what it is. There's nothing to understand. However, I would appreciate it if you could keep what you saw between us.'

Her eyes went wide. 'They haven't seen it?'

I shook my head.

Sky stayed quiet for a while before she spoke up. 'You know, you don't need to worry. Everyone can see that Cassie and Leah love you. Even though you look scary as hell, it wouldn't change how they feel about you. They know the true you – what's in your heart. Just think about the werewolves. They look scary when they shift, but we all know they're just people like everyone else.'

My lips turned up in a smile. 'Sky, are you comparing me to a werewolf?'

'Well, you aren't that different.'

I tried to contain my laughter but failed. 'I really need to give you some history books when we get back.'

Sky eyed me for a while.

'I'm sorry we didn't get much information from Abigail,' I said. I should have pushed harder, but I had been close to losing control.

'It's okay. I think I know which book she's talking about. It's in the temple.'

I smiled. 'That's great. Come on, let's go home.'

She frowned. 'We're not going back to Nick's?'

I shook my head. 'No. I can teleport us out of here by myself. We only needed Nick to get into here.'

Sky let out a breath. 'Good. I don't think my heart can handle anything else right now.'

'Tell me about it. That's one demon you don't want to get on the wrong side of,' I said with a smirk. I offered her my hand. 'Come on, let's get out of here and tell the others what we discovered.'

Sky nodded and hesitantly grabbed my arm. I guessed she still wasn't sure about me, but at least she trusted me enough to get her back home.

Sky bolted to the bathroom as soon as we arrived. I followed her and held her hair out of the way as she dry heaved over the toilet. 'I'm so sorry. I know how much you hate teleportation.'

'It's okay. I asked for it,' she answered. I conjured a bottle of water and handed it to her.

We walked back to the living room and sat down on the sofa. Sky let out a yawn as Leah burst into the room. 'Sky, are you okay? Did the spell work?'

'Yeah, I'm fine. Just tired,' she said as she leaned her head against the back of the sofa.

'What did you find out?'

Sky remained quiet.

Leah walked towards us. 'Sky?'

When she still hadn't answered, I moved over to check on her. Her eyes were closed, but she was still breathing and her heart was beating.

'Is she okay?' Leah asked.

I nodded. 'Physically she's fine. She's been through a lot. I'm sure it's just exhaustion.'

Leah gently shook Sky, and she started to stir but fell back to sleep again. 'I think you're right.' She picked up her phone. 'I'll get Mark to watch over her.'

Cassie entered the room and came over to kiss me. 'I'm so happy you're finally back. I know time moves faster there, but you've been gone for most of the day.' She gestured towards Sky on the sofa. 'Is she okay? Did anything happen to her? Did the spell not work?'

'She's asleep,' I answered. 'I think the teleportation and dimension hopping became too much for her.' Not to mention her reaction to seeing my demon form.

The back door flew open with a bang, and Mark marched up to us. 'She'd better be fine.'

'Nothing happened to her. She was fine when we got home,' I said defensively.

'I think it's just exhaustion. Remember how tired I was after my and Jax's trip to the witch village?' Leah said.

Mark gave a grunt as he made his way to the sofa and sat down next to Sky. He stroked her hair and kissed her forehead before whispering things into her ear. She stirred and opened her eyes.

'Are you okay?' Mark asked, stroking her hair.

Sky let out a yawn. 'I'm just tired. I'll be fine once I've rested.'

Mark picked her up in his arms. 'Let's get you home.' He gave us all an annoyed stare as he walked out of the house.

After Mark had left with Sky, I apologised to Cassie and went outside and transformed into a crow. I needed a moment to myself to recharge mentally. I had been so close to letting the demon take over interrogating Abigail. What would have happened if I had lost control? Would Abigail have been dead? I shook my head and concentrated my mind on the cool air that rushed between my feathers as I circled over the treetops. The sun had started to go down, painting the sky in various shades of pink and orange. I kept flying until the stars came out.

When I got back, Leah and Cassie had already ordered takeaway, which we shared in front of the TV. Cassie cuddled up to me and I put my arm around her, overwhelmed with joy at how strong our relationship was becoming. But would it be strong enough if she saw what I truly was?

'I have a surprise to show you,' Cassie said as the TV programme finished.

'What is it?'

'You'll see, but you have to close your eyes and trust me.'

I looked over at Leah to try to get an indication of what Cassie wanted to show me, but she kept her poker face.

We got up from the sofa, and Leah gave Cassie a scarf to tie over my eyes. What could the surprise be? She led me upstairs, and by my calculations, we were standing in my bedroom. Or, more correctly, *our* bedroom now, since she had agreed to move in with me.

She kissed my nose and removed the blindfold. Why were we here? I scanned the room and a feeling of happiness entered my chest. She had moved all her stuff in. There was even some furniture I'd never seen before. But the best part was the shelves above the bed that contained several framed photos of us together.

'What d'you think?'

'I love it,' I said, giving her a kiss.

'Good. It was hell moving everything around,' Leah shouted from outside the room. Cassie rolled her eyes, which made me laugh.

Later we went to bed together in our bedroom and I fell asleep with a smile on my face.

SKY

NIGHTMARES FROM HELL

Mark walked all the way back to the cabin with me in his arms. I tried to tell him that I could walk, but he insisted on carrying me, so I nuzzled into his chest. The warmth of his body mixed with his familiar smell made me feel safe.

He placed me carefully on the bed and kissed my forehead. 'Just rest. I'm right outside if you need me.'

Before he moved away from the bed, I grabbed his arm. 'Please stay.'

His eyes met mine. 'Are you sure? Leah said you needed to rest.'

I nodded. He got onto the bed, and I cuddled up next to him with my head resting on his chest and he put his arm around me. It was exactly what I needed, and I couldn't imagine not having him by my side.

I shifted my head and gazed into his eyes. 'When we get our magic back, I will accept you as my mate.'

Mark stroked my hair. 'Let's talk about it later when you have your strength back. Try and get some rest.'

I closed my eyes and fell asleep. The next thing I knew I was transported to a strange and unfamiliar place. A heavy veil of dust obscured the sky, and the sun cast an eerie orange glow over the surroundings. The atmosphere was oppressive and suffocating, with the scent of sulphur thick in the air. My throat felt raw and scratchy, and a hacking cough or gag followed every breath.

I tore a strip of fabric from my shirt and tied it around my face, desperate for some relief. It helped a little, though the air still smelled like rotten eggs. Where the hell was I?

My eyes roamed around the barren, rocky landscape, searching for anything familiar. But all I saw was emptiness and uncertainty. There was no vegetation to be seen anywhere, not even a single blade of grass. I tried to piece together how I'd got here, but my memories were foggy. The last thing I remembered was being asleep in my bed. Could I be dreaming? I shook my head. This place felt too real to be a dream.

As I stumbled across the porous rocks, the hot ground scorched the soles of my bare feet. Sweat dripped down my spine and I struggled to keep going. I needed to find shelter, shade and a source of water, or I wouldn't survive. How had

I got here? And how would I get home?

I set off down a path, searching for any signs of life. Moving was a struggle and my lungs were screaming for clean air, but I pushed on. I was ready to give up when I caught sight of a moving shadow in the distance. A flicker of hope lit up inside me. Someone else was here. I quickened my speed, eager to catch up with them and ask for their assistance. Maybe they knew how to get out of here. As I drew closer, I realised the silhouette wasn't human. It reminded me of Jax's monstrous demon shape. Was Jax here too?

I shouted, but my voice came out as a hoarse whisper, unable to travel through the thick dust and reach the being in front of me. The earth beneath me trembled, causing me to stop and regain my balance so I wouldn't fall. As I had to move more slowly, the distance between us grew. The creature started climbing up a massive mountain, and a bad feeling overcame me as the ground growled underneath me.

The ground shook violently and cracks appeared in the porous rocks. Hissing sounds echoed around me. I dropped to my hands and knees to maintain my balance. As the cracks between the stones grew, burning red liquid filled them. An explosion caused me to cover my ears with my hands. The mountain the being was climbing was spitting out a red, glowing liquid from the top, which was making its way downhill.

Panic rose inside me. My heart pounded in my chest and my breathing became shallow. The red liquid was close to reaching him now. I had to warn him. I got to my feet, screaming my lungs out while moving as quickly as I could manage between the cracks. I wasn't sure he could hear me, but as I got closer, he turned around. And I realised it wasn't Jax. The creature was something else. Its malevolent force consumed me as its black, piercing eyes fixated on me. My body froze, making me unable to move. I gazed up pleadingly at the creature, but it just gave me a sinister smirk.

The landscape shook again, creating a crack in the ground underneath me and sending me hurtling towards the red liquid below. Panic consumed me, and I screamed in terror as I plummeted towards my fiery fate.

'Shh. It's only a dream. I'm right here.' Mark's soothing voice rang out. Relief flooded through me and I tried to open my eyes, to tell him that I was okay, but they wouldn't open. I tried to move my hand, open my mouth to talk, but my body did not respond to my commands. Somehow I'd become trapped inside myself. My heart pounded in my chest. What was happening?

JAX

REPERCUSSIONS

The sound of the phone woke me up. I looked out of the window as I answered the call. It was still dark outside, with no sign of dawn brewing. Who was calling at this time?

'Hello?'

'Something's wrong with Sky. She won't wake up,' Mark said in a panicked voice.

I sat up in bed. 'What do you mean, she won't wake up?'

'Something's happened. She screamed, and ever since then, I can't get her to wake up. It's like she's not even there.'

'What do you mean, she's not there?'

'I don't know. Like someone took her soul away from her body or something.'

'Hold on. Let me teleport over.' I ended the call.

Cassie looked over at me with worried eyes, biting her lip. 'What's happened to Sky?'

'I'm not sure. I'm going over to check.' I kissed her and teleported to the cabin.

When I arrived, Mark was pacing back and forth in the bedroom. He stopped and looked up as I entered. 'What happened when you went to talk to Abigail? You promised you would keep her safe.'

'I did. Nothing happened while we were there.'

Mark walked over and removed some hair from Sky's face. 'Then why is she like this?'

I shook my head. 'I don't know. There could be a million reasons.'

'Well, she was fine before you took her to see Abigail, so you need to fix her.'

I nodded. 'I will try, but if it's something spell related, it may be worth getting Leah.'

'I'll text her.'

I bent down and looked at Sky. There didn't seem to be anything physically wrong with her; all her limbs were there and her heart was beating steadily. I sent out my energies to pick up on anything supernatural. I detected nothing unusual. Why wasn't she waking up?

'Can you fix her?' Mark asked with tears in his eyes.

I glanced over at him. 'I've found nothing that can explain this. She seems fine, and there's no foreign or supernatural energies around her.'

'Well, she's not fine. You need to do something. This is all your fault. You should never have taken her with you.'

My gaze went to Sky again. Her face was relaxed and her breathing was deep and even. Anyone would have thought she was just sleeping. Her eyelids caught my attention, and on closer inspection, I noticed they were moving, almost like she was having a dream. I lifted her eyelids; her eyes were all glazed over. It reminded me of Freya and how her eyes changed when she zoned out. Was that what was happening? Was Sky having a vision?

I shook her lightly, but she didn't respond. I looked up at Mark. 'Did she ever mention anything about visions to you?'

'No. Why?'

'Her eyes are glazed over like she's having one.'

'You're telling me she's been having a vision for the last half hour?'

'I don't know.' That was a long time. Freya's ones usually only lasted a few moments. Something else must be going on. Why wasn't she waking up? I thought back to the collapsed horse in Edmond's stable. He had thought it was going to die, but somehow I'd used my energy to heal it. Maybe I could try something similar on Sky.

I held Sky's hand in mine, took a few deep breaths to centre myself and closed my eyes, visualising a bright light flowing from my core and into Sky. I had always envisioned it as sharing part of my life force, but I didn't know if that was true. The charge of the energy tingled as it moved down my arm and onto Sky's.

I opened my eyes when something pushed me to the side. Mark towered over the bed and cupped her face. 'Babe, I'm right here.'

Sky slowly opened her eyes and tried to sit up. Mark helped her and placed a pillow behind her back.

I caught Sky's gaze. 'What happened?'

She shook her head. 'I don't know. I had this horrible dream about being burned alive. When I woke up, I couldn't move or open my eyes. It felt like I was trapped, and no matter what I did, I couldn't break through. Until I saw this light. It flowed into me, gave me strength, and helped me to finally break through to the surface.'

I gave her a smile, happy my energy had helped her.

'You are never to go to the demon realm again. I don't know what I would do if I lost you,' Mark said to Sky before turning to me. 'It's all your fault.' His chest puffed up and his eyes dilated.

I prepared for the impact. I deserved it. After all, I had let Sky come along, even though it was against my better judgement. No one but demons should travel to demon realms.

'Stop it. This is not Jax's fault. It was my choice. I chose to go. Besides, we don't even know if it's related,' Sky said.

She was right, but it didn't help my guilty conscience. It had happened right after we'd got back, so the chances it wasn't related were slim.

Watching Mark fuss over Sky made me feel like I was intruding. 'I'm going to leave you two to catch up. Maybe we can figure out our next step when you feel better,' I said as I made my way to the door.

'I'm fine. Get Cassie and Leah and we'll meet you in the living room in a bit.'

'Okay,' I said as I left the bedroom and walked out to the living room. Cassie, Leah and Seth looked up from the sofa. 'You're here?' I asked.

'Of course. If Mark's worried enough to ask you for help, it's obviously not good,' Leah said.

'Is she going to be okay?' Seth asked.

I nodded. 'I think so. She's up and awake.'

'Thank you.'

I sat down next to Cassie and leaned my head on her shoulder. Using a lot of energy always came at a price, even for me. Only I recovered quicker from it.

'Are you okay?' Cassie asked. 'What did you do to make her wake up?'

'I gave her my energy.'

Cassie looked at me with a crease on her forehead. I was about to explain it when Sky and Mark walked into the living room.

'Great – you're all here,' Sky said with a smile. She looked energised and rested, with no sign of what she just been through. 'Anyone know of a way we can get back to Whitelake village?'

Everyone stared at Sky, and she glanced down at the floor. Mark wrapped an arm around her shoulder. She cleared her throat. 'So that we can get the book.'

'What book?' Leah asked with a frown.

Sky met her gaze. 'The one with the spell in.'

'I haven't told them what we discovered yet. I wanted to wait until you were rested,' I said.

Sky gave me a nod. 'We spoke to Abigail. She told us the spell she used on Mark was in a book that's kept at the temple. If we can get our hands on it, we're one step closer to figuring out how to get Mark's shifting back and mine and the other witches' magic.'

'Maybe we can go through the portal Jax and Leah went through to get to the village,' Cassie suggested.

I shook my head. 'We can't go back to Whitelock Unlimited. They would have been alerted about what is going on by now. If nothing else, they would know Abigail is missing. It's likely to be crawling with people.'

'How else do you expect us to get it? It's in another realm. It's not like we can just drive there,' Cassie said, defeated.

'Maybe we can get Leaf to create a connection circle that you can teleport to. It worked to teleport out of there. Maybe it works to teleport back,' Leah said.

Sky hesitated. 'I'm not sure if that works. But it's worth talking to Leaf. Maybe she knows some way to get me back into the village.'

'Not happening. I don't want you to go anywhere. You almost got yourself killed last time you went to another realm,' Mark said sternly.

Sky threw her arms up in the air. 'This is not the same. This isn't some demon realm. It's my home. Nothing's going to happen.'

I could tell she was eager to go, but for once I agreed with Mark. 'Mark's right. We don't know what caused you not to wake up. It's too risky. It's probably better if I go.'

'You?' Sky said, cocking an eyebrow. 'No offence, but you don't know the village as well as I do. You don't even know what book you're looking for. I do.' She gave me a pleading look.

I let out a sigh. 'Let's get all the facts first. You can talk to Leaf and see if she knows a way to get back to the village. I will talk to Freya. Once I'm back, we can come up with a plan. Sounds good?' I glanced around at everyone, making sure they understood. My eyes settled on Sky. 'I mean it. Do not do anything until I get back.'

I teleported to Freya's realm. The journey to her house was uneventful. Grey clouds filled the sky, and the light rain continued for the entire journey. I landed on the veranda and transformed into my human form before walking into her cottage. I didn't bother knocking. She knew it was me – she always did.

I heard Freya's voice as soon as I stepped inside.

'Come join us for some tea. It is a new herbal mix I am trying out.'

I entered the living room. Freya sat on a chair next to the fire, with one cat in her lap and the other curled up by her feet. I kissed her cheeks and sat down in the chair next to her. I stretched my feet towards the fire, appreciating its heat, and took in the comforting smell of burning wood. 'Us?' I said with a smirk. 'Is there someone else here?' Even though I knew she was referring to the cats.

She rolled her eyes and gave me a warm smile. 'What can I do for you, Jax?' she said as she handed me a cup of tea.

'We figured out where the book is kept, but we need to go back to the witch village to get it.'

Freya tilted her head. 'But that is not why you are here.'

I met her gaze. 'No. Something happened to Sky after we got back from Nick's.'

'And you want to know if I know something about that.'

I nodded in response.

Her breathing became slower and her eyes glazed over. I took a sip of tea while I waited for her to come back to reality. The flavour surprised me. There was a taste I couldn't place. It almost tasted like peach, but with the aftertaste of something tangy. I was deep in thought when Freya gasped. My attention darted towards her. 'What did you find out?'

'The realm unlocked something inside Sky.'

'So it was my fault she couldn't wake up?'

Freya placed her hand on mine and gave me a sad smile. 'So quick to blame yourself. It would have happened whether she went with you or not. The journey only accelerated the inevitable.'

'What do you mean?'

'The visions she had are a part of her. They have been and always will be part of her.'

'But she couldn't wake up.'

Freya let out a breath. 'It is because her body lacks the

strength to restore itself without magic coursing through her veins. A witch is never supposed to be without her magic.'

'So it will happen again?'

'I do not know. Your energy gave her the tools she needed to recover. It may be enough for now.'

I nodded as I tried to take in everything she had said. The cat in her lap meowed.

'Yes, Amber. I know I should, but now is not the time.' Freya looked up at me. 'What did you think about the tea?'

'It was interesting. What's it made from?'

'Oh, just some fruit and herbs from the garden.'

'Should I be worried I'll end up with an extra arm or something?' I said with a smirk.

She laughed warmly. 'It will help replenish your energy. You will need it after giving away all that energy to Sky. Speaking of Sky. I think it is time for you to go. She is an impatient one, and you would not want her to do anything foolish that she will regret.'

The cat jumped down and Freya got up and walked over to me. I rose in my chair, and as she hugged me, I bent down to kiss her goodbye.

'Remember to follow your instincts,' she said as she let me go.

When I got home, Leah and Sky were mixing herbs together and looking through a spell book. They didn't acknowledge me.

'Leah, we need something that belongs to Whitelake village. But I belong there, so maybe some of my hair would work,' Sky was saying as I arrived.

'You're home,' Cassie said with relief in her voice. She made her way over and kissed me. 'Maybe you can talk them out of it. I tried, but they aren't listening to me.'

'Talk them out of what? What are they doing?'

'They spoke to Leaf and she told them how she got Leah and her father out of the village all those years ago and said maybe the same spell could help get Sky back to the village. So Leah is helping her prepare for the journey,' Cassie said.

'They're doing what?' Heat was flowing through my veins, feeding the sleeping demon inside. Was this what Freya had wanted me to stop them doing?

Mark walked up to me. 'Nice to see that you agree it's a stupid idea for her to go all by herself. I couldn't get through to her, but maybe you can ... But then again, you let her come with you to the demon realm, so I guess we're doomed.'

I wasn't sure what he wanted me to reply. Was he joking? Was he being serious? Did it even warrant a reply?

Leah looked up from what she was doing and smiled. 'Good. You're back. We can use your help.'

I glared at her. Hadn't she realised I didn't agree with what they were doing?

Her smile faltered. 'Or maybe not. What did Freya say?'

'She said I should go home and stop you from doing something you'll regret.' I shook my head in defeat. Why didn't anyone ever listen to me? 'I told you not to do anything until I got back.'

'You're back now. And we haven't done the spell yet,'

Leah said with a cheeky grin.

'And that's the best way to get there. Even Leaf agreed,' Sky chimed in before eyeing me up. 'If you know a better way, I'm all ears.'

I ground my teeth, trying to control the frustration inside me. 'Not yet.'

'So it's settled, then,' Sky said.

'If Freya didn't think it was a good idea, maybe we should find another way,' Cassie said.

'No. Time is running out. We need to get our hands on that book, and this is the best way to do it.' Sky turned towards Leah. 'How's the preparations coming along? Are we almost ready?'

Leah looked around, indecisiveness in her eyes. She took a deep breath and closed her eyes. The contents of the bowl made a puffing sound, and smoke appeared from it. 'Yeah, I think we're ready. All you have to do is place the quartz crystals in a circle around you, pour some of the potion on your skin and think of home.' She poured the contents into a vial and handed it to Sky. 'It's your choice, but maybe you should listen to Jax.'

Sky huffed. 'Why don't any of you understand? It's not your future that's at stake here. It's mine and all the other witches' who had their magic sacrificed.'

'How about we all go?' I asked, trying to meet them in the middle. At least I would be around to protect them if anything happened.

Sky shook her head. 'We can't. It's only built for one

person. The only reason Leaf managed both of them was because Leah was a toddler.'

I took a seat next to Mark. It was obvious nothing I said would make Sky change her mind. 'Mark, why don't you do something?'

He gave me an annoyed glance. 'You don't think I've tried? Short of holding her down, there's nothing I can do to stop her.'

I let out a sigh, and Cassie walked over to join us. 'It'll be fine.'

I took her hand in mine. The tension eased from my body as my fingers drew circles on her palm. 'I hope you're right.'

We watched as Leah and Sky set everything up. When they were done, they came over. Sky embraced Mark, and Mark's eyes became watery.

I squeezed Cassie's hand, happy she was safe by my side. Would I have been as understanding as Mark? No – I would probably have locked Cassie away to keep her safe.

Sky said bye to Leah and Cassie and turned to me. 'Don't say I didn't warn you,' I said before giving her a hug. 'Please be careful.'

Leah performed the ceremony, and as she continued to chant, Sky disappeared from inside the circle. Leah thanked all the elements and opened the circle before taking a seat next to us.

'How do we know she got there okay?' Cassie asked.

'I would have felt it if something had happened to her,'

Mark said.

'How? I thought you hadn't mated yet.'

Cassie's choice of words made me chuckle. Mark shot me a glare, and I quickly covered my mouth with my hand and pretended to cough. Now was not the time for jokes.

'She's my mate and she hasn't rejected me. Trust me, I would know.'

Cassie nodded as Leah came and joined us. 'What do we do now?'

'Now we wait. Though she probably won't go looking for the book until tomorrow,' I said, not knowing what else we could do.

'Maybe we can contact Leaf and see that she got there okay,' Cassie said.

'Do you know where she put the stone?' Leah asked.

Cassie shook her head. 'No, but we can't just sit around worrying.'

Mark got up from the sofa. 'You're right. I'm going to go and look for the stone in the cabin.' He walked out and left the three of us.

'I'm going to have a nap. I'm exhausted.' Leah left the room, and the stairs creaked as she made her way up to her bedroom.

I turned to Cassie. 'What would you like to do?'

She hesitated. 'Maybe we can practise my teleportation? I don't know if I'll be able to concentrate, but anything is better than just sitting here. Besides, we haven't done any practising since before Sky got here.'

'Okay. But we're starting small.'

Cassie nodded in agreement.

'First thing, you need to picture the place you want to go, every tiny detail, and then imagine that you're already there. Let's think of our bedroom.'

Cassie closed her eyes. 'I'm picturing it now.'

I watched her closely, confident she wouldn't be able to do it on her first try. My heart almost stopped as she started to flicker.

Paranoia hit me. What if she teleported somewhere I couldn't find her, or worse, get stuck somewhere in between, if that was even possible?

'Cassie?'

She became solid again and opened her eyes. 'What?'

I took her hand. 'Are you sure you want to do this?'

She looked up at me with big eyes. 'Yes.'

'But what if you get stuck somewhere and I can't get to you?'

She gave me a reassuring kiss. 'But how am I going to learn if you won't let me try?'

She had a point. I was being overprotective. I needed to let her try. I needed to believe she could do it.

'Besides, you'd always find me,' she said with a smile.

She closed her eyes again and flickered. I held my breath, not sure if I wanted her to succeed or not. A moment later, she disappeared. My heart started racing until I heard her shout from upstairs. 'I did it!'

I teleported myself to our bedroom. Before I'd even

looked up, Cassie threw herself at me. 'I did it!' Light beamed from her eyes.

Her touch smoothed my tense muscles, and my shoulders relaxed. I gave her a kiss. 'Yeah, you did.' Pride engulfed me. I couldn't believe she had managed it on the first try.

'Let me try getting back downstairs again.' She closed her eyes, and this time there was almost no flicker before she disappeared from sight. I joined her downstairs.

'I can't believe I can really teleport. Let me try one more time,' she said with a smile. She closed her eyes. There was a small flicker, but she stayed where she was. She opened her eyes and bit her lip. 'Why didn't it work this time?'

I walked up and hugged her. 'Teleporting takes energy. Sometimes your body needs to recharge before you can teleport again.'

Cassie sighed before looking up at me with hopeful eyes. 'Maybe we can try again tomorrow?'

I smiled. 'Sure.'

22

SKY

Whitelake Village

Energy entered my body. I let it consume me as I thought about the excitement of telling Leaf everything that had happened since I'd left. I could feel a shift in the air, and when I opened my eyes, I was sitting in the courtyard. The sun cast long shadows as it descended in the west. Looking around, I caught sight of Leaf standing by the house with a warm smile on her face.

I ran over and hugged her. 'How did you know I was here?'

'I felt a change in the air and thought it was you. I'm happy it worked,' Leaf said. 'Come on, let's have some supper and you can tell me about your plan.'

We walked into the cottage, and I sat down in the common room and Leaf went to get some soup from the kitchen. How I had missed her cooking.

'Hi,' Eva said as she took a seat next to me. 'I'm glad you came back. I wasn't sure if you would. You left so suddenly.'

I gave her an apologetic smile. 'I'm sorry I didn't say goodbye.'

Leaf came back to the table with two bowls of soup. 'Hi, Eva. Do you want me to get you some soup too?'

Eva shook her head. 'I've already eaten.' She turned back to me. 'Tell me what you've been up to.'

I told them everything that had happened since I'd left. Both of them listened, intrigued. 'Anyway, after we questioned Abigail, she told us the spell was in the grimoire.'

'You mean the book that never leaves the temple?' Eva asked with wide eyes. I nodded.

'That's great news. It means the spell can be cast using elemental magic,' Leaf said.

I nodded. 'Yeah, but by the sounds of things, we need to jumpstart the regeneration to get the magic back.'

'How are you planning on getting your hands on the book? It's not like they will let you walk up to it and take it during a ceremony,' Eva said.

'True, but it has to be somewhere around the temple when it's not in use.'

'How will you get into the temple to look? I know it is open to everyone, but people may recognise you from the sacrifices,' Eva said.

'Are you sure? It's been more than a year. I never really paid any attention unless it was someone I knew.'

'The High Priestess will know.'

'Then I guess I need to avoid her and hope the Fates are on my side. As long as she's not around, I can pretend to be one of her students or maybe even one of the servants.'

'You're not planning on going now, are you?' Leaf asked. 'It's quite the trek, and it's dark outside. Better to get some sleep first.'

I nodded and muffled a yawn. 'I could do with some sleep.'

I said good night to Leaf and followed Eva to our sleeping quarters. My bed and everything else was as I had left it, but it didn't feel like home anymore.

I spent some time catching up with some of the other people in the house before I went to sleep. And though I had been around these people for more than a year, our conversations felt shallow and it was clear to me I didn't belong here anymore. My home was with Mark in the human world.

I woke up with a gasp. I'd been dreaming about the volcanic place again, but luckily I hadn't been trapped this time. Looking around, everyone was still asleep, and it was still dark outside, but the sky had started to brighten. Unwilling to go back to sleep, as the dream still lingered, I got up. The faster I could get my hands on the grimoire, the quicker I could go home. I left Leaf a note so she wouldn't worry and set off on my journey to the temple.

As Leaf's house was on the far outskirts of the village. It was quite the walk, but it felt excruciatingly slow. I was trudging along, debating if I had been stuck in an endless loop, when a few houses appeared in the distance.

I continued on the path that would become one of the main roads leading to the temple as the sun peeked up over the horizon. The houses towered on both sides of me now, and I couldn't help but think back to all the times my family had gone into the village together. My life hadn't been great, and I'd often felt like I didn't belong, but I still missed them. Were they still wondering where I'd gone?

I stopped outside the temple and caught my breath. It was a chilly day, but my fast pace had sped up my circulation and sweat dripped down my back. The last time I'd been inside the temple was the day they'd stripped my magic away.

Anger filled me, and I did my best not to take it out on the stairs. There weren't many people about, and it was still too early in the morning for any ceremonies to be happening, but I needed to remain inconspicuous. I entered the temple, which appeared to be empty, and made my way to the back, where the ceremonial altar was located. If I was a spell book, where would I be?

I searched around the altar and lifted the cloth covering it to see if there was a cupboard underneath. No luck. They obviously stored the book somewhere else when it wasn't in use. I went over to the side and opened one of the doors. It was a utility room. I doubted they would hide the book between the brooms and mops, so I tried the door next to it.

This was more like it. My eyes caught sight of different stones, and several herbs were hung up to dry. There were even a few athames and other ceremonial objects lying on a table. I opened the drawers and the cupboards along the side, looking for the book.

As I rummaged through a drawer, someone tapped me on the shoulder. I froze, and my heart stopped for a moment. I hadn't heard anyone opening the door, but I'd obviously been busted. *Think.* Maybe I could pretend to be one of the students who worked under Hecate. I picked up some candles from the drawer and turned around, preparing what to say, but the moment I laid eyes on my sister, my mouth went dry.

Her eyes were enormous with shock, and a second later she almost tripped me over as she jumped me with a big hug.

'Oh my gods, I thought I would never see you again. Where have you been and what are you doing here?'

'I'm sorry,' I said as guilt overtook me. 'How is everyone?'

'Mum took it very hard when you ran away. She blamed herself. She kept hoping you would come back. But after a couple of weeks she realised you weren't, but she still leaves the outdoor light on just in case.'

I sucked in a breath. 'What about Night?'

'He thinks you abandoned him. We knew you were unhappy about losing your magic, but it was for the greater good. Running away from everything was childish. Did none of us matter to you?'

I scratched my head and stared at the ground. 'It's not like that. Of course you matter, but I had to do it.'

Dawn rolled her eyes. 'You've always been selfish. Only thinking about yourself. What reason did you have to run away?'

'I needed to find out the truth.'

'The truth about what?'

'The sacrifices. Everything you think is for the greater good – well, it isn't. The High Priestess and Hecate take people's magic, but for what?'

She sighed. 'You know why. It's to keep us safe from the demon.'

I cocked an eyebrow. 'Yeah? Well, I've met the demon you're talking about, and believe me, he has no intention of destroying our village.'

'You're talking rubbish. We both know demons are evil and can't be trusted,' she said with narrowed eyes.

'You may be right about other demons, but I trust Jax with my life.'

She took my hands in hers and looked at me with concern. 'I will pray for you. You're obviously under some kind of spell.'

I removed my hands and took a step back. 'I'm not under a spell. You are. But I'm going to fix it.'

'Fix what?'

'Hecate has taken magic that isn't hers to take. Lives have been ruined. So I need to find the grimoire so I can make things right.'

Dawn's eyes went wide. 'You can't be serious!'

'I am. You're working for a liar. I'm not sure why Hecate is pretending to help the village, but you don't need protection from the demon we've all been told to fear growing up. He's not evil, and he's not after revenge.'

Dawn stared at me with furrowed eyebrows. 'I will not help you destroy your life. Stealing the book is a death sentence. You need to leave, or I will call the High Priestess.'

'Fine. I'm leaving,' I said, holding my hands up. 'But losing my magic was a death sentence. And this is a chance for me to set things straight. I'm dying anyway so may as well give my life for this cause.' I turned and dashed out of the room, closing the door on my sister before she had a chance to say anything else.

My heart was racing. I snuck through the door on the other side of the altar to the room that was used as a holding place before the ceremonies. Hopefully Dawn wouldn't find me. I took a deep breath to clear my head. I needed to focus on the book. Where should I look next?

Another door caught my eye. I opened it and was met by stairs. I followed them down into a long corridor and tried the first door on the right. As I stepped inside, a smile formed on my lips. The room was full of ceremonial artefacts. The book had to be in there.

I scanned the room more closely. A big glass display table was located at the back. I walked up to it and there, underneath the glass, was the grimoire I'd been looking for, bound in leather, with the symbol of the Triple Goddess within a pentagram on the front.

Full of anticipation, I tried to open the cabinet with trembling fingers, but to my dismay, it was locked. I looked around for the key. Where would they keep it?

'I see you found the grimoire.'

I turned around and came face to face with a young lady I'd never encountered before. She wore a long white dress and had a circle of white flowers on top of her blond hair. 'Are you looking for this?' She held up a large key.

I nodded.

She gave me a sly smile. 'Why would you need the key? It's not like you could do any of the spells.'

'Why do you say that?' I asked.

'Your magic was taken away from you, wasn't it, Sky?'

I jerked at the use of my name, uneasiness filling my body. How did she know who I was? 'Who are you?'

She smiled. 'I'm someone that can get your magic back. You just need to trade for another magic. And I'm sensing you have something else to trade with.'

I glanced around the room, unsure what to say. Who was this person?

'I can get your magic back. All you have to do is give up your mate bond.'

My eyes went wide. 'How do you know about that?'

'Oh my dear, I could sense it a mile away,' she said with a sly smile.

'What about my mate? What would happen to him?'

'Don't worry about him. He will continue as normal,

oblivious to what has been taken.'

'Can you give him his ability to shift back too?'

'Sorry. It doesn't work that way. Either you get your magic back or he gets his magic back. I cannot create magic, only change its form.'

My heart beat faster. I could have my magic back. I opened my mouth to say yes but hesitated. I would lose Mark in the process. A person I'd come to love. Could I really give him up to get my magic back? No. He meant too much to me now. Maybe there was another way. 'I need to think about it,' I finally replied.

'What is there to think about? I know your deepest desire is to get your magic back, and I'm offering it to you.'

'What about the others?'

'They are not your problem now, are they?'

I wasn't sure what to say to that. Maybe it wasn't my problem, but I still cared about the other witches who had lost their magic.

'Very well, I'll give you an hour. When the time is up, I will come and see you for your answer. Now leave this place.' She dismissed me with a wave of her hand.

A second later, I was standing outside the temple and she was gone. Witches could not teleport. A weird numbness spread over me as the realisation I'd just spoken to Hecate, but in her younger form, seeped in. I could have my magic back or I could get Mark's ability to shift back, but either way I would have to give up my mate bond. Indecisiveness weighed heavy on my heart. What was I going to choose?

I sat down on a bench at the edge of the market, the temple looming over me to the left, reminding me I had a choice to make. The turmoil inside me was overwhelming. My eyes wandered to the market in the courtyard, where people were setting up their stands and getting ready for a new day of customers. They all seemed so carefree. I wished I could be one of them.

I desperately wanted my magic back, but my reason for it had changed since I'd met Mark. If only I could talk to him, feel his warm embrace and the safety of his love. But I knew what he would say. The mate bond is holy. He wouldn't want me to give it up. But I wouldn't allow myself to mate with Mark until I got my magic back. There was no way I would send Mark to an early death. He meant too much to me, but if I sacrificed the bond, he wouldn't be my mate anymore.

The wind picked up, whipping my hair across my face, and I shivered. I was stuck between a rock and a hard place. The weight of my decision lay heavily on my chest. Whatever decision I made, I would end up losing Mark one way or another.

I was lost in thought when a surge of energy enveloped me, and before I knew what was happening, I was standing in front of the temple. Footsteps echoed over the water flowing from the cleansing pond as Hecate made her way down the stairs. She had returned to her better-known form, a woman in her thirties with a black dress and black hair.

When she stopped in front of me, a mixture of fear and awe entered my body.

'Have you decided what you want to do?'

'I can never betray Mark like that.' My voice came out strong and confident. I'd thought about getting my magic back, but my love for Mark went beyond that, and I knew I would rather die than do something to hurt him.

'You're saying your mate bond is more important than your life?'

I nodded. This was what Mark would have wanted. There were only a few more days until the full moon, but if I told him my worries, maybe we could come up with another solution to be together.

'You're condemning both of you to a short life. You need magic for your body to remain healthy.'

'Then why are you taking it? We both know the sacrifices aren't needed.'

Hecate tilted her head. 'But aren't they? They are the reason your village is still safe.'

'No they aren't. The demon you're pretending to protect this village from isn't evil.'

'How can you be so sure.'

'Because I know him.'

Hecate's eyes went wide. 'You trust a demon over the protector of your village?'

'You're not our protector. If you were, you wouldn't take our magic and condemn us to an early death.'

'Some actions are justified. Would you not sacrifice

yourself for your mate's life?'

'Of course I would. It's why I won't accept him as my mate until I get my magic back, but ..."

Hecate waved her hand. I felt something inside me break, and an emptiness filled my soul. Tears fell down my face. 'What did you do?'

'I gave him his wolf back in exchange for the bond.'

Anger boiled up inside me. 'I never asked you to do that.'

She smiled coldly. 'But you did. You said you would sacrifice yourself for your mate. However, there is another way for you to get your magic back. You're special and can be of use to me. I'm not sure why I didn't feel it before. I will give you your magic if you agree to work under me.'

'I thought you couldn't create magic.'

'I can't, but there's a loophole. I will transform some of my magic to enable it to flow in your veins, and it will restore your own magic and you won't fade, but you would have to work under me and the High Priestess, staying and studying in the temple with the other students and learning to hone your craft.'

Could it really be that simple? 'I need to talk to someone first,' I said. There had to be a catch, but if I worked in the temple, maybe I could find a way to destroy Hecate for what she'd done and get the magic back to everyone who had had their magic sacrificed.

'I've already given you more than enough time. Agree to work for me or perish like the rest of the people that have lost their magic. It's a simple choice, don't you think?'

'Okay. I'll do it,' I answered, sounding more sure than I felt.

'Great.' She waved her hand and some sort of bracelets made of purple light appeared in the air. They floated towards me and attached themselves to my wrists. I watched as they disintegrated into my skin. 'What was that for?'

'You belong to me now.' She looked at me, an evil smile forming on her lips, and I knew I'd made a terrible mistake.

'Make sure you are in the temple within the hour, or you will realise the consequences of your defiance,' she said and disappeared in a cloud of smoke.

I slumped down on the ground, my legs too weak to support my weight. Everyone would be so worried when I didn't come back, and Mark would never forgive me for breaking the bond.

I brought my hand to my face and cried silently. How had I got myself into this mess? Why hadn't I listened to Jax when he'd said Freya had warned him we were about to do something stupid?

JAX

Mark's Wolf

I flew over the forest, enjoying the cold air and the view of the sun moving up from the horizon. A few hours later, as I was making my way back to the house, a scream echoed through the air. I darted towards the sound. Mark was hunched over on the ground, screaming in pain. What was going on?

I landed and took on my human form. 'Mark, are you alright? What's happening?'

'The bond. The bond is breaking,' he said between clenched teeth.

I grabbed him and teleported us back to the house.

'Leah! Cassie!' I shouted as I carefully placed Mark on the sofa, scared I would cause him more pain. Leah and Cassie came rushing down the stairs.

'What's happening?' Leah said as Cassie rushed to Mark's side.

'He said the bond is breaking. I'm assuming he meant the bond between him and Sky.'

A growl escaped Mark's lips. Cassie held his hand. By the look of it, he had her hand in a tight grip. Her fingers were almost white, like he was cutting off the circulation, but her face did not portray any pain, only worry for her brother. I took a step towards her, but she shook her head.

Leah looked at me with wide, worried eyes. 'Something must have happened to Sky.'

Helplessness filled me as Mark bent over in pain again. Cassie sat next to him, trying to soothe him with no luck. Leah had sprung into action and was currently creating some sort of potion.

I thought about the energy I had given to Sky that had woken her up from her sleep. Maybe it would work on Mark? As I neared the sofa, Mark growled at me, a clear sign he didn't want my help. I backed away. I wouldn't force him to do anything.

'Here, get him to drink this,' Leah said as she handed Cassie a bottle. She carefully poured some into Mark's mouth. A moment later, his body relaxed.

I looked over and gave Leah a smile. It died on my face as Cassie shrieked and the sounds of bones popping filled the air.

I rushed towards the sofa to grab Cassie away from harm.

When she was safely behind me, I turned back to face Mark. In his place was a massive wolf, baring its teeth with a deep growl. The only sign of Mark was his ripped-up clothes on the floor.

Making sure Cassie stayed behind me, I backed away slowly. 'Leah, get behind me.' I kept my eyes on the wolf but avoided eye contact, knowing it would be seen as a threat – I didn't want to give him any reason to attack. I had no idea whether he had any control over what was happening, but I wanted to avoid a fight.

'I'm going to teleport us out of here so we are safe,' I told them, without removing my eyes from Mark.

'No. Mark needs our help. We can't just abandon him,' Cassie answered.

'Fine. Does anyone know what might be happening?'

'He obviously got his ability to shift back somehow,' Leah answered.

'You think?' I said sarcastically.

The large grey wolf jumped off the sofa and came closer to us in a crouching position, its hackles raised. Its ears were pulled back flat against its head, and its green eyes followed my every move. Its teeth were clearly on display as it let out another deep growl that caused the surrounding air to vibrate. There was no doubt in my mind that it was going to attack me.

It jumped, and within a second I had conjured my sword, ready to defend myself, when Cassie barrelled into me. I fell to the floor, not prepared for the impact.

'You can't kill him,' Cassie said.

I looked over at her, the wolf now between us. Indecisiveness weighed me down. Cassie and Leah were all that mattered. I'd rather have them alive but mad at me than watch them be devoured by Mark's wolf. 'I don't care that he's your brother. If he lays a finger on you, he's dead.'

'He won't,' Cassie answered confidently.

I took a step towards Mark. His posture became rigid and his eyes glared into mine. He bared his teeth, growled and started snapping the air. I maintained eye contact but backed away, hoping he would follow me so Cassie and Leah could get to safety. But after a few steps, Mark turned and made his way towards Cassie. My heart raced. I darted towards him, ready to defend Cassie.

'Stop,' Leah shouted. 'He's not going to hurt her.'

I stopped in my tracks and realised Leah was right. Mark was licking Cassie's hand.

'Are you okay?' I asked Cassie.

She smiled. 'Of course. Why wouldn't I be?'

'We need to calm Mark down, and he seems to see you as a threat,' Leah said.

I nodded and kept my distance, fighting the urge to rescue them. Mark wouldn't hurt them. Cassie stroked Mark's fur as Leah gazed into his eyes. 'Remember who you are.'

We waited in silence for what felt like forever, but eventually Mark turned back into his human form. I conjured some clothes and threw them at him as I made my way to Cassie.

'Sorry about that,' Mark said calmly. 'My wolf's instinct took over for a moment.' He looked over at me. 'You have such a threatening scent. All I could think of was to protect Cassie and Leah from you.'

I shrugged. 'No harm done.'

'What happened?' Cassie asked Mark.

'Sky. She broke the bond,' Mark replied.

'How? Is she okay?'

Mark shook his head. 'I don't know. At first I thought she may have died, but considering I have my ability to shift back, I'm not so sure anymore. We need to talk to her.' Mark's voice was agitated, and I understood why he was worried.

'If we could find the stone, we could talk to Leaf. She may know what happened,' Cassie said.

'I found the stone in the cabin. It's in my pocket. I was about to bring it over when this happened,' Mark said. 'But it doesn't make any sense. Why would she break our bond?'

Cassie looked over at Mark. 'I'm sure she had her reasons.'

'That's what I'm worried about. What mess could she have got herself into where someone was powerful enough to break our bond and get my ability to shift back?'

Leah walked over to the sofa and took the stone from the pocket of Mark's ripped trousers. 'Let's ask her.' She grabbed the scrying bowl from the bookcase, filled it with water and placed the stone in it. A moment later, Leaf's face appeared.

'Hi, Leaf,' Leah said.

'Hi, my darling. How are you?'

'I'm okay, but we have some unexplained things happening here and we think it may involve Sky. Do you know what's going on?'

'I'm afraid not. Sky left early this morning, but I haven't seen her since. I expected her to be back by now.'

'We need to get there. Sky could be in trouble,' Mark said in an agitated voice.

'Unfortunately, I do not know how to get you all here. If I did, I would have suggested it in the first place, but as I told Sky, the spell requires a lot of energy. It's too much for any witch to cast it more than once without a proper rest in between,' Leaf said. 'I'll keep my ears open and let you know as soon as I know something.'

Mark paced back and forth. 'What now?'

'We'll think of something,' Cassie said.

'Why did I let her go? We could have found another way.'

Hearing Mark this upset gave me a new appreciation for him. Even with the mate bond gone, he clearly still cared for her.

Mark stopped, his body stiffening. He turned to me with a frown. 'I didn't know you had a cat.'

'I don't,' I said as one of Freya's big grey cats jumped up on the table next to us.

Cassie walked over and gave the cat some cuddles. 'There's something stuck to its collar.'

I looked over at her. 'What does Freya want?'

'What does Freya have to do with this?' Cassie asked as she got the note from the collar.

'It's her cat.'

The cat meowed.

Cassie unfolded the paper. 'It says to use the cat.'

'How?' Mark said.

I held up my hand. 'Let me think. Freya's cats can move between different realms with ease. Maybe this is our way to get to the witch village.'

'I guess they're not really cats, then,' Cassie said.

I shook my head. 'Not really. They are some sort of magical being. Freya keeps them around as familiars.'

'How did she know we needed to get there?' Leah asked.

'Better not dwell on questions like that. She knows far more than she'll ever tell.'

The cat meowed and jumped off the table. Cassie looked over at it as it made its way towards the back door. 'I think he wants us to follow him.'

The cat turned around and meowed once more before walking through the closed glass door leading to the garden like it wasn't even there.

'I guess it's worth a try,' I said as I caught up with Cassie and opened the door so we could go after the cat. I was intrigued to see where he would lead us.

SKY

IMPRISONED

Someone cleared their throat behind me, interrupting my crying. I turned around and the High Priestess stood in front of me.

'I have directions from Hecate to show you to your room. You must be very special to her. Normally we don't let any of the students stay at the temple.'

She offered me her hand and pulled me up from the ground. 'I hope they are happy tears. It is an honour to work with such a powerful Goddess.'

She walked away, and I followed her up the stairs that led to the entrance of the temple with heavy steps. I paid little attention to where we were going, my mind preoccupied with fear and guilt over the choices I'd made. Eventually we stopped in front of a door in a corridor.

'This is your room,' the High Priestess said as she opened the door. 'You are excluded from the studies today to allow you to adjust to your new living arrangement. Lunch will be served in an hour.'

The door closed behind me and I let out a breath. My eyes scanned the room. It wasn't big by any means, but it seemed to have all the necessities: a bed, a desk, a wardrobe and a small bathroom.

I sat down on the bed with an empty feeling in my heart. A book caught my attention, and I reached over to the bedside table and picked it up. Maybe I could pretend I was someone else for a while. To my disappointment, the book was a leather-bound notebook with nothing written in it. As I flicked through it, a piece of paper fell out. I picked it up from the floor.

Dearest Sky.
Your dreams are special; add them to this book.
—Hecate

Why would Hecate want to know about my dreams?

I put the book away and lay back on the bed, trying to come up with a plan of action. I was stuck here, but maybe I could try to find out some information that could help reverse the sacrificial magic spell. Maybe I could try to get the grimoire again, or at least look through it.

I opened the door and scanned the corridor. It was empty. The windows on the opposite side told me it was still before noon. They overlooked the resting area for the horses, and next to it was the bike station.

I tiptoed towards the room where I'd found the grimoire. Hopefully this time Hecate wouldn't be around to stop me.

I closed the door quietly behind me. The glass cabinet remained locked. There had to be a spare key somewhere. I spent some time looking without any luck. How could I get to the book? I hit the cabinet as hard as I could with the corner of another book, but nothing. Not even a crack. Had it been magically reinforced? Defeated, I slumped down on the floor. What was I going to do? The solution to reverse the spell was less than an arm's length from me and still I couldn't get to it.

Wait. I straightened my body. I didn't need the book; I only needed the spell. Maybe I could use wind to flip the pages. Hecate had said that I had got my magic back. I reached into myself to connect with my magic and stared at the book, willing it to open, but it remained closed. Maybe my magic hadn't fully returned or maybe I needed to concentrate more. After all, it had been a long time since I'd had my magic.

A noise outside got my attention. It sounded like someone walking in the corridor. Would they know I was in here? I stopped what I was doing and placed my ear against the door to listen, but whoever had been in the corridor was gone. Maybe now was not the right time. I could always come back at night when everyone was asleep.

I opened the door and had started walking back to my room when someone entered the corridor. I held my breath, worried they were going to tell me off for wandering around. A guy around my age, with brown hair, stopped next to me. 'When did you decide to start working at the temple?'

I studied him. He seemed familiar. Wait – was it the guy who had had his magic sacrificed with me and Aurora? 'Heath?'

He smiled. 'You remembered me.'

'What are you doing here?' I asked, wondering if he'd made some deal with Hecate too.

'I work here.'

'Why? Did you get your magic back?'

He shook his head. 'Don't be silly. They're sacred sacrifices. But working here is amazing. Come on, I'm on my way to get some food. Let me introduce you to my friend.'

We walked into a room at the end of the corridor, which appeared to be a kitchen.

'Are you hungry? Miriam here is the main chef. She's been working here for almost ten years. She's an amazing cook. The best food I've ever tasted.' Heath made his way to a table and pulled two chairs over for us to sit down on.

Miriam smiled. 'You're always so kind. I saved you some leftovers.'

'Thank you,' Heath said. 'This is Sky. She had her magic sacrificed at the same time as me.'

'Welcome to our group,' Miriam said and brought over two plates of food for us.

'Your group?' I asked in confusion.

'Yes. Everyone that works here has been part of the sacrifices.'

'But you're old. How come you're still alive?'

A frown formed on Miriam's face. 'I'm only twenty-seven. Why would I not still be alive?'

'Our bodies can't handle the lack of magic and slowly fade away. I've seen it happen.'

'It must have been because of something else. Our stable keeper turned forty last year,' Miriam said.

This didn't make any sense. Why were they still alive when most of the people at Leaf's house had started to fade away at around the age of twenty? And Aurora hadn't even lasted a year without her magic. Hecate had even said herself that a witch needs magic to remain healthy.

Dizziness engulfed me, and it was becoming harder to breathe. 'I'm sorry. I need to get some fresh air,' I said as I rushed out of the kitchen. Heath followed me but grabbed my hand as I was about to run upstairs.

'This is quicker,' he said as he opened another door that was hidden at the base of the stairs. Fresh air blew into the corridor and my breathing settled down.

'Thanks.'

'No worries. It gets a bit stuffy being stuck here all the time.'

'You're not allowed outside?' I asked.

'Of course we're allowed outside. We have to look after the horses. But we're advised to stay in the temple as much as possible. It's why we all live here.'

Maybe there was something special about the temple. 'Do you think that's why the others haven't faded away yet?'

'I honestly have no idea what you're talking about.'

I shook my head. Heath had been excited to be picked. I didn't think anything I said would make him think badly of Hecate. I scanned the outside. This was the entrance leading directly to the horses and the stables. In the distance a brown horse stood eating some hay. As its mane shifted, a scar in the shape of a lightning bolt became visible. Lightning?

I straightened up. Could it really be Lightning? I hadn't seen her in more than a year. I stepped out of the door but quickly rushed back in as my skin burned. 'What the hell?' The skin on my arms had blistered.

Heath's eyes widened. 'Are you okay?'

'What do you think?' I said, holding my arms up for him to see.

'Did that just happen? That looks painful. Let me get some water,' he said and started down the corridor.

Water. I closed my eyes and thought of water, sending my senses out. Next to the horses was a large water bowl. I concentrated on that and visualised the water moving towards me. I was deep in concentration when a glass shattered.

I looked up to see Heath with an expression of shock on his face and shards of glass on the floor in front of him. 'Why do you have magic?'

I shrugged, pretending it wasn't a big deal. 'Hecate gave

it back to me.'

'That's why you burned. The universe is punishing you for withdrawing the sacrifice you made. You're a disgrace. I will not be seen by the likes of you again.' Heath let out a quick disgusted snort, turned on his heel and walked away.

I sat there for a while, staring after him. I guessed we weren't going to be friends after all. Oh well.

I went back to my room and washed my arms in cold water in the sink before putting on a long-sleeved shirt. I lay down on the bed and let out a yawn.

Before I knew it, I was back in the volcanic place and so was the other creature. I knew it was a dream, but there was an urgency inside me that said I needed to catch up with him and see his face. It was easier to run this time. My lungs were less affected by the dust in the air. The creature in front of me started climbing a mountain. I tried to shout to get his attention, but he didn't seem to hear me. I closed the distance.

The creature was black like charcoal, with horns on its head. Streaks of ember and cyan ran through the blackness. I stared at it, hypnotised by the web of colours. It almost seemed like the colours were fighting each other. I reached up and touched his shoulder. He turned around, and I froze. His eyes were pitch black. They reminded me of something or someone. Only I didn't know who.

I woke up with a jolt. When I realised I was back in the room at the temple, I relaxed. A light glow seemed to come from the book Hecate wanted me to write my dreams down in. I picked it up and opened it. It felt like it was pulling energy from me, and before my very eyes, black letters in my own handwriting appeared on the pages. I dropped the book in a panic. It remained open, and letters filled the page. From the safety of the bed, I peeked out over the edge and stared at the writing in fascination. It was writing down my dream.

I picked up the book and ripped the pages out, only for them to reappear in the book. This was far beyond normal witch magic, but then again, Hecate was a goddess, so maybe it wasn't weird.

If I couldn't destroy it, maybe I could hide it. I looked around the room and walked over to the wardrobe. A few skirts and shirts were inside. I shoved the book to the bottom and pulled some clothes off the hangers and placed them on top. Hopefully Hecate wouldn't find it.

Unsure what time of day it was but feeling too claustrophobic to stay in my room, I stepped outside. The High Priestess had said I was excluded from the studies today, but I was curious to see how they were being conducted, so I made my way upstairs to the temple hall. As I entered the main area, I could see several girls standing around. I scanned for my sister and caught a glimpse of her as the High Priestess entered the room.

We bowed our heads in respect, and the High Priestess started talking about the different affinities and what she expected from us during the session. She divided the girls into small groups and demonstrated the exercise she wanted them to try, which was to create an electric current by using two affinities at the same time.

She walked around the groups and made her way over to me. 'You had been excused from today's session, but as you are here, you may as well get started. I won't place you in one of the groups. They have been given advanced exercises that are beyond your current ability. Not to mention you only have two affinities. The Fates only know why Hecate wanted you here.'

She walked over to a refreshments table at the side of the room and picked up two glasses. She poured some water into one and marked the level of the water on the glass. 'The most important part of magic is control. It does not matter how powerful you are, if you can't control it, the magic is useless or even dangerous. Maybe someday you will control lightning, but until you can move this water to the other glass and back again without losing any of it, this is what you will do.'

I nodded, happy to have my magic back. The exercise did not bother me at all.

I practised making the water move from one glass to another. At first I struggled, but with each try, it became easier and easier. At the end of the session, my sister came over to me.

'I'm happy you came to your senses. And you got your magic back. That's so amazing. Why don't you come home with me and we can have dinner as a family again?'

I shook my head. 'I'm not allowed to leave the temple.'

She narrowed her eyes at me and placed her hand on her

hip. 'You know, if you don't want to see our parents, that's fine, but at least have the spine enough to say so instead of making up excuses.'

She wasn't getting it. 'I'm not making up excuses. I would love to see our parents, but I can't leave the temple. Hecate made sure of that.'

She sighed, crossed her arms and stormed off.

I stared after her until she disappeared out of the entrance. Some other girls were packing up and leaving too. But I stayed, hoping I could show the High Priestess my success with moving the water so she could see I wasn't useless. But she wasn't around anymore.

'I wouldn't bother. The High Priestess doesn't care until you've proven yourself worthy.'

I turned around and came face to face with a girl with long brown hair with blue streaks. 'But how can I prove I'm worthy if she doesn't care about the result?'

The girl shrugged. 'Beats me. I'm Naia, by the way. Are you staying at the temple?'

I nodded. 'I'm Sky.'

'Come on, Sky, let's get something to eat,' she said as she pulled me with her to another room. The smell of newly baked bread entered my nose as we stepped inside. There were several containers of different vegetables. Plates were on the side next to a hamper of bread.

'How long have you been studying under the High Priestess?' I asked Naia as I dished up some food.

'All my life. But I'm a disgrace to the family, as I only

have three affinities.'

'What! I would have killed to have three affinities,' I answered.

She smiled. 'You would have thought it would be good enough, but when your mother is the High Priestess, it's not.'

My eyes went wide. 'She's your mother?'

She nodded. 'Yeah, but she likes to pretend I don't exist.'

'I'm sorry,' I said as I thought about my own family.

'No worries. How come you're here if you have less than three affinities?'

I debated how much to tell her but thought I might as well be truthful. 'It's a long story. I had my magic sacrificed but made a deal with Hecate to work under her in exchange for my magic back.'

'I thought I recognised you from somewhere. It must have been horrible without your magic for you to make a deal with her.'

Her words surprised me. 'You don't like Hecate?'

Naia looked around before lowering her voice. 'It's not so much that I don't like her. I'm just not buying what she's selling.'

'Me neither. I don't know what the sacrifices are for, but it's not to keep the village safe.' I hesitated. Could I trust her? 'Since Hecate restored my magic, I can't leave the temple.'

Naia looked shocked. 'Are you sure?'

I nodded and pulled my sleeve up to show her my burn.

Her eyes went wide. 'And I thought my mother was bad.'

'Maybe she's punishing me. I was trying to get to the

grimoire. There's a spell in there that I need. But it's locked in the cabinet and Hecate has the key.'

Naia gave me a devilish smile. 'You don't need the key. It can be opened by anyone who possesses all four elements. It's the reason my mother won't let me become a High Priestess in training.' She let out a sigh. 'They already started training my baby sister, even though she's too young to have her magic. They have no idea if she will even have an affinity for all four elements, but according to my mother, the Fates will make sure the High Priestess role stays within the family.'

'What happens if she doesn't?'

Naia shrugged. 'I don't know. I just know that to be High Priestess you have to possess all the elements, or the grimoire would be useless.'

I thought of Leaf and Leah. They both had an affinity for all four elements and carried Whitelake blood. 'I'm sure the Fates have a plan,' I said with a smile.

We continued to eat in silence. When we were done, I excused myself and went back to my room.

As I opened the door, I realised someone had been inside. They'd placed a few books on my desk and hung towels over the chair.

I rushed to the wardrobe to check if the dream notebook was still hidden. Nothing had been touched, and the clothes were still in a pile on the floor. Relief flooded through me.

I sat back on my bed and looked over the books I'd been given. There was one about water and another about air. The third book contained ceremonial magic. I picked the one about ceremonies and started reading. A yawn escaped me, my mind tired from everything that had happened. I set the book aside and allowed myself to close my eyes for a moment.

I woke up in a forest. It seemed vaguely familiar, but I couldn't quite remember where I recognised it from. A twig snapped, making me jump. I hid behind some bushes, hoping no one would find me. A large grey cat became visible. Was it the same cat that had accompanied me to Leaf's? Several wolves followed behind the cat, and I finally remembered where I was. I was in the human world. I got out of the bushes and made my way towards the wolves. Maybe they could give Mark a message. That was when I saw all of them: Mark, Leah, Cassie and Jax. I shouted, but they didn't hear me. Were they in some sort of trance? I rushed over to them and tried to touch them, but my hands went right through them like I wasn't even there.

Then I remembered. I was stuck in the temple. This must be a dream. But why did it feel so real? I followed them until they came to a lake. They stopped for a while before marching right into the lake, where the water swallowed them whole. I screamed after them, terrified of what I had just witnessed.

My screams echoed in my head, and before I knew it, I was back in my bed, the sheets glued to my sweaty body. I jumped out and started pacing the room. It had only been a dream, right?

A blue glow from the wardrobe got my attention, and I felt compelled to pick up the dream book. Again it felt like my energy was taken away from me as I watched the letters appear on the pages.

.

JAX

Follow the Cat

The cat walked into the forest, past the cabin and further into wolf territory, where he stopped and let out a meow. A moment later, five wolves appeared. The Alpha turned into his human form. However, the others remained in their wolf form.

'I got told you needed assistance, I'm not sure by who, but here we are. Happy to help,' the Alpha said.

A smirk appeared on my face. 'Don't you know better than to listen to voices you don't know? You'll never know whether it's a friend or a foe leading you to your death.'

'Very true indeed,' the Alpha responded.

The cat meowed, and the Alpha turned towards him.

'Yes, very well. We're all here, so let's go.' The Alpha turned back into a wolf and followed the cat.

Had he been able to speak to the cat? I'd never heard them talk, but then again, I wasn't really a shifter, and who knew what type of creatures the cats truly were?

We followed the cat and the wolves. Knowing it was Freya's familiar somehow put me at ease. She wouldn't lead us astray. The trees became sparse and the reflection of a lake came into view. The cat stopped and gave one last meow before jumping into the lake and disappearing. It was obvious he wanted us to follow. The water rippled and the surface turned into a picture of fields and houses.

'It's the village,' Mark said as he started walking towards the water.

How he knew it was the witch village, I didn't know. Sky had probably told him about it.

Leah grabbed his wrist before he could enter the lake. 'You mean you want us to walk into the water and drown ourselves?'

I turned to Leah. 'Have a little faith. Freya wouldn't send us to our deaths.'

Leah rolled her eyes. 'You just said not to trust anyone.'

I smirked. 'But Freya's familiar isn't anyone.'

She shook her head and let go of Mark, who quickly waded into the lake. 'Come on, we're wasting time,' he said before the whole of him disappeared under water.

I grabbed Cassie's hand and led her into the lake. The wolves were close on our heels.

When the water touched my torso, I turned around and gazed at Leah. 'Come on. The water's not that bad.'

Leah muttered to herself as she hurried to catch up with us. She took Cassie's other hand.

'Take a deep breath before you go under. You never know how long it will take until we're on the other side.' I waited for both Leah and Cassie to take a big breath before I dragged us under.

A bright light overtook us, and a moment later we were standing in a different lake – one that belonged in the witch village. We waded out of the lake, and as I waited for the wolves to arrive and catch their breath, I scanned the area to get a sense of where we were. There were trees all around us. Freya's cat caught my eye as he let out a meow and disappeared behind some bushes.

When we had recovered, we continued toward where the cat had disappeared and entered a field. Before long, Leaf's house came into view. But this time it didn't look abandoned. Instead there were several people walking about, both young and old.

Leaf was standing in the courtyard talking to some people when she spotted us. She waved and started walking towards us. 'Hi, my dearest. I see you found a way to cross over.' She gave me, Cassie and Leah a hug before giving Mark and the wolves a courtesy nod. 'A lot of things have changed in a short space of time. I'll try and catch you up.'

She led us towards the house. 'I had a dream a couple of days ago where the Goddess told me it was time to get our village back so I could get back what was mine by birth. I never cared much for that, but I want it to be a place where people feel safe and where everyone gets to keep their magic. As you know, Hecate has been using them for her gain. She doesn't need the magic she is taking. Maybe she did once when she moved the village to another realm, but now I think she is just collecting it for herself.'

She gestured to the courtyard and all the people there. 'I wasn't sure what to make of the dream, but people from the village turned up shortly after Sky left for the temple. They said they had come to help me set things straight.'

I looked around. There were at least thirty people. 'How did they all know to come here?'

'I'm not sure how much Sky told you about her time here, but a young lady whose twin sister died due to the withering set out on a mission to tell people about what the sacrifice does and to find people that were willing to fight on our behalf. But some people said they'd had a dream that told them to come here and fight for the cause. Most of them know someone that has had their magic stripped.'

Gasping noises made me turn around. The witches were keeping their distance from the wolves. The Alpha transformed into his human form, and someone quickly tossed him a coat so he could cover himself.

Mark, who had been walking behind us, spoke up. 'Where's Sky?'

Leaf turned to Mark. 'I haven't seen her since she arrived a few days ago.'

A frown appeared on Mark's forehead. 'A few days ago? But she just left this morning. We talked to you less than a couple of hours ago.'

'I'm afraid you are mistaken. It has been several days since I last spoke with you. I tried to contact you several times, but I got no response, and then everything has been so crazy around here that it slipped my mind.'

That was strange. The last time we had been here, time had moved parallel to the human realm. Maybe the portal jumping had altered the time.

'Do you think Sky would still be in the temple?'

Leaf nodded. 'I believe so. Maybe she got caught. It's the only reason I can think of as to why she's not back.'

Mark pulled on my arm. 'We need to go. Sky might be in danger.'

'You should come with us,' I asked Leaf.

She nodded. 'We were just getting organised to set out, so we'll be right behind you.'

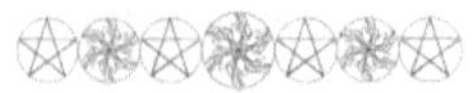

We made our way towards the village. The wolves were running ahead, scouting out the area, but stopped at the edge of the village.

When we had caught up, Cassie turned to the Alpha. 'Maybe they should turn back so we don't scare the people.'

He shook his head. 'They would feel too vulnerable. It's better if they stay in wolf form. I would have preferred it too, but this is the only way I know how to communicate with you all.'

He had a point, so we left it at that and continued walking. The wolves had taken up positions all around us. It almost looked like they were herding us. A few people came out of their houses to see what was going on, confusion written all over their faces, but none tried to speak to us.

We stopped in front of the temple, unsure what to expect or what we would walk into.

'You guys distract them and I'll search for Sky,' Mark said as he started walking up the stairs leading to the entrance.

I sped up to catch up with him. 'Be careful,' I said as I overtook him.

When I walked through the entrance, the High Priestess stepped into my way. 'You do not belong here.'

'You're right, I don't, but I'm looking for someone that I believe is inside,' I said as I moved aside. Cassie and Leah came and joined me, and Mark passed us, but the High Priestess didn't notice as she stared into my eyes. The demon inside pushed itself to the surface, turning my eyes red.

She released my gaze and crossed her arms over her chest. 'Demons do not belong here. You are an abomination that should never have existed. Your kind are the reason we have to keep this village safe.'

I smirked. 'And what a great job you're doing. All their sacrifices and I can still get into this village as I please. It makes me wonder why you even bother with them. Clearly the sacrifices aren't to keep me out. But don't worry. If I wanted revenge for what was done to me, your village would have been destroyed by now.'

Her face went pale as the realisation of who I really was sank in. She glared at me with hatred in her eyes. 'I will not let the temple be tainted by your presence. Hecate will not allow it.' She moved her hands like she was preparing to draw upon her magic.

'Then how about you fetch our friend and we'll be on our way?'

'Demons don't have any friends.'

'He has us,' Cassie spat out and hooked her arm in mine.

'If you don't let us in, we will use force to get inside,' Leah said.

The High Priestess laughed in our faces. 'You may be a witch, but your magic is no match for me. I'm a descendant of the Whitelakes.'

Leah swirled her arms and threw some air out, which pushed the High Priestess back before she created a shield around her.

'Like I said, I am above you. You can't touch me. This is my temple.'

'That's where you're wrong. The temple is mine by birthright,' Leaf said as she took the last step and joined us by the entrance.

The High Priestess frowned at her. 'And who are you?'

'I'm Leaf, or more correctly Layla Fey, daughter of Katie Whitelake.'

Shock became evident on the High Priestess's face for a second before she corrected her poker face. 'But you're supposed to be dead.'

'As you can see, I'm very much alive. Now please let us inside so we can discuss matters.'

The High Priestess stared at us for a moment but didn't bulge.

'Let them pass.' Freya's voice sounded from inside.

I guessed we were late to the party after all.

The look of distaste on the High Priestess's face was priceless as she stepped aside and let us inside.

SKY

The Reunion

I'd been sitting in my room for a few hours, studying the books they had given me, when I heard a bang. My concentration shattered and curiosity got the better of me. I put the book away and listened for more sounds. A second later it sounded like a door was slammed open, causing the walls to vibrate from its impact. Why was someone looking through the rooms? And why weren't they being more careful? I was trying to think of who it could be when the door sprang open. In walked a massive grey wolf.

I jumped up from my chair, ready to use my magic to escape until I glanced into the wolf's green eyes. A moment later I ran towards him and threw my arms around him. 'You came for me. I can't believe you came for me.'

Mark responded by licking my face.

I was so happy. I buried my face in his fur. 'I'm sorry for everything. I never meant for any of this to happen. But I'm glad you can shift again.'

Mark transformed into his human form and embraced me. 'I'm just happy you're okay. I should never have let you out of my sight.'

My cheeks filled with heat. I'd never seen Mark naked before. I desperately wanted to take a peek, but I didn't want him to know, so I maintained eye contact. 'I'm sorry about the bond, but it's better this way. At least you can shift and be free.'

Mark put his finger over my lips. 'Shh. Let's talk about this later when we're home. Come on, we must hurry.'

'If you're planning on walking out of this room, I suggest you put some clothes on,' I said, staring at the floor.

Mark glanced down at himself like he wasn't even aware that he wasn't wearing clothes. 'Sorry. I'd forgotten about that.' He reached over for a blanket and tied it around his waist.

'The grimoire. I found it.'

Mark smiled. 'That's great news.'

'Yeah, but we can only get it with the key Hecate has or by someone with the four elements.'

'Leah's upstairs with the others. Let's go and get her.'

Mark transformed back into his wolf. His body changed form, and he went down on all fours. His arms became legs and his hands became paws. His skin sprouted grey fur. It looked gruesome.

He lowered his chest to the ground so I could climb up on him. I locked my arms around his neck, and he left the room and trotted up the stairs. The door to the holding room was ajar, and I could hear voices coming from the other side.

'It's ironic how you are preaching peace when you're the one responsible for a never-ending war.'

'I have spent all the time since trying to reverse it. I was stuck between a rock and a hard place and chose to save myself.'

I recognised the first voice, knowing it was Hecate speaking. However, I didn't know who the other person was, but it sounded like an old woman.

I told Mark to stop so we could listen.

'Excuses, excuses,' Hecate said.

'I have grown a lot since then. I am not the same person anymore. I left my people, left Odin and created a life for myself where I offer refuge to anyone who is looking for it. I am asking you nicely to leave these people alone. No more sacrifices.'

'But how will I be able to keep the village safe without them?'

'We both know the one you are pretending to protect this village from will never destroy it.'

'Are you sure about that? It was foretold that the being who set it in motion would be the end of it.'

'That can mean so many things. It may not even be about

Jax.'

The mention of Jax piqued my interest, and I gestured for Mark to get closer. He quietly moved through the door, keeping next to the wall. In front of us were Hecate and a short, petite elderly woman with white hair. They were so immersed in their conversation, they did not seem to notice us.

'O powerful Freya, why don't you enlighten me, considering you can see the future?' Hecate said in a mocking tone.

'We both know it is not that easy.'

A big, evil smirk appeared on Hecate's face. 'Oh, I forgot – you tried to change the future once, and look what that got you. Not only did you lose your precious daughter, but you ended up with a demon as a grandchild. How ironic.'

Freya raised her voice. 'You shall not speak about things you know nothing about. Now I am asking you nicely – stop stealing others' magic.'

'Then get my hellhounds back and I won't need to,' Hecate retorted.

Mark took a step forward, and as much as I wanted to continue listening to their conversation, our chances of being detected were high, and I didn't want to risk their wrath from eavesdropping on their private conversation, so I signalled for him to continue. We followed the wall until we entered the main hall.

Several people were in the temple, and it looked like more were arriving at every moment. What was going on?

I caught sight of Leaf, who was heading our way. 'What's happening?' I asked her.

She placed a hand on my knee. 'I'm happy you're okay. I've come to speak to Hecate to end the sacrifices. I hope she will agree, but if not, we might have to do it by force. But because of Star's help, we have the numbers.'

'Please be careful. If there's one thing I've learned about Hecate, it's that she's deceiving.'

She nodded. 'I will. Go and find the others.' She squeezed my knee and entered the room behind us.

The people moved away and gave us a wide berth as we moved further into the main hall. I skimmed the crowd for the others and my eyes landed on my sister. I told Mark to stop so I could jump off him. I started walking towards my sister, but Mark grabbed my hand carefully in his mouth.

'It's my sister. I need to talk to her,' I pleaded with him. I met his gaze, and he released my hand but stayed at my heels.

I gave my sister a hug. 'I don't want to fight with you. Please leave the temple while you still can.'

She glanced past me. 'Hecate and the High Priestess will protect me,' she sneered. 'I thought you had come to your senses, but clearly I was wrong.'

'Dawn, please.' I grabbed her hand. 'I don't want anything to happen to you.'

'Get your hand off me.' She zapped me with a small bolt of electricity.

Mark took a step towards her and bared his teeth. Dawn summoned up fire in her hands.

I stepped between them and used water to demolish her fire. I was about to tell her to back down when bells started ringing above us. Mark nudged me with his head. His eyes were telling me we needed to make a move. The witches had divided themselves into two groups, and we were in the middle of the opposing one.

Once the bells had stopped, Freya's voice echoed through the temple. 'If you are not willing to give this place up and leave the witches alone, we will fight you for their freedom.'

Everyone fell dead silent, and the two groups stared at each other for a while before they all started using their magic at once. It was complete mayhem as the room filled with colourful blasts created by the four elements. Mark pushed me to the ground, and I barely escaped the fire that had been coming towards us. I looked pleadingly at my sister one more time before jumping up onto Mark's back. He started running. His reflexes were amazing. He dodged and jumped and avoided several different elements coming towards us. I thought about using my magic, but it was hard to concentrate while holding on to him.

I spotted Jax and the others by the entrance. 'They're over there,' I said as I pointed towards them. Jax was standing in front of them with a sword, deflecting the magical beams coming towards them. Leah was standing behind him, chanting and moving her hands around.

Something cold hit me, and I almost fell off Mark's back. Fighting through the burning pain that exploded in my shoulder, I held on tighter, urging Mark to run faster. I thought he was taking us to the others, but he made a beeline for the exit.

'Stop. I can't go outside!' I screamed over the commotion. Mark made a sharp turn a few steps shy of the entrance but tripped over a vine on the floor. He lost his balance, and we tumbled to the ground outside.

Excruciating pain erupted all over my body, and I screamed. Two wolves ran towards me, but on closer inspection I realised it was just Mark. He dragged me back into the temple. The pain eased slightly. Mark looked into my eyes with worry.

'Hecate did something to me. I can't leave the temple.'

Mark nodded at me and bent down so I could get back up on him, but the blisters on my skin made it too painful to move. He let out a howl before turning back into his human form and picking me up. I wanted to scream from the pain, but I tried to keep a brave face as we navigated through the fight towards the others. We were almost there when a bolt of fire flew towards us. Without the reflexes of Mark's wolf, there was no way we could escape it. I closed my eyes and prepared for the impact.

# JAX

THE WRATH OF JAX

I summoned my sword and tried to keep Leah and Cassie away from the chaos in the temple as Leah worked to get a defensive barrier up. The thought of grabbing Cassie and running away crossed my mind, but she would hate me for it. I had to trust that she could hold her own.

Leah erected a transparent protective barrier, and relief crashed through me when Cassie got behind it. Being the caring person that she was, Cassie monitored the fighting from behind the safety of the barrier, and if she saw someone from our side who had been injured, she would ask the wolves to fetch them so she could triage them.

It worked well for a while, but the protective barrier

wasn't that large, and as the number of people needing protection increased, it became clear that it was insufficient, not to mention the strain it put on Leah to keep it up. Where were Sky and Mark?

A scream came from the entrance, and I looked over. Mark was dragging Sky back into the temple. Why had they not been able to escape? Mark turned back into his human form and started carrying Sky towards us. They were almost at the protective barrier when a blast of fire hurtled towards them. I jumped in front of them and deflected it with my sword. 'Get behind the barrier,' I called.

When they were safely behind it, I looked around the temple. The two groups were fighting each other, but I wasn't sure the other group knew why except to defend Hecate's honour. However, one thing was certain: this fight had to end, preferably before the witches killed one another.

The easiest way to do that was to locate Hecate and Freya, because at its core it seemed to be a fight between them, though I wasn't sure how any of this connected to Freya or why she was here.

Because we were in the witch village, I couldn't teleport, but my fighting skills were better than those of these people. It seemed like most of them had no clue what they were doing and just randomly spewed magic towards the opposing group. I took my time getting to the back of the temple, deflecting magic as I went and jumping over vines and people that had fallen to the ground. Cassie would have been disappointed in me for not helping them, but I had my eyes set on the bigger picture. The faster I could get to Freya and Hecate, the faster the fighting would end.

I made it to the platform at the back, where Freya and Hecate were fighting each other with magic. Despite the inappropriateness of it, it was a beautiful display of smoke, teleportation and magic all mixed together. Anyone would be foolish to underestimate Freya because of her appearance. She might look old, but her graceful movements rivalled those of Hecate, and she matched her advances perfectly.

My eyes met Freya's, which distracted her from Hecate's attack. She shielded herself at the last moment, but it caused her to stumble and fall.

I dashed over to help her up. 'It's mayhem out there. We need to stop the fighting before more people get hurt,' I told her as I turned towards the crowd.

My gaze landed on Cassie, who was helping a witch lying on the floor. What was Cassie doing in the crowd? Why wasn't she behind the barrier?

Something flashed in my peripheral vision. Hecate held a set of daggers. 'I may not be able to physically hurt you, but she can't stop me from hurting the ones you hold dear.' An evil smile slid across her face as she threw a dagger at Cassie. My heart stopped as I sprinted towards Cassie, but I knew I wouldn't be able to make it. My eyes traced the dagger through the air until it hit Cassie's heart.

Blood streamed down her body as she collapsed on the floor. I reached her and clutched her in my arms. Tears burned in my eyes as I pressed my hand to her chest to try to stem the bleeding, but there was too much blood seeping between my fingers. I didn't know what to do. Her wide eyes stared back at me as the life drained out of them. A scream left my lungs. I had nothing left to fight for.

My will to live diminished, and when the demon inside me pushed to the surface, I did not fight it. I didn't care if my demon side took over and killed everyone. I'd already lost Cassie. Rage bubbled up inside me and I slammed Hecate into a wall with my mind. The walls shook and she collapsed on the floor. I hoped it had killed her, even though I knew it wouldn't, but she deserved it for what she had done to Cassie. The temple was completely silent. All the fighting had stopped, and all the attention was on us.

Cassie let out a gasping sound and brought my attention back to her. My senses detected a faint heartbeat; she was still alive, but barely.

I looked around for Freya. 'Save her,' I begged quietly as tears streamed down my face.

Hecate got up from the ground. She let out a malicious laugh and turned towards Freya. 'Did I not say that he would be the one to end it?'

Freya ignored her and rushed to my side. She put her hands over my claws. 'I cannot, but you can. There is so much untapped power inside you. Open your heart and think about love, but whatever you do, do not give in to your hatred. I believe in you.'

I closed my eyes and prayed to the Fates not to take Cassie. I listened to Freya's soothing voice and shut the hatred from the demon inside me away. Instead I thought of Cassie, of everything we'd been through together, the laughter and love we'd shared, the moments that were perfect just because she was there with me, the moment when we were standing on the cliff and told each other 'I love you'.

A light of energy built up inside me. I welcomed it, and when I couldn't contain it anymore, I opened my eyes and guided it into Cassie. The bright light exploded all around me, blinding me for a moment.

I gazed down at Cassie, holding my breath until she stirred. The bleeding had stopped, and the wound knitted itself up. She tried to sit up, but before she even had a chance to move, I scooped her up in my arms and kissed her.

She pulled away, and I could see fear in her eyes, along with the reflection of my demon form. I had been so caught up with everything, I had forgotten I was still a monster.

'Jax?' Her voice came out in a confused whisper.

I nodded but made no sudden moves, terrified of what she would think of me. A moment later, she threw her arms around me and kissed me.

'I love you.'

'I love you too,' I answered with relief.

Knowing she loved me despite seeing the monster inside me filled my heart with joy, and a weight lifted from my shoulders. Sky had been right.

I let my love for Cassie shine out of me, and somehow it engulfed her in a protective bubble of energy. She looked around with a smile and laughed.

Now that I knew she was safe, I turned my head to face Hecate. 'I will not let you take her from me again,' I said, glaring into her eyes.

Hecate took a step forward, towards the crowd. 'This is the horrible demon I have tried to keep you safe from – the reason you need to sacrifice your magic. Freya let him into our realm, a goddess whom I do not have enough magic to disobey. She is nothing but a fa—'

Anger and rage rose up inside me, and the next moment, the dagger next to me that Hecate had thrown at Cassie flew through the air towards Hecate. I wasn't even sure how I had made that happen. I just couldn't let her get away with insulting and degrading the only person who had been like a mother to me. Unfortunately, Hecate deflected it.

I turned and faced the people. There were a lot of gasps and whispers. 'I know what it looks like, but she has deceived you all. The stories you know about me are not true. Let me show you what really happened.'

Freya placed her hand on my shoulder, giving me strength to open my heart to the witches and show them all the memories I had of me and Katie and what had actually happened. They deserved to know the truth of what their old High Priestess had done to me.

SKY

VISIONS FROM THE PAST

My mind was inundated by memories of Katie's and Jax's lives.

A slightly younger-looking Jax was walking in a field. A girl in her late teens came into view. She looked like she'd been crying. Jax asked her if she wanted to come and collect a horse with him, and she nodded slightly. As they walked, Jax told her jokes to cheer her up. When they reached the horse, she was smiling and laughing. The scene quickly changed to another. They were sitting in the field talking and laughing. Katie rested her head on Jax's shoulder, and it was easy to see they were growing closer.

The next scene showed the same field decorated with

candles during sunset and Jax on one knee proposing to Katie. It was beautiful. I couldn't help the tears falling down my cheeks. This was far from the story we'd been taught.

We followed Jax as he walked to the place where they used to meet up. He picked up a letter from behind a stone. The letter stated Katie was pregnant, and we watched as Jax ran towards the village.

The images changed again. Jax and Katie embraced each other, and he put his hand on her stomach and told her how the three of them belonged together and that he was going to fight for them so they could stay together.

Katie's mother, Elise Whitelake, the High Priestess at that time, listed a lot of conditions and had Jax promise not to use any powers if he stayed with their daughter in the village. He agreed, and the scene moved on to their wedding day. It was easy to see the love they shared with each other was special.

It flashed forward. Jax was sitting next to a very pale Katie in the healing ward, where she told him she was ready to die for their baby as long as he promised to keep her safe. He told her she and the baby were his everything and he would fight to the end of time to keep the baby safe.

I felt his agony over losing his soulmate and the love he had for his daughter. The indecision about leaving his baby to go to Katie's funeral. The vision flashed forward and showed us the betrayal from the High Priestess – how they drugged him and told him his daughter had died before they made him forget everything about his family. Anger bubbled up inside me. How could any living being be so cruel?

The images stopped. But the temple remained quiet.

'Don't listen to him. Demons can't be trusted,' Hecate shouted as she stepped up and faced the crowd again.

'But you can?' Freya said, facing Hecate. 'Then let us show the people how they treated Jax's daughter after Jax had been exiled.' Leaf placed a hand on Freya's shoulder. And once again my head was assaulted with memories.

A girl no older than five was begging to get a toy. The High Priestess at the time, Katie's mother, told her no, but a moment later the girl had somehow conjured the toy in her hand. She seemed confused but happy with what had just happened and turned to the High Priestess. 'Mummy, look.' The High Priestess's face showed fear and distrust.

The scene changed to a scared little girl in a ring of fire – the same fire that had been used to take our magic. Hecate started an incantation while the girl begged her mother for help. As the fire swept closer to the girl, she disappeared.

The girl, still visibly upset, was now standing in an unfamiliar room with tears streaming down her face. She looked around with wide eyes. Where was she and where did the fire go?

An elderly man stepped into view and bent down to her level. 'What's your name, little one?' he asked her calmly.

The little girl mumbled between her tears, 'Layla Fey.'

The man cupped his ear. 'Did you say Leaf?'

The girl nodded and smiled.

'What a wonderful name. My name is Edmond,' the elderly man said. The little girl ran towards him and he held his arms out in anticipation. He embraced her and wiped her tears away. 'You are safe here. I will not let anything happen to you.'

The scene disappeared from my head, and Freya spoke up. 'This is the person you give your magic away for, for protection. A goddess that does not even hesitate to take the powers of a young girl instead of teaching her how to use them. Now, as you all saw, Leaf managed to survive and teleport herself to her father's old house. And she was lucky that Edmond was still around to look after her. She learned how to embrace her powers and has given refuge to the young witches that have had their magic taken ever since. She has dedicated her life to precluding the withering that befalls all witches without magic.'

Freya glanced over at Hecate. 'Hecate has not been very forthcoming about what happens to a witch when they sacrifice their magic. For a witch to be healthy, magic must flow in their veins; without it they will perish. However, Hecate has delayed the inevitable by forcing the sacrificing witches to live in the temple, which stands on sacred land.'

Freya took a moment to look out over us before she continued with authority in her voice. 'Leaf is the daughter of Katie Whitelake and therefore the rightful heir to this place. However, all she wants is for people to live in peace and for no more sacrifices to be made. Are you willing to agree to this and bow down to her, or do we need to continue fighting?'

Men and women glanced at one another. It was hard to

tell what was going through their minds. After a painful moment, Naia knelt down on the temple floor and bowed her head. I hadn't seen her in the crowd earlier and wasn't sure which side she had been fighting for. But I was grateful for her nonetheless. A second later, another person did the same, and like a slow wave, everyone in the temple followed suit.

JAX
The Wolves Sacrifice

I scanned the temple, amazed to see all the witches bowing before us. Bowing before Leaf. Tears streamed down her face and my heart filled with pride. She was finally where she belonged.

It had been hard to learn what had happened to Leaf. I should have been there to protect her. But I was grateful to Edmond. He had been like a father to me when I'd lived in the witch village, and I was happy to learn he had been looking after my daughter. I would forever be in debt to him.

I was lost in thought, too caught up with everything. Freya and Leaf's attention was on the crowd. In the corner of my eye, I saw Hecate move. A dagger materialised in her hand, and she threw it at Freya.

I shouted as I charged at Hecate and drew my sword, stabbing her in the chest. Her eyes went wide before she pulled the sword out and teleported away.

The whole temple shook.

I turned to Freya. The dagger was embedded in her arm. 'Freya, are you okay?'

'I will live,' she said as she pulled out the dagger and placed her hand over the wound to stop the bleeding and heal the skin. 'Which is more than can be said for the village now that Hecate has abandoned it.'

The entire building continued to shake, and I staggered to catch my balance. 'What do you mean? What is happening?'

She gave me a haunted look. 'The realm is crumbling without Hecate's magic. Unfortunately, I do not have enough power to stabilise this realm or to move it somewhere else. We must try to gather everyone and escape.'

Mark, Leah and Sky made their way over to us though the crowd of witches trying to escape the temple.

'Hecate used the bond of a mate to restore Mark's magic. She said it was one of the most powerful magics there is. Maybe you can use that,' Sky said.

Freya nodded in agreement. 'She is right, but I cannot ask the wolves to give that up. It is part of what they are.'

The Alpha came up to us and transformed into his human form as the temple shook again. 'If it means saving all these people, it is a worthy sacrifice. I give you my permission to take the magic of the mate bonds from us.'

Freya looked at the Alpha. 'Are you sure? We can find another way.'

The temple shook vigorously and large cracks appeared in the stone walls. Screams echoed around us.

'There's no time for courtesy. We both know there's not enough time. It's a price we are willing to pay to prevent genocide,' the Alpha said.

'Very well. Please come over here,' Freya said.

Mark looked at Freya with worried eyes. 'What do we do about Sky? She can't leave this temple.'

'It is not the temple she cannot leave. The sun is the problem.'

The stone roof cracked and large blocks of stone crashed to the ground.

'You all need to get out of here.' Freya turned to the Alpha. 'Are you sure about this? It is an immense sacrifice to make.'

The Alpha nodded as Leaf spoke up. 'I'm staying. I can't leave my people.'

Freya gave an understanding nod. 'Take my hand. I will use you as a conductor, as you are part of this world. I am not sure what will happen, but I will try to move us to my domain and keep everyone intact.'

She extended her other hand to the Alpha. 'Because you are the Alpha, I should be able to syphon the magic from everyone in the pack through you, but the rest of you should go.' As she held both their hands, she looked over at me. 'Jax, get everyone else out of here before the temple collapses.'

'We need to get the grimoire,' Sky said.

Freya gave her an apologetic smile. 'I am afraid there is no time. If we do not leave soon, there will be no one left to save.'

Sky nodded and made her way over to me.

Mark lingered by Freya. 'What will happen to Sky when we get back?'

'She will be fine. Just keep her out of the sun and I will come and find you afterwards. Now go with Jax.'

I scanned the area. Most of the witches had left the temple, but there were still far more people than I had ever teleported before.

'You only need to teleport the ones who do not belong to this world. My magic should be strong enough to carry everyone else over with the help of the Alpha and Leaf,' Freya said.

That left nine people, including myself. It was still more people than I had ever tried to teleport at once.

Frustration mixed with guilt overcame me and I shook my head. 'I can't do it. I don't have the power,' I said as the temple shook once again.

Freya gave me a loving gaze. 'You need to believe in yourself. Tap into your powers. You are not just a demon. You are a god too.'

'A what?' I gaped at Freya. She graced me with a quick smile and closed her eyes, beginning to recite an incantation.

I shook my head. When we got out of this, Freya and I were going to have a serious heart to heart. She had obviously been keeping things from me.

'You can do this,' Cassie whispered to me through her protective bubble.

Leah squeezed my arm. 'We believe in you.'

'Okay, everyone grab hold of each other,' I said as Leah and Cassie took my hands. Mark placed a hand on my shoulder, his free arm draped protectively over Sky. The wolves huddled closer to me, and one of them placed a paw on my foot.

I closed my eyes and thought of home. A bright light entered my head. I heard a final rumbling as the wall of the temple seemed to fall in on us.

I hit the ground hard and slowly opened my eyes. We were back in the woods outside the cabin. I tried to get up, but exhaustion held me down.

A loud scream echoed through the trees, and I caught sight of Sky writhing in pain from lying in the sun in front of me. Before I even knew what I was doing, my instincts kicked in and I teleported her into the cabin.

Mark ran to me. 'Where did she go?'

'She's in the cabin,' I said before everything went black.

SKY

Reconnecting

I was standing in the temple with everyone else, and the next moment, excruciating pain consumed me and I screamed. When it stopped, I opened my eyes and looked around. I was inside our cabin. Tears of relief fell down my face. Freya was right. I could leave the temple.

Before I had any more time to think, Mark rushed into the cabin and cradled me in his arms. 'I was so scared,' he said.

I knew he would never admit it to anyone else. He preferred people to view him as tough and without emotion. However, as our bond had grown, I had learned so much more about him, and the big tough guy that didn't care was nothing but a front.

I was worried, though. I'd broken our bond so he could get his ability to shift back. He'd said we would talk about it later, and then everything had exploded, but now we were back in our world. Without the bond, I could no longer feel his emotions. Would he hate me for what I'd done?

'I'm sorry.' It came out as a whisper, but to be fair, Mark had squeezed me so tightly, I struggled to get any air into my lungs. That I even managed to say anything at all was impressive.

He stroked my hair away from my face. 'Don't be sorry. You did what you thought was best.'

There was a moment of silence before he kissed my forehead. 'Just know that even though we're not bonded anymore, I still care for you deeply.'

I looked into his eyes. 'I care about you too.' Tears threatened to break through. I had never completely felt like I belonged or that anyone truly appreciated me growing up. But now I'd met the most amazing person, and despite breaking our bond, he still cared for me.

I wasn't sure how long we just stared into each other's eyes, embracing each other, but all the fear and tension from the fight slowly disappeared.

'How did all of you get into Whitelake village?' I asked after a while.

'Freya's cat led us into the lake and we turned up there.'

'So my dream was real, only you didn't drown yourself like I thought.'

Mark frowned. 'What are you talking about?'

I shrugged. 'I had a dream that you were following a big grey cat and then you walked into a lake and drowned yourself.'

Mark was about to say something when two wolves in their human form walked in through the door carrying an unconscious Jax to the sofa. 'We're not sure what happened. We can't seem to wake him.'

I went to check on him, but I wasn't too worried. He'd exerted himself. Not only had he fully transformed into his demon form for everyone to see, but he'd also healed Cassie from the brink of death, fought Hecate and transported us all back here to the human world. If I wasn't completely mistaken, he'd also had something to do with my quick teleportation to safety after we'd all ended up in the woods.

'Does anyone know where Cassie and Leah are?' I asked the wolves. Why weren't they by Jax's side? Had something happened to them?

The wolves stared at each other, frowning, before meeting my gaze.

'I'm sure Jax is fine. He used up a lot of energy in the last few hours and needs to recover. However, I know the first thing he'll ask about when he wakes up is Cassie. So if you don't mind bringing them here, that would be great. I'm sure they're worried about Jax as well.'

The wolves nodded and walked outside.

'Bossy woman much,' Mark joked before he became all serious. 'I really thought I had lost you. I'm happy Freya was right. Staying inside with you all day won't be that bad.' He gave me a cheeky wink.

I hit him light-heartedly on his chest and shook my head. Boys would be boys.

'Let me see your hands,' Mark demanded.

'They're fine,' I said as I waved them in his face.

'Why didn't you tell me you were hurt?'

'Because I'm fine. It doesn't hurt.'

'I find it hard to believe. Your skin is all red and blistered.'

As bad as the burns might look, they weren't that painful – not since I had got out of the sun. 'I'll be fine.'

What was that about, anyway? Hecate had told me not to leave the temple, but she'd said nothing about not being able to be out in the sun. I looked down at my hands, remembering the handcuffs of energy she'd put around my wrists. There wasn't anything indicating they were still there, but I couldn't shake the feeling they were responsible for my condition.

Mark grunted. 'Why are you staring at your wrists? Are they hurting?'

I shook my head. 'No. I was just thinking about the magical handcuffs Hecate put on me.'

Mark furrowed a brow. 'Handcuffs? I don't see any handcuffs.'

I rolled my eyes and sighed. 'They're magical – you won't be able to see them.'

'Maybe we should ask Leah. She may know what to do,' Mark said.

'I don't think there's anything she can do. I deserve this

for not listening to Jax.'

Mark placed his finger over my lips. 'Shh ... you did what you thought was right. No one can blame you for that.' He gave me a hug and planted a kiss on my forehead.

JAX

Waking Up

My body was resting on soft padding instead of the grass outside. I could hear someone moving about, shuffling their feet, and I tried to sit up to see who it was, but my body wouldn't oblige.

'Cassie?' I said as Sky came into view. 'Where's Cassie?' My voice came out as a whisper, so I wasn't sure she had heard me.

'The others are getting her for you.'

I lay back down on the sofa. Every movement was tiring. It felt like a mountain had hit me. The sound of the door opening got my attention, and I fought my body to open my eyes.

'Jax.' Cassie's voice rang out, and a moment later, she was by my side. She gave me a kiss on my forehead. I closed my eyes, relishing the feel of her lips on my skin.

I must have passed out again, because the next time I opened my eyes, my head was in Cassie's lap.

'Cassie,' I said as I looked up at her face.

'It's okay, I'm here,' she said as she stroked my face. 'Just rest.'

'The others?'

'You got us all over to the human world safe and sound. But me and Leah ended up at the house. It's why it took me some time to get here.'

I took a deep breath and relaxed. At least everyone here was safe, and hopefully Freya had managed to move the village.

'How are you not scared of me?'

Cassie bit her lip. 'Why would I be scared? I know you would never hurt me.'

'But you all saw—'

She placed a finger on my lips, interrupting what I was going to say. 'I don't care what you look like. What I saw was a beautiful creature that would risk everything for the people he loves.'

My eyes became watery, and I looked away so she wouldn't see how weak I was. How could she accept the demon part of me so easily when I couldn't accept it myself? I'd always suppressed the demon inside, terrified it would take over and hurt the people I loved – only it hadn't.

'I only have one question.'

I blinked away the tears before facing Cassie again. 'And what's that?'

'What would I look like?' she said with a gleam in her eyes.

It caught me off guard, and I pushed myself up into a sitting position next to Cassie. 'What do you mean?'

'Well, you once said we were the same and that I'm part demon, so doesn't that mean I should have another form too?'

I shrugged. 'Your father is half demon, but I've never seen him in his demon form. I'm not even sure if he has one, and your mother was something else entirely. So I'm not sure if you'll have another form, or what it would look like if you do. I guess we'll just have to wait and see.' I stifled a yawn. 'If you want, I can try and find out if your mother had another form than her human-looking one.'

Cassie smiled. 'I think you should rest. We can talk about it more later.' She got up from the sofa and gently pushed me so I was lying down once again.

'If you're going to force me to sleep, then I think you should do the same.' I lifted my arm and waited for Cassie to lie down next to me. When she did, I put my arm over her and snuggled into her, placing my head by her neck and breathing in her flowery scent. This was my type of heaven. It wasn't long before I was asleep again.

When I woke up, Cassie was sleeping by my side, and I smiled. Despite seeing what I was, she still loved me.

Getting up from the sofa without waking Cassie was a challenge I failed. She turned to face me and opened her eyes.

'Hello, beautiful,' I said as I kissed her. 'I didn't mean to wake you.'

'How are you feeling?'

'Tired,' I said as I gave her a smile.

'Why don't you rest a bit more?'

'I can't. I need to find out what happened.' I hated feeling weak and not in control. I had been too exhausted to think about anything, but now, as the tiredness had started to wear off and my mind had cleared, there was a knot in my stomach and I couldn't help but worry. I had no idea what had happened to Freya or Leaf – or any of them, really. Had they managed to save the village? To save the witches?

'Everyone will be asleep.'

'We both know they won't.'

Cassie sighed and got up. She offered her hand to help me off the sofa. I would have been fine on my own, but I took her hand so as not to offend her. My legs were shaky, but after a few steps, I got my balance back.

Cassie put her arm around me like she thought I was going to collapse at any moment. I held my tongue. I knew she was just trying to help, but it was my job to look after her, not the other way around.

We left the cabin and walked outside. The air was chilly, and I glanced over at Cassie, happy she had put a coat on. I wasn't sure what time it was, but it was dark and the stars were sparkling in the sky. I scanned the area and spotted some wolves patrolling.

'Hey, you guys have some news?' I shouted out.

One wolf broke away and marched towards us, changing form. 'No news yet, but the Alpha told us not to worry.'

My eyes went wide. 'You can still talk to your Alpha?'

'Yeah, but I don't know where he is.'

That was interesting. The fact they still had their Alpha link must mean he was at least alive, which meant the likelihood of Leaf and Freya being alive was pretty high.

'Has he said anything to you?' I asked eagerly.

'Not really, only that he's sorting things out and we shouldn't worry. Before they broke our mate bonds, he told us we may experience pain, but that it was for the greater good; however, no one has told us exactly what happened.'

I looked over at his sad expression. 'There was a massive fight, and the Alpha gave up your mate bonds to save a population of witches that would have died if he hadn't.'

The wolf nodded at me and transformed back into a wolf. He ran back to the others and they continued their patrol.

Worry about Freya and the others and the frustration of feeling powerless built up inside me and the need to be alone and recharge surfaced, but at the same time I was worried about leaving Cassie alone, knowing there was still a possibility something else might be after her. 'Cassie, why don't you go back to the cabin?'

'And leave you out here?'

'Please, Cassie. I don't want to worry about you too.'

'But it's okay for me to worry about you?'

'You know that's not what I meant.'

Cassie gave me a sour expression and crossed her arms over her chest. 'You don't get to make all the rules. Where you go, I go.'

I looked at Cassie, lost in her bright blue eyes.

'Fine, but we're going home.' I grabbed hold of her and tried to teleport us to the house, but nothing happened.

'See, you need me,' she said with a smug smile. 'Let me give it a go.'

She closed her eyes and a moment later, we landed in our bedroom. Leah came rushing in, hands raised like she was ready to use her magic.

'Oh, it's you,' she said as her hands dropped to her sides. 'Ever heard of using a normal door? Or maybe even considered appearing during normal waking hours instead of in the middle of the night? I thought something had come to kill me.'

I rolled my eyes. 'The house is shielded.'

Leah threw her hands in the air. 'You keep saying this, but I have no clue what it actually means. Our other house was enchanted, but evil still got in.'

'It stops anyone from teleporting inside unless I have invited them. And if anyone who wasn't invited breached the perimeter, it would alert me.'

'Okay, but alerting you isn't really going to help me.'

'Then cast your own protective spells over the house.'

Leah's eyes went wide. She opened her mouth to say

something but I cut her off.

'I'm sorry,' I said as I walked out of the room, leaving Cassie and Leah behind. I needed to reel in my frustration at feeling powerless instead of taking it out on everyone else. My body was still drained. I hadn't even been able to teleport us to the house, so I doubted I could turn into a crow. The only other place I could be alone was the bathroom.

I stripped down and got into the shower. The water around my feet was the colour of blood and dirt. I had completely forgotten I was wearing the same clothes as I had been when the fight went down. It felt like such a long time ago. When I got out of the shower, I looked around. I usually conjured clothes for myself, but I couldn't do that at the moment. At least there were towels. I grabbed one, wrapped it around my waist and returned to the bedroom.

Cassie and Leah were still there, but their hushed conversation came to a stop as I entered. Leah looked me over before giving Cassie a smirk and practically running out of the door.

I looked after Leah before turning to Cassie. 'What was that all about?'

'Nothing. She's just tired.' Cassie shrugged. Her eyes flickered over my bare torso before quickly returning to the floor. The pink of her cheeks darkened, and she cleared her throat. 'I think maybe I should have a shower too.' She grabbed a change of clothes and slipped out without a second glance.

SKY

The Dream

I ran fast through the forest. Much faster than I'd ever run before. But I was aware of everything around me – the smells, the light movement of the wind, the sharpness and colours of the trees.

I gracefully swerved in and out between the trees, the placement of my feet precise. I looked down and saw my paws connecting with the ground. It was a chilly day, but the coldness didn't bother me. My fur kept me warm.

The sun was peeking out above the horizon, but I felt no fear. The sunlight could not hurt me in this form. I continued running. I heard a twig break behind me and tried to run faster. But eventually a massive grey wolf jumped me and I stopped in my tracks. I looked up and saw Mark in his wolf form.

'You may be fast but you can't outrun me,' he said playfully in my mind as he licked my muzzle.

I opened my eyes. I was still in bed next to Mark. The sound of his snoring kept me from getting back to sleep. Instead, I cuddled up to him.

The thought that Mark didn't hate me and still cared for me, despite everything, left a warm feeling in my heart. He had his ability to shift back and I had my magic back. But I still felt guilty. I hadn't managed to get the grimoire. Not to mention we didn't know if everyone in Whitelake village was even alive. Getting the book wouldn't matter if they weren't.

'Morning,' Mark said as he put his arm around me.

I smiled. 'I just had the most amazing dream.'

He opened his eyes and met my gaze. 'Was I in it?'

'Yeah – well, you were, but you were a wolf. I was one too. We were running in the forest and the sun was out.'

'Sounds like a lovely dream.'

'What if it wasn't a dream? What if I could become a werewolf like you?'

Mark sat up in bed and looked at me seriously. 'I've never heard about anyone becoming a werewolf. I don't think it's possible. It's something you're born into.'

He must have seen the sadness on my face. 'Come here,' he said as he put his arms around me. 'We'll find a way for you to be out in the sun again. I promise.' He kissed me. 'Now we can either stay in bed or get up and get some breakfast. I vote for staying in bed.'

I threw a pillow at him as I got out of bed. He gave me a mocking look of surprise. 'Breakfast it is.'

When I walked into the living room, I expected Jax and Cassie to still be on the sofa, but they were gone. I gave Mark a questioning look.

'I think they left sometime last night. I heard the door open and close. I'm sure they're fine, though. Jax probably just wanted to get home. That's what I would have done if I was stuck at his house.'

I nodded. 'Anyone else been in touch?' I asked, hoping he had received some news about Whitelake village on his phone. We hadn't heard anything before we went to bed, but who knew how much magic it took to move an entire village to another realm? I liked to think they had succeeded and were resting and recharging before coming back here.

He shook his head. 'Just Seth to say he's staying at Mike's still, but other than that, nothing. But I can check with the wolves after breakfast.'

I gave him a smile and went to the kitchen to make some breakfast for us.

A while later, Mark came up behind me and put his arms around me. 'It smells delicious. I knew sorting the extension out was a good call.'

I dished up the eggs and bacon and sat down at the kitchen table. Mark took a big chunk of bacon from his plate before speaking. 'What do you want to do today?'

'I have my books and my research. Hopefully I can figure

something out regarding my situation. Or maybe Leah has found something.'

'I'll text Leah to come over and keep you company. Maybe Jax has some books she can bring that might be helpful.'

After we had finished eating, Mark left the cabin. I'd just washed up after us when the door opened and Cassie and Leah walked in. 'Where's Jax?' I asked, a bit confused.

'He left early this morning. Something about clearing his head and finding out what happened,' Cassie said.

'And you let him go?'

She bit her lip. 'I didn't really have a choice. He was gone when I woke up. If he hadn't left a note, I would be out looking for him, but I guess with everything that happened, I can't blame him for needing some time to himself.'

I nodded. 'That's true. And you can't blame him for being worried about his daughter and grandma.'

'Grandma?' Cassie asked with a frown.

'I overheard Hecate and Freya talking, and Hecate said he was Freya's grandson. I don't see why she would lie about that.'

'That definitely explains a lot. Though Jax always refers to her as a friend. I wonder if he knows?' Cassie said thoughtfully.

There was a moment of awkward silence.

Leah cleared her throat. 'I can see your skin has healed. I'm happy the herbs helped.'

'Yes, thank you. It's like it never happened.' I lifted my

arms up. 'But I still can't go out in the sun because of these stupid handcuffs that Hecate placed on me. It's a good thing Freya figured out it was the sun or I would have been stuck in the temple forever.'

'Well, Hecate is the Goddess of the moon and the underworld, so I guess something happened when she tied you to her. Let me see if I can sense the handcuffs,' Leah said.

She placed her hands over me and closed her eyes. It seemed like forever before she opened her eyes and spoke up. 'There's some foreign energy around your wrists. I guess the magical handcuffs she put on you have something to do with it.' She met my gaze. 'Can you remember anything else she said or did to you?'

I shook my head. 'Only that she wanted to know all my dreams because they were special.'

'That's strange. Why would she want your dreams?' Cassie asked.

I shrugged. 'I don't know. She even gave me a notebook that wrote my dreams down every time I opened it.'

'Maybe she thought they were visions,' Cassie said.

I nodded. 'Maybe. One of my dreams did turn out to be true. Speaking of that, I had a dream of me being a wolf and the sun didn't bother me. So maybe there's a way to become a werewolf? Mark says I'm wasting my time, but I'm stuck in here until the sun goes down anyway.'

'Mark's probably right. But maybe we can find another way. I raided Jax's house and brought some books that seemed promising,' Leah said.

She placed all the books from her bag on the kitchen table. We spent the next few hours looking through them.

Mark walked through the door and I looked up from the book I was flicking through. 'Any news?'

He looked over at all of us. 'Not really. The Alpha has spoken to them via the mind-link and told them not to worry, but that's all I know.'

'At least we know he's alive,' I said as I walked over and gave Mark a hug.

'We should probably be going,' Leah said from behind.

I said bye to her and Cassie before getting comfortable on the sofa with Mark. 'So what do we do now?'

Mark wiggled his eyebrows at me.

'I'm serious, Mark. It doesn't look like Leah has any clue how to fix me. Maybe you should just get on with your life without me.'

'Don't say that. First of all, it has only been a day. Give it time. If Freya is as powerful as Jax makes her out to be, she'll get here soon and I'm sure she'll have a solution.'

'You don't know that. What if I can never be out in the sun again?'

Mark embraced me. 'Freya just moved an entire village to a different realm. She will know what to do.'

JAX

The Proposal

The fog lay thick over the landscape, almost like smoke. It was impossible to see anything below the treetops, even with my enhanced eyesight. I flew high in the sky, enjoying the chilly wind under my wings. The sky had turned a lighter shade of blue; the sun would be up soon. I thought about Freya and teleported to her realm. Maybe she was at home. I slowly made my way over to her cottage.

When I got there, no one was there. Freya usually knew I was coming, but there was no welcome, no freshly brewed tea. I checked the house, but I didn't even see her two cats that were always hanging around. She must still be busy with the witch village. I hoped she was okay.

There was nothing left for me to do but fly back home, as I wouldn't get any answers from staying here. While flying back, I replayed all the recent events in my head. Cassie had seen the monster I truly was but had chosen to stay by my side despite everything. How could I show her how much that meant to me – how much she meant to me?

I got home in the late afternoon. Cassie and Leah were watching TV.

Cassie got up from the sofa and walked over to me. 'How are you feeling? I was worried about you.'

'I'm fine. Just needed to clear my mind.'

She kissed me before making her way back to the sofa. I grabbed her hand. 'How would you feel about going on a date?'

She turned to face me. 'Now?'

'Yeah. Why not?'

She glanced over at Leah, who put her hands up in a shrug. 'Don't mind me. I'll be fine here on my own.'

Cassie looked back at me. 'Okay. Let me just freshen up and change clothes. Where are we going? What type of clothes should I wear?'

'Just pick something comfy.' I gave her a kiss and watched as she left the room.

'Should I wait up?' Leah said.

I ran my hand through my hair. 'It depends on how well the date goes.'

'Just give me a heads-up if you decide to come home in the middle of the night. I don't need another scare.'

I gave her a tight nod.

'You seem nervous. This isn't a random date, is it?'

I was about to answer when Cassie walked back into the room in a pair of jeans and a top. 'I'm ready. Do I need a jacket?' I shook my head.

Leah gave me a knowing smile before Cassie and I teleported away.

We arrived by a lake with a massive waterfall. It was truly beautiful, and I was happy Freya's domain didn't have the same laws of seasonal weather.

'Where are we?' Cassie asked as she looked around with wide eyes. 'It's warm, and everything is so green and colourful.'

'We're in Freya's realm. I can't tell you where, exactly; I found it by accident a long time ago.'

'It's beautiful.'

I took Cassie's hand and led her along the path that led into a little cave behind the waterfall. I had thought about bringing her here for the longest time, but it had never seemed like the right time. The moment when she had got deadly injured was still fresh in my mind, and I couldn't go through that again – not without her knowing just how much I loved her.

I wasn't completely sure if Nick would approve, and in an ideal world I should have asked for his blessing first, but I didn't care. Immortal or not, life was precious, and I was planning on making the most of it.

I led Cassie into the crevice right behind the waterfall and kissed her. 'Close your eyes.'

'What's going on?'

'Just close your eyes.'

Cassie finally closed her eyes, and I conjured some rose petals and candles to make the place more romantic. I double checked I had the ring with me.

'Okay, you can open your eyes,' I said as I went down on one knee in front of her.

She put a hand over her mouth; her eyes became watery.

I hadn't prepared a speech, so instead I spoke from my heart.

'Cassie, you are the most amazing woman I have ever met, in this life and in the past. I would love nothing more than to have the chance to show you every day just how much I love and care for you. You are everything to me, and without you, life is not worth living. I told you once that a lifetime with you wouldn't be enough, and now I have been blessed to share my life with you for eternity, if you'll have me. My love for you has no boundaries. You are the missing part of my soul, and with you by my side, I feel like I am finally whole. So Cassie, will you marry me?'

Tears fell down Cassie's face as she nodded happily. 'Yes. Yes, I will marry you.'

I placed the sapphire ring on her finger and blinked away some happy tears before I got up and kissed her passionately.

We spent the next few hours behind the waterfall making love to each other for the first time. It could not have been more perfect.

SKY

The Portal

Mark and I stood by the window in the living room and watched the last bit of sun disappear below the horizon.

'It's a good thing we're in the winter months and the sun goes down early,' Mark said. 'Where would you like to go for dinner?'

'The pack house is fine,' I said as I looked at my hands. My skin was still red, but the blisters seemed to have gone away. I wouldn't want to be out around humans looking like this. Even if it wasn't painful, I was bound to get some funny stares. At least the wolves wouldn't give it a second thought. Some of them had some gruesome scars on display themselves.

'Ready to go outside?' Mark asked.

I nodded and got my coat and scarf before opening the front door. I stood there for a moment, breathing in the brisk air. My heart beat faster. What if Freya had been wrong and I couldn't be outside at all?

Mark rested his head on my shoulder before stepping outside. He turned and offered his hand. 'Take your time. Though I'd prefer to leave the house before the sun comes up again,' he said with a smirk.

I closed the gap between us so I could give him a playful slap for being cheeky. 'I'm sorry for taking a moment to appreciate the surrounding nature.'

Mark gave me a wide smile. I looked around and realised I was now standing outside.

'How are you feeling?' he asked as he placed his hand in mine.

'I'm fine,' I answered, relief flooding through my body.

'Good.' We started walking towards the pack house. I let Mark lead the way, knowing his eyesight was superior to mine, especially in the dark.

When we got there, Mark picked up a bag that was next to the wall by the exit. I looked at him curiously. 'We're not going inside?'

He shook his head. 'I thought you'd appreciate being outside after being stuck in the cabin all day, so I asked Seth for a favour.'

We walked away from the pack house and further into the trees.

He got undressed and placed his clothes in the bag before handing it to me. A moment later he was in his wolf form. He lowered his head as if to tell me to jump on.

When I got onto his back, he started running. The trees passed us in a blur. The chilled air hit my face, making my eyes water. I held on tightly to his fur, scared that if I relaxed even a tiny bit, I would fall off. It was petrifying and amazing at the same time.

He came to a stop and I got off his back. He shifted back and threw some clothes on before taking two containers and two big blankets out of the bag.

He spread one blanket out on the ground and handed me the containers of food before taking a seat. After we had eaten, he laid the other blanket on top of us. I cuddled up to him for some warmth. He'd been like a human furnace since his ability to shift returned, and I gladly sank into the comfort of his warmth.

The stars and the moon shone brightly, and I thought about everything that had happened.

'I'm sorry about everything,' I said to Mark.

He shrugged. 'There's nothing to be sorry for.'

I'd never expected to grow this close to anyone, and the fact I had completely doomed this relationship before it had even properly started wasn't lost on me. I'd given up everything to get my magic back and now I couldn't even walk in the sunlight anymore. What life would that be for Mark? He'd told me nothing had changed, that he still cared for me and was happy to spend the rest of his life with me, bond or no bond. But he had a chance to become Beta – a chance to be part of the pack. I would only hold him back. I wasn't a wolf. I couldn't even be out in the sun. Mark deserved someone who was his equal.

We continued to stare at the sky in silence. Guilt tugged at my heart. I deserved happiness too, but could I really be that selfish? I snuggled into him further. I would do what was right for Mark, but for now, I would enjoy being close to him.

Mark jerked up from the blanket, a growl escaping his lips.

I sat up and turned towards him. 'What is it?'

'Something is happening. I'm not sure what.'

A moment later I heard a noise as well. It was hard to distinguish where it was coming from. It sounded almost like a massive heartbeat echoing through the woods.

'I'd better get you to safety,' Mark said and changed before my eyes. He nudged me with his nose. As soon as I'd climbed onto his back, he took off, but we didn't get very far. An invisible force, like a shock wave, knocked me off his back. He circled back and I climbed back up.

To my surprise he turned and ran towards where the shock wave had come from.

'What's going on?' I asked without getting an answer. How I wished I could talk to him while he was in his wolf form.

After a while, we came to a stop in a glade. The Beta and several other wolves stood in a circle, staring at what looked like a rift. No one seemed to have approached it yet.

It pulsated, causing ripples of energy in the air that moved outward like rings in the water. The hair on the back of my neck stood up. This was not natural. It reminded me of something I had read about. 'I think it's a portal,' I whispered to Mark.

He nodded, and a few wolves looked my way.

A rustling sound coming from the rift got our attention, and after a moment the Alpha and Leaf stepped out of it. Relief flooded through me; I was happy she was still alive. All the wolves bowed down. I took that opportunity to get off Mark and run towards Leaf.

Before I reached her, she put her hand up, signalling for me to wait.

The Alpha took a step towards the wolves. 'I'm happy that you are all here. We have much to discuss, but first Leaf would like to say a few words.'

Leaf walked past me and assumed a position next to the Alpha. 'I'm truly sorry for what you have all gone through because of me and my people. I know we did not ask every single one of you. There just wasn't time, but I'm truly grateful for the sacrifices you made. The magic from your mate bonds saved my village and my people, and I'm forever indebted to you. This portal is a way into my village, and every single one of you is welcome to come and see what you helped us save. A lot of buildings have collapsed and several people got injured; however, because of you, we can start over.'

The Alpha looked over at Leaf and then continued with a speech of his own.

'It was not a decision I made lightly, and I'm sorry I didn't have time to discuss it with you, but under the circumstances, giving up our mate bonds to save thousands of people seemed like a simple choice. However, I apologise for the pain it caused everyone. But know that your pain helped to avoid a genocide.'

He took a moment to look out over the audience.

'All the established mate bonds have been broken, and we all have to learn to live with the void it caused, but rest assured I'm very much in love with your Luna. Mate bond or not, I feel like I would have made the same decision. Hopefully you will all feel the same, despite being unable to feel your mate's emotions. For everyone who hasn't found their mate yet, I'm sorry. Because the bond is gone, it's no longer up to the Fates to decide who you are with. And though you might not have as strong of a connection, you are free to decide yourself who you want to spend the rest of your life with.'

He signalled for the Beta to step forward.

'I will shortly discuss the matters of the portal with my Beta and the other guardian wolves, but we are to become the witches' new guardians and help guard this portal from outside threats. Leaf and I have decided our species are to live as one, side by side, helping each other.'

The Alpha took a moment to collect himself before he continued. 'Because of everything that has happened in their world, a lot of things need rebuilding. Please volunteer if you want to help and we can organise a joint effort. The witches on the other side of this portal have been told everything you have, and I have asked everyone to make sure that everyone feels welcomed.'

As he stepped away, the wolves howled, most likely waking up everyone who may have been asleep.

I finally got to give Leaf a hug. 'I'm happy you're safe.'

She returned the hug. 'Me too.'

'Have you seen my sister and family?'

She shook her head. 'I haven't had a proper look around. A lot of buildings collapsed, and the witches are working hard to find people and heal them.'

'I should look for them.'

Mark grabbed my hand. 'You can't. The sun will be up soon.'

I looked at the sky and realised it had started to brighten. 'But it's my family.'

'And they wouldn't want to lose you over something as silly as sunlight. Come on, let me get you back to the cabin and we can come back tomorrow night.'

I sighed but agreed with Mark. I wouldn't be any help to my family in the sunlight.

JAX
The Day After

I woke up to the sunlight reflecting from the waterfall, causing flecks of light to appear on the stone walls of the crevice. I looked over at Cassie, still peacefully asleep. A big smile formed on my lips. I wasn't ready to go back home to reality, so instead of getting up, I put my arm around Cassie and pulled her closer to me, kissing the back of her head as I breathed in her scent. It felt like a weight had been lifted from my shoulders, and I was overflowing with happiness.

Eventually Cassie stirred and we reluctantly got up. 'How about a swim before we go back?' I said with a smile.

'Won't it be cold?'

'There's only one way to find out,' I said as I offered my

hand. She took it and gave me a nod and we jumped into the water.

The water was cold enough to wake us up but still pleasant. We spent some time playing around in the water, but eventually we got out and sat down on a rock next to the waterfall to dry off.

'It's beautiful here, but maybe we should head back. You said time moved differently here, so who knows how long we've been gone for?' Cassie said.

I met her gaze, and as much as I wanted to stay here with her and forget about the world, she was right.

'Yeah, we probably should. We can always come back another time.'

'I would like that,' Cassie said with a smile before taking my hand.

I teleported us back to the house. When we arrived, I tensed up. Something was different – there was a weird energy in the air that hadn't been there when we left.

'Let me see it,' Leah said as she burst into the room.

'How did you know?' Cassie asked as she showed Leah the ring on her finger.

'Jax was acting nervous, so I had my suspicions, and then when you didn't come home, I thought it could only mean one thing.' She grabbed Cassie's hand to examine the ring. 'Wow, you really went all out, Jax.'

'Sorry. Something's wrong. Can you watch Cassie for me?'

Cassie crossed her arms. 'I don't understand why you

always ask Leah to look after me. I can look after myself. I'm not helpless. You know I've been practising my powers.'

'Mind reading and empathy is hardly going to keep you safe.'

Cassie hit me lightly on the arm. 'You know I can do more than that.'

I gave her an apologetic smile. 'I feel safer knowing the two of you are together, looking after each other.'

I turned into a crow and flew out of the window. I needed to find out what was going on. The energy increased and vibrated in the air, telling me I was close to its source. I picked up on noises and movements. Several wolves and humans were walking around in the forest. Something was definitely up.

The intensity of the energy made it challenging to maintain a steady flight. Scanning the area, I finally saw where it was coming from. There was a portal in the middle of a clearing. Could this be from the witch village?

I flew closer to examine it. Two wolves were standing guard next to the portal. As I approached them, Leaf stepped out. Relief flooded through me, and I descended from the sky. I transformed into my human form before walking up to her.

'I'm really glad you made it,' I said as I gave her a hug.

'And you. I'm happy you got everyone to safety before the temple collapsed,' Leaf said with a smile.

'What happened after we left?'

'Freya managed to move the village to her realm, but she

couldn't save the buildings, and several of them collapsed. We are still going through it all, digging out people from the ruins.'

'I'm sorry, but at least you don't need to worry about Hecate anymore.' I knew I hadn't killed her, but I had weakened her enough that she had retreated. It would take time for her to regain her strength. Maybe we would see her again, or maybe she had learned her lesson. Either way, she wouldn't be bothering the witches ever again. They were under Freya's protection now.

She nodded. 'The people have assigned me as their new High Priestess, at least until further notice,' Leaf said.

I smiled. 'Congratulations. I'm happy you finally got your rightful place in the village.'

She gave me an awkward look. 'You know I don't care about that. I just want peace. The true High Priestess would be Leah. After all, I'm way too old for this and she would be next in line, but I have yet to talk to her and my people about it.'

I grinned. 'Good luck with that. It's impossible to get Leah to do anything she doesn't want to do.' I looked around for Freya, but she was nowhere to be seen. 'How come Freya isn't here? I need to talk to her, especially after she told me I was part god.'

'She had other things to attend to. You know her, always a hundred irons in the fire.'

'That's very true,' I said as I gave her another hug. 'I'm happy you're safe. I'll come back a bit later to help.'

'Thank you.'

I turned back into a crow and flew back to the house. At least I knew where the strange energy was coming from and that it was nothing to worry about.

When I got back to the house, Leah was in the kitchen, cooking by the looks of it, and Cassie was setting the table. 'Everything's okay?' Cassie asked.

I nodded. 'The energy I felt was from a portal to the witch village.'

Leah rolled her eyes. 'I could have told you that if you had given me a chance to talk earlier. The portal appeared early this morning while you were away. I'm going to go and help them later.'

She brought the food to the table and Cassie and I took a seat. We ate in silence for a while, enjoying the rich flavours of the casserole Leah had made.

'So, how did Nick take the news?' Leah asked.

I swallowed before meeting her gaze. 'I haven't told him yet.'

'Scared he'd kill you?' Leah said with a smirk.

'He wouldn't kill his best mate,' I said with confidence. At least, I hoped he wouldn't.

'Well, you're marrying his daughter.'

I looked up at Leah with confusion.

'I'm not saying he'll kill you. I'm just saying it's different. He may view this differently.'

I grimaced. 'I guess there's only one way to find out. Wish me luck,' I said before teleporting myself to Nick. This was going to be one awkward conversation, especially considering I hadn't even mentioned anything about me and Cassie to Nick.

SKY

REUNITED

I was interrupted from my reading when I heard the door to the cabin open and close. Mark had left earlier that day to attend to some pack business. Technically, he wasn't part of the pack yet, but he'd told me the Alpha had plans to perform the initiation ceremony as soon as things had calmed down.

I got up and walked into the living room, hoping Mark would have some news, but instead Cassie was there. 'Hi,' I said.

She smiled and waved. A massive blue rock on her hand almost blinded me. 'Holy Goddess,' I said as I made my way towards her to inspect the ring. 'When did this happen?'

'A few hours ago.' She beamed with happiness.

'Between everything that's been going on, I'm surprised he found the time.'

'He said he had been waiting for a special time and hadn't wanted to rush it, but after almost losing me the other day, he felt like he couldn't wait any longer.'

'Yeah, he went crazy when he thought he'd lost you. I almost peed my pants the first time I saw his demonic form. Weren't you scared?'

'How can I be scared? I love him. All of him. What he looks like doesn't matter to me. I see his heart, his light. Besides, seeing him like that made me feel safer. I'm sure you know what I'm talking about, seeing Mark in his wolf form for the first time. Were you scared?'

When I thought about it, I had to admit that Mark's wolf form didn't scare me at all. I'd known instantly it was him, even though I'd never seen his wolf before. I wondered how, as it was after our bond had been broken. 'Okay, you have a point.'

We made our way over to the sofa. 'So where is your knight in shining armour? Is he helping at the portal?' I asked.

Cassie shook her head. 'He's gone to see Nick. But I'm sure he'll help once he gets back.'

'I can't wait until the sun goes down so I can go over and look for my family.'

Cassie nodded. 'It must be hard not knowing whether or not they're alive.'

The way they used to treat me entered my mind, but I

also remembered all the small things they'd done for me – things that made me realise they did actually love me in their own way. I may not have been their favourite daughter, but Dawn had told me how devastated they'd all been after I left.

I let out a sigh. 'You have no idea. Seeing Dawn brought all the feelings I have about my family to the surface. I love them, but their favouritism towards Dawn drove me mad and made me feel insignificant, like they never cared about me or could be bothered to get to know me, but maybe I didn't put enough effort into it either.'

'Do you regret running away?'

'I don't know. But I think it's what the Fates wanted. If I hadn't run away, none of this may have happened.'

'That's true,' Cassie said thoughtfully.

The door opened and Mark walked in. He came over and gave me a kiss, then did a double take as he turned to Cassie. 'That is one big rock. Who's the lucky guy?' he asked with a smirk.

Cassie just stared at him.

'I'd ask you to tell us all about it, but I don't really want all the details. There's no denying how crazy Jax is about you. So if you're happy, I'm happy for you.'

'Thanks, Mark. That means a lot coming from you,' Cassie said as she gave him a hug.

Mark turned to me with a loving gaze. 'Don't get any ideas. There's no way I can compete with that rock.'

Cassie laughed. 'Mark, it's not the size of the stone that matters but the size of your heart and commitment to the person.'

I nodded in agreement. 'Cassie's right.'

'Really?' Mark asked with a frown. 'You wouldn't care if I made a ring out of wood?'

'If you put your heart and soul into making a ring out of wood for me, I would treasure it more than anything bought in a shop.'

Mark shook his head. 'I will never understand women.' His gaze went to the window and back to me. 'The sun is about to go down. Are you ready to head out?' I nodded in response.

'I should probably head back to the house to check on Leah,' Cassie said. 'She's trying to figure out a way to get the witches' magic back.'

'She is?' I should have gone back to doing the same now that we knew they were all alive. 'Has she found anything? Maybe we can compare notes tomorrow.'

Cassie nodded and said goodbye.

Mark and I walked towards the portal. I was nervous and restless and couldn't wait to see my family to make sure they were okay. I hadn't seen them in a long time, but seeing my sister had ignited a longing to see them again. But how would they react to me?

We stopped next to the portal, and Mark squeezed my hand. 'Are you ready for this?'

I nodded. 'Yeah. Let's find my family.'

Leaf came up to us before we stepped through. 'Sky, I must warn you, it's in an awful state and I'm not sure if your sister made it out alive.'

'I don't care. I need to see it,' I said, with an empty feeling in my heart. I pulled Mark to the portal and we stepped through.

We ended up in the middle of the market square and were met by rubble and ruins. The temple was a heap of large pillars and broken cement, and most of the houses around us had collapsed too. We followed the path someone had cleared between the wreckage which led to a large orb of light that shone above the temple in the sky. A group of people were working to move rubble out of the way while searching for survivors.

They had just dragged a person out of the ruins and several witches were working their healing magic on them. Would my mother be around here somewhere? She was, after all, a healer. I scanned the area again, and my heart stopped. There, in the middle of it all, was my mother. I spotted my dad as well, using our horses to help carry the rubble away from the area.

'Mum,' I shouted as I ran towards them. She looked towards me. Her dark eyes filled with warmth and a smile appeared on her lips.

I stumbled a few times on the uneven surface but eventually made it to my mother's side.

'Sky? My precious Sky. We have been so worried.' She hugged me tightly. 'I'm so happy to know you're okay.'

'What about Dawn and Night?'

'Night is helping your father. We haven't had any sign of

Dawn yet. She was in the temple when it collapsed. But we have found a few witches that are still alive, so hopefully we will find her soon too.'

Tears threatened to escape my eyes. 'I tried to save her. I tried to get her to leave the temple.'

'I know, honey. It's not your fault,' my mother said as she hugged me again.

When we broke the embrace, my father was by our side and grabbed me in a tight bear hug that lifted me off the ground and made me struggle for air.

'Who's your friend?' my mother asked, her gaze set on Mark.

'This is Mark,' I said as I stepped over to him. I gestured towards my parents. 'Meet Gina and Fergus, my mother and father.'

Mark stretched his hand out to them. 'It's a pleasure to meet you.'

My father shook his hand. 'Any friend of my daughter is a friend to this family.'

My mother called my brother. 'Night, get over here and say hi to your sister.'

A moment later, a taller, older version of Night walked up to us.

'Hi. I'm happy you're alive,' he said without emotion, his voice sounding much deeper than I remembered.

'I can't believe how grown up you look,' I said with a smile. Night made a face and walked away.

My mother turned to me. 'Don't worry about him. He

will come around. He took it hard when you left.'

Someone shouted and my mother turned around. 'I think we'd better get back to work. Sounds like they have recovered another body.' She hurried off towards the person who'd been shouting.

I looked around. 'What can we do to help?' I asked my father.

'We need to clear everything. Pick a spot and start moving the rubble to the cart.' I nodded, and he went back to the horses.

When I turned to Mark, his eyes were focused and he was tilting his head. 'What is it?' I asked.

'I think I can hear someone. Hold on.' He moved around and stopped in front of a pile of rubble. A marble cooler was visible, but it was covered by broken cement blocks. 'I think someone's inside it,' he said as he pointed towards the cooler.

'Okay. Let me use my magic to get it free.' I took a deep breath and called on air to help me move it, but nothing happened. Why wasn't it moving? I closed my eyes and concentrated harder. Still nothing. What was going on? Why wasn't my magic working? It had been working in the temple.

'What's taking you so long?' Mark asked.

I looked up at Mark with tears in my eyes. 'My magic's gone.'

Mark frowned. 'You don't have any magic? But Hecate gave it back to you.'

'I know, but it's not working.'

He wrapped his arms around me. 'Do you know when it happened?'

'I don't know. I could use it in the temple.'

'Have you used it since you got back?'

I shook my head. 'No. Last time I used it was during the fight in the temple. Do you think Hecate took it when she left?'

He shrugged. 'I don't know. Maybe.' He wiped a tear from my cheek and kissed my forehead. 'Don't worry. We'll get your magic back again.'

He released me and looked over at the other group of people. 'Can we have some help?' he shouted. 'I think someone's trapped inside the box.'

Two witches rushed over, cleared the rubble on top of the cooler and opened the door.

A dirty but seemingly intact person was inside. I offered them my hand and helped them out. As I got a better look at them, I realised it was Miriam from the kitchen in the temple.

She let out a cough and sat down on the ground. 'Thank you. I thought I would die in there.'

'How did you end up in the cooler?'

'I was cooking food when the temple started shaking, and I thought the cooler would be the safest place for me.'

My mother came over and ran her hands over Miriam. 'I don't think anything's broken. The cooler may have saved your life, but let's get you to the healing centre.' Miriam got up and my mother walked off with her.

We continued working on clearing the rubble, and we

found a few more witches. They were all alive, but some had sustained quite severe injuries and it was unclear if they were going to make it. I wasn't sure if I was worried or relieved none of them had been Dawn.

JAX

Nick's Blessing

I reluctantly walked up to the door and rang the doorbell. Surely he would be happy for us? He hadn't been in a great mood the last time I'd seen him, but I was still his best mate.

Nick opened the door. 'Social call or business?' He sounded annoyed, like I was interrupting something important.

'Hi to you too.' I looked around uncomfortably. 'I guess it's more of a social call.'

He smiled. 'Very well. I guess I have some time.' He opened the door further to let me inside. 'Sorry about the other day. I wasn't expecting you to drop by, and I was waiting to hear back from my scouts. I'm getting closer, you know.'

I furrowed my brow. 'Closer to what?'

'To figuring out who's responsible for Lily's death. Just waiting for my source to confirm it.' He sat down on the sofa. 'So how is Cassie doing? Any new abilities I should know about?'

'Her main ones are still mind control and empathy. But she has been practising her telepathy and teleportation skills too.'

He tilted his head. 'Anything else you want to tell me?'

I took a moment to collect myself. 'We ran into some trouble with Hecate and I almost lost her.' I glanced over at him, waiting for him to become angry because I'd let someone get their hands on Cassie, but he stayed calm – almost too calm.

'It's a good thing you were there to protect her, then. Maybe I need to pay Hecate a visit.'

'No need. She's gravely injured.'

He nodded. 'So why are you here? Because we both know it's not to tell me about everything that went down with Hecate, because if it was, you would have come sooner. Don't think just because I'm not around that I'm not up to speed with what's happening.'

I had temporarily forgotten he could see the present and the past in the fire. It always confused me, as it made more sense to scry in water. But then again, he was the son of Surtr, the fire giant.

When I'd first met Nick in school, he had just found out

about his powers and concluded that his father, whom he had grown up with, wasn't his biological father. Figuring out who his father was had got me trapped in the hell realm in the first place.

Nick cleared his throat, and I got back to reality. I glanced over at him. 'I have some news about me and Cassie.'

'Oh. You mean my daughter you were supposed to look after, not fall in love with?'

I held my breath. I should have known he would know about us. Why hadn't I told him sooner?

He gave me a smile, and I could feel my body relax as I exhaled. 'I want her to be happy, and even though I'm not sold on the idea that my best friend is planning to spend eternity with my daughter, I can't blame either of you. The heart wants what the heart wants. After all, I would be foolish to tell you otherwise. I wouldn't have been with my beautiful Lily had I added logic to the equation.'

'Thank you, Nick. It really means a lot to me.' I guessed Leah was wrong. I wouldn't get killed today.

Nick's smile dropped and he glared at me, his eyes turning black. 'However, if you hurt her, I will hunt you down.'

'I will protect her with my life.'

'Good. I do have one request. I would like to see my daughter first and personally give you both my blessing. It was a tradition Lily's people used to do, and as they denied her it due to marrying me, it would mean a lot to me if I could do it for you to carry on the tradition in Lily's honour. It's what Lily would have wanted.'

'It would be my pleasure. Like you said, we have eternity together, so there's no reason to stress anything,' I said with a smile. 'I'll bring Cassie with me once it's safe.'

Nick suddenly went quiet and distant, looking towards the door. He got up from the sofa. 'Duty calls. My scout's back with confirmation and Corson's whereabouts.'

I froze. 'Corson, as in the demon keeper of the west?'

'Yes.'

'The keepers are forces that shouldn't be messed with.'

'If Corson is responsible for Lily's death, they will pay.'

My mouth went dry. 'You ... you can't kill him.' Not only was he a true immortal, but killing the keeper of the west would cause mayhem in the demon realms. And if all keepers were killed, it would destroy the universe.

'I'll find a way.'

'Please be careful. No revenge is worth ending the world for.' I patted him on the shoulder before stepping outside and back to the human world. I was worried about him and what he may do, but I knew there would be no way of stopping him. He was a powerful demon, more powerful than me. What I had gained in experience over the years, Nick made up for in pure strength. Immune to my powers and a powerful fire demon at that.

'You're back,' Cassie shouted in excitement as she made her way towards me.

'And you're not dead,' Leah chimed in.

'Did you ever doubt it?' I said with a smirk.

Cassie ignored Leah. 'What did he say?'

'He wants to personally give us his blessing.'

'Does that mean I get to finally meet my dad?' Cassie said, a wide smile appearing on her face.

I shook my head. I hated to burst her bubble.

The smile on Cassie's face faded. 'Why doesn't he want to see me?'

I embraced her. 'He does want to see you, but it's not that simple.'

'But Sky went to the demon realm and met my dad. Why can't I?' She looked up at me with tears in her eyes.

'Because it's not safe. If Nick is right about who is behind all of this, it's important that no one finds out you're his daughter. I would do anything to keep you safe, but there are a lot of demons that are more powerful than me. I wouldn't stand a chance.'

Cassie bit her lip. 'You mean he knows who killed my mother?'

I nodded.

'Does he know why?'

'I don't know. Nick's not really forthcoming with information.'

SKY

The Ceremony

I kept going back and forth to help in Whitelake village. It was comforting seeing my family again, but Night still avoided me. One afternoon Leaf came by the cabin. She let out a sigh and gave me a sympathetic smile. 'I have some bad news, but I think it's better you hear it from your mother.'

My heart stopped beating. This couldn't be good. Leaf got a scrying bowl out and placed a calling stone in it while I processed what she'd said.

A moment later, my mother appeared. Her eyes were red and swollen from shed tears. 'Hi, Sky. We found Dawn.'

I stared at my mother, scared to ask about Dawn's condition. From the state of my mother, I knew it was unlikely to be good news.

'She's gone. It looks like she sacrificed herself to save the High Priestess.' My mother let out a sniffle. 'I know you can't be here right now, but I wanted you to know.'

Tears stung my eyes and it took a while to sink in. 'And the High Priestess?' I asked coldly.

'She's alive but sustained a head injury. They're not sure if she'll make it.'

I nodded, feeling a growing emptiness in my chest. 'Thank you for telling me.' My mother gave me a sad smile before vanishing from the water.

A void opened in my stomach. It wasn't fair. My sister was dead, but the High Priestess got to live?

'I'm so sorry,' Leaf said and wrapped her arms around me. Tears streamed down my face. Why did it feel like the world was ending? I didn't even like my sister that much, but despite all the moments I'd wished she was dead, I hadn't actually meant it. I'd even tried to get her out of the temple.

I let go of Leaf. 'Would you mind giving me some space? I need to be alone.'

She squeezed my shoulder and wiped the tears from my chin. 'Take all the time you need. I'm here if you need me.'

Ever since I'd found out that Dawn had died. I had refused to go back and had just been moping around in bed, grieving. What was the point of anything?

Cassie, Leah and Jax had all come around to check up on

me, but I hadn't been in the mood and pretended to be asleep. Mark picked up on it and asked them to give me time.

I was lying in bed, too exhausted to get up but too awake to go to sleep, when Leah walked into the room. 'Sky, you need to pull yourself together. I know losing someone you care about is hard, but the world doesn't stop because of it. You've been in here for weeks. It's time to face reality again.'

'You don't know what it's like. She was my sister.'

'Maybe I don't, but I lost my dad, so I know what it feels like to lose someone you love and feel like it's your fault. And it sucks, but at some point you need to stop blaming yourself and get on with life. Dawn made her choice, and you are not responsible for the outcome. You have so many people that care about you. So many people that still need your help.'

'I only make things worse.'

'That's not true and you know it,' Leah said as she threw some clothes on the bed. 'A friend of yours is here to see you, and she brought something with her.'

'What did she bring?'

Leah gave me a wry smile. 'Why don't you get out of bed and join us in the living room to find out?'

I let out a deep breath and fell back down on the bed as she closed the door. I closed my eyes as tears burned behind them. I hoped she was right. That this feeling of emptiness inside me would go away. This feeling of guilt.

I got up and got dressed. I didn't really feel like seeing anyone, but she hadn't mentioned the person by name, so curiosity got the better of me – and what would she have brought?

As I stepped into the living room, Leah was sitting on the sofa with Naia, the grimoire between them. It was in great condition considering everything it had endured. The glass case must have protected it.

'Hi. How are you doing? I'm sorry about Dawn,' Naia said.

'I'm sorry too.'

Naia shook her head. 'Don't be. I told you we weren't close. She always treated me like I didn't exist.'

'She's still your mother. Do they know if she's going to make it?'

'She's in a coma. The healers are doing everything they can, but they don't know if she'll wake up. But I didn't come over to talk about my mother. We found the grimoire in the ruins, and Leaf said you needed it to reverse the withering.' She handed the book over to me. 'It's affecting the people that worked at the temple too, and a lot of them have already died.'

'I'm sorry,' I said as I started flipping through it. It was full of different spells and ceremonies, all written in different handwriting.

'My mother said it once belonged to Elise Whitelake and was handed down to the next generation's High Priestess. All the spells are useless unless you have an affinity for all four elements.'

Leah winked. 'I guess it's a good thing I'm here.'

I stopped on the page that showed how the magic had

been taken from the witches. Leah looked over my shoulder. 'Do you think we will be able to reverse it?'

I shrugged. 'It's a complicated spell. We have to overload everyone with magic to restore the regeneration, but without Hecate we don't have the magic that was taken. So we have nothing to draw upon unless we can find another source that contains enough magic.'

'What about nature? Can't we take magic from there?' Leah asked.

I shook my head. 'I forget you didn't study magic. Nature does hold magic – it is what helps us create – but we also need to use our magic within, because the magic in nature doesn't have a high enough concentration. It's why it tires us out, but both can be replenished, so the negative effects aren't severe. But with the extent of magic we need, you would end up with a dead wielder and a dead land – and it probably still won't be enough.'

Leah became thoughtful. 'What about the witches that died in the temple? Leaf had me looking into funeral ceremonies. I found a funeral spell in my book. I don't know if it's the one you normally do, but Jax said it was a beautiful ceremony. He witnessed it when he lost Katie. I thought maybe if we tweaked it, we could use the magic from the ones who got caught in the crossfire or when the building collapsed to restore the magic to the ones who had theirs sacrificed.'

'But that would stop their souls from moving on. It would trap their magic inside the other witches,' Naia said.

Leah shook her head. 'Not really. It would delay them from being reborn until their magic becomes free again. But don't you think it's something worth considering?'

I shrugged. 'I don't know. It's a lot to ask.'

'Maybe. But it would mean their deaths wouldn't have been for nothing. This might be the way to reverse all of Hecate's influences. You might even be able to go out into the sun again. Don't you think Dawn would have wanted to redeem her sins?'

'I can't speak for any of the others, but if Dawn hadn't been brainwashed, I'm sure she would have been on our side.' I thought back to some childhood memories of a time when me and Dawn had been close. She'd always looked out for me when we were younger. I blinked away some tears.

'It's settled, then,' Naia said. 'I will ask for the families' permission.'

'And I'll talk to Leaf and see what she says,' Leah said with a smile.

A couple of days later, we were getting ready for the funeral when someone knocked on the door. Jax and Cassie stepped inside. 'Are you guys ready to go?'

'Yeah.' I looked around. 'Where's Leah?'

'She's already there. Leaf thought it would be a good idea for her to lead the ceremony, as she's the one that came up with it.'

I nodded.

'Want me to teleport us over?' Jax asked.

I shook my head. My stomach became uneasy just thinking about it. 'We have time. Why don't we just walk?'

'Walking sounds good to me,' Mark chimed in. He turned to Seth. 'Ready?'

'I don't understand why it has to be in the middle of the night or why I have to come.'

'Because the witches are part of our people now, and we're there to show our respect. Besides, it's Sky's sister's funeral. Don't you want to be there for Sky?'

He shrugged. 'I guess.'

We made our way to Whitelake village in silence.

The debris had almost completely been cleared, and several houses had been rebuilt. If it wasn't for the ruins of some houses, it would have been impossible to tell something bad had happened.

When we arrived where the temple used to be, it had been stripped of everything but its foundation. It had taken the biggest hit, and it was almost a miracle the foundation was still sound. They were planning to rebuild it, as it had been built upon sacred land. That was also the reason the funeral had to be there. They'd placed all the bodies of those who had fallen in a circle on the foundation, with a spell cast on them to preserve them, so everyone could come and pay their respects.

We separated from Jax and Cassie and went to seek out my family. I gave my mum a hug as tears streamed down her face. Dad squeezed my shoulders before turning back to console my mother. Night acknowledged me with a nod but remained quiet. I would have to think of some way to make it up to him. It was hard to believe my sister was gone. I wasn't sure what was worse, the feeling of loss or my mother's heart-racked sobs.

I gestured toward Mark and Seth. 'You already met Mark, but this is Seth, Mark's brother.'

'What a pleasure to meet you,' my mum said between sobs. 'You look to be the same age as Night.' She turned towards Night. 'Night, why don't you come here and introduce yourself?'

He sighed but walked over to us again. 'I'm Night.'

Seth gave him a sad smile. 'I'm Seth. I'm sorry for your loss.'

Night shrugged. 'Is your brother really a werewolf?'

Seth nodded, and they drew aside together.

'I should probably go and see Leah and get ready for the ceremony.' I said bye to my parents and to Mark and made my way over.

Leah offered me a white robe before joining Leaf by the altar. Leaf started talking. 'We have gathered here today to say goodbye to everyone that passed during the battle with Hecate and to give back the magic to the witches who had it sacrificed. This day will mark the beginning of our new ways, and as the sun rises, creating a new dawn, so will we.'

I walked up to the foundation with several others wearing white robes. These were the people who had lost their magic. I recognised most of them from when I lived with Leaf, but there were a few new faces. Maybe they were the people who had lived in the temple. I looked for Heath, but I couldn't see him. Had he fallen victim to the collapsed buildings?

Leah started walking around the bodies, and we followed, creating a circle.

Once Leah got back to the top, Leaf took a step towards the crowd. 'Inside this circle are all the people that have given their lives for what they believed. We have contacted all the families of the ones that have passed, and they have given us permission to allow them to live on in the people that had their magic sacrificed and therefore restore them to what they once were. Like everything in nature, life goes in cycles, and their sacrifice will not be forgotten. Once their new cycle comes to an end, their energy will be released and be reborn in the natural order.'

Leah walked over to the north quadrant of the circle. 'I call upon the power of Earth for your protection, nurture and prosperity. Please join our circle.'

Before my eyes, vines appeared from the ground and grew over the bodies.

Leah continued to the east. 'I call upon the power of Air for your protection, wisdom and knowledge. Please join our circle.'

Wind grew around the circle, caressing everyone inside it, and leaves floated around freely in the light breeze.

'I call upon the power of Fire for your protection, strength and rebirth. Please join our circle.'

A small fire moved around the bodies and created a mini circle within the large one.

'I call upon the power of Water for your protection, patience and healing. Please join our circle.'

Water appeared from nowhere and swept over the fire, causing smoke to rise in its place.

Leah walked back up to the top of the circle. 'I call upon the power of Spirit for your protection, balance and guidance. Please join our circle.'

The smoke changed colour and created a purple haze inside the circle.

'I welcome you all into the circle and ask you to help us right a wrong.' Leah walked towards the bodies on the floor and placed an amethyst in the middle of them all. 'Merry meet, merry part and merry meet again.'

As she stepped back, all the bodies became engulfed by the fire. At first it was a normal orange flame, which changed to pink, purple, and finally blue. As the bodies ceased to exist, the blue flame became glowing smoke. It lifted from the ground and circled me and everyone else in the circle before entering our bodies.

A lightness overcame me, filling me with safety. I tingled from its touch as it moved through my body. When it left, my body felt strengthened. And everything became still.

Leah lifted a goblet from the altar and raised it in the air. 'Blessed be.' She thanked all the elements and opened the circle.

As the ceremony finished, food and drinks were brought

out, and people started mingling.

Eva walked over to me. 'That was amazing. And I have my magic back. Look,' she said as small vines started growing on the ground next to her. She let out a laugh. 'Thank you, Sky. I know this would not have been possible without you.' She bowed her head and walked off.

Several of the witches who had their magic back tried it out with various degrees of success. Everyone around was laughing and cheering them on. I was happy for them, but I didn't feel like joining in. I walked away from the festivities and sat down by a tree. Mark joined me.

'Did it work? Did you get your magic back?'

I nodded and made the leaves rustle in the wind. 'I'm not sure if it solved the sun problem. I thought I would feel something, but I don't.'

'I'm sorry,' he said. He looked around as Cassie and Jax joined us.

'Where's Seth?' asked Cassie.

'He's still with Sky's brother,' Mark answered.

She nodded and turned to me. 'How are you feeling?'

I shrugged. 'I don't know. I'm not sure the ceremony helped me.'

'Why'd you say that?' Jax asked.

'Just a feeling I have.'

Jax stepped in front of me. 'Hold your hands out and I'll see if I can feel anything.'

I did as I was told, and he placed his hands over my arms. He gave me a sad smile. 'I think you're right. I can still feel interference.'

I sighed. 'I guess I'm just not meant to walk in the sun again.'

Mark nudged me with his side. 'Don't say that. We'll find a way.'

I woke up to the light coming into the room. Mark was still asleep next to me. As I debated whether I had the energy to get up, something jumped onto the bed. I looked up and saw a big grey cat walking towards me – the same one that had helped me get to Leaf's house.

'Hi there, handsome,' I said as I stroked him behind the ear. A growl from behind made me look around.

Mark had jumped out of bed and made his way towards the cat. 'Get your filthy paws off my woman.'

'It's just a cat,' I said calmly, unable to understand his anger. I knew he was technically a dog and that cats and dogs didn't really get along, but it seemed very exaggerated.

'That's what you think,' Mark spat. 'I happen to know he's not a cat at all.'

I looked at the cat again and he meowed in agreement before jumping off the bed and walking through the closed door. I stared at the door, wondering if I had imagined it.

'Come on. Let's get dressed. I have a feeling someone's here to see you,' Mark said.

We walked into the living room and were joined by Freya.

Mark kissed me. 'I need to see the Alpha and talk about the pack ceremony. I'll be back as soon as I can,' he said before heading out of the door, leaving me alone with Freya.

'Please come and join me and have some tea,' she said as she poured another cup.

I wasn't sure what was going on, but I did as I was told. 'Thank you,' I said as she handed me the cup.

She took a long sip before she spoke up. 'I am truly sorry for everything you have endured. I wish I could remove the bond Hecate placed on you. Unfortunately, I do not have the ability to do so. But because you are a chosen one, there is another way. Your human form cannot cope with the sunlight, as it is tied to Hecate and the underworld, but I can give you the ability to transform into an animal. While you are in the animal form, Hecate's bond is temporarily voided and you can be outside in the sun.' She took another sip of her tea. 'I understand you and Mark, despite losing your bond, are still very much in love, therefore my gift to you would be the ability to turn into a wolf at will. It will not interfere with your own magical abilities, but you may not be able to access them as a wolf.'

'A chosen one? What does that mean?' I asked.

'The Fates have granted you visions of what is to come. Please be vigilant.' Freya looked into my eyes. 'Are you ready?' I nodded, though I was still trying to comprehend everything she'd said.

She took my hand and whispered something in a language I didn't understand. Some foreign energy washed over me, creating a feeling of light inside me.

'Now, think about being a wolf.'

I did what she said, and a bright light flashed before me, causing me to close my eyes. When I opened them again, I was closer to the floor and everything seemed sharper.

'Here, let me help you,' Freya said as a big mirror appeared in front of me. Looking back at me was a beautiful white wolf. I walked up to the mirror in awe and pressed my nose against it. It was really me.

Freya chuckled in the background. 'I think my job here is done. If you need to turn back, just visualise yourself as a human, and the same goes for turning into a wolf.'

I practised it a few times. 'How come I get to keep my clothes when the wolves don't?'

'Because you turning into a wolf works by a different magic. The shifters physically change, but your change is a magical one.'

'Thank you.'

'You are very welcome, my child,' Freya said before disappearing.

I stood by the mirror inspecting my wolf for a long time, coming to terms with the gift Freya had given me.

Mark walked in through the door. 'Sky? Are you—' He stopped in his tracks and stared at me. 'Is that you?'

I tried to talk to him, but all that came out was howling noises.

'I can't believe you're a wolf,' he said with a smile on his face.

JAX
The White Wolf

For the last couple of weeks, we had been helping the witches clear the village. It was refreshing knowing that despite seeing me in my demon form, none of them had shielded themselves from me. I'd also got the chance to get to know my daughter better. It was strange. She was wise beyond her years and more mature than I was. To be fair, I had spent a lot of my life as a crow avoiding reality, whereas she had been thrown into the deep end early on.

It had been amazing seeing Leah and Leaf working the ceremony together. It was clear they were in their element. Everyone was thanking them for getting the magic back to the people who'd had theirs sacrificed. I couldn't have been more proud of them. However, I felt sorry for Sky, because we hadn't managed to break the bond between her and Hecate.

Cassie and I were walking toward the cabin to check on Sky when Freya appeared from nowhere, greeting us with her presence. 'I believe congratulations are in order.' She gave me a warm smile. 'I am happy you are finally whole.'

'Thank you.' I reached out and grabbed her hand. 'Freya, I really need to talk to you.' Not only did I want to know what she meant when she'd said I was a god, but I also needed to discuss what Nick had told me.

She placed her hand over mine and met my gaze. 'I know, but now is not the time.' She released my hand and smiled before walking away, leaving us standing there in confusion as she disappeared between the trees.

'What was that about?' Cassie asked.

I shrugged, and we continued walking.

As the cabin came into view, we saw Mark and a white wolf outside. I had never seen this white wolf around, but it seemed familiar. We closed the distance.

'How is Sky doing?' I asked Mark, and his gaze went to the wolf.

He smiled. 'I think she's okay.'

The wolf came up and licked Cassie's hand. I gently pushed her to the side. 'What'd you do that for?' she asked.

I looked at her with a questioning expression. Why would I let some random wolf lick her?

As I was about to answer, she spoke up. 'It's Sky. The

wolf is Sky,' she said with a smile.

My eyes went wide. *No, it can't be.* I scanned her closely and threw out my energy to examine hers. She didn't have the same energy as the shifters, but it was indeed Sky.

'How ...' I started, but I already knew the answer. Freya.

'Freya gave her the ability to turn into a wolf so she can be out in the sun,' Mark said happily before he continued. 'We're making our way over to the Alpha. My initiation to the pack is today, but after all of this, I want to ask him to include Sky as well. You guys should come and join the celebration.'

'We would love to,' Cassie said.

'Great. The ceremony starts after sunset by the massive oak tree. Guess we'll see you then,' he said before he and Sky disappeared behind the trees.

'Come on, let's tell Leah,' Cassie said as she grabbed my hand. I expected us to walk back to the house, but the next moment we arrived in our bedroom.

'Woah. A bit of pre-warning would have been nice,' I said as I collected myself.

'I thought you'd be used to teleportation by now,' Cassie said with a smirk.

'I am if I'm prepared for it. When did you become this good?'

She smiled and walked out of the room. I caught up with her as she knocked on Leah's door.

'Come in.'

As we walked in, Leah looked up from the desk. There

were books everywhere. 'Did you raid the library?' I asked her with a smile.

She met my gaze. 'Well, between Sky and Leaf wanting me to become High Priestess, I thought maybe I could find something that could be helpful.'

'And have you?' I asked.

'No, not yet. But I'm hopeful.'

'I don't think Sky needs your help anymore,' Cassie said.

Leah cocked her head. 'Why not?'

'She can turn into a wolf now,' Cassie said with a big grin.

Leah's eyes grew big. 'A wolf? How is that possible?'

I shrugged. 'Freya.'

'Oh ...' Leah answered.

After a while, I cleared my throat. 'We came to tell you that Mark invited us to his initiation today. It starts at sundown. I'm sure he would like you to be there.'

Leah nodded. 'Of course I'll be there.'

A few hours later, the sun was setting, and we were making our way to the big oak tree. There were several wolves around, some in their wolf form and some in their human form. There were even kids running around. Seth was there with Night and Sky's parents. I guessed the Alpha had agreed to initiate Sky too.

They had built a little stage next to the tree. The Alpha stepped up onto the stage and everyone went quiet.

'Hi, everyone. It is my honour to initiate two new

members of the pack tonight; however, Freya has a few words she'd like to say before we start.'

SKY

Initiation to the Pack

I was standing next to the makeshift stage by the big oak tree in my wolf form, watching as the Alpha entered it.

It amazed me how everything had turned out. Not only did I have my magic back but I was also standing next to the love of my life and Freya had gifted me with the ability to turn into a wolf.

After Mark had seen me in my wolf form, he had insisted we go to the Alpha to ask if I could join the pack as well. The Alpha had agreed, and we were now waiting for the pack ceremony to start.

My thoughts were cut short when I heard the Alpha mention Freya's name, and I moved my attention to the stage.

'Thank you, Alpha Derek,' Freya said as she bowed her head before turning to the audience that had gathered in front of the stage.

'Your sacrifice to save another magical species was exceptionally noble and heartening. Heroic acts like this give me hope that one day there will be peace amongst us all. I have a gift for you to show my appreciation for what you gave up. Even though I cannot restore what was lost, I am able to give you the choice of creating new mate bonds. They will be similar to what you are used to, but there will no longer be a destined mate. You are free to enter this bond with whoever holds your heart.'

What? Me and Mark can bond again? I looked up at Mark and caught his gaze. A wide smile covered his face and he bent down to scratch me behind my ear.

'I love you,' he whispered. I wanted to tell him I loved him too, but my wolf form prevented me from being able to talk to him, so I licked his face instead.

He laughed, and it looked like he was about to say something else when the Alpha continued. 'Anyone who wishes to reunite their mate bonds, come and see me or Freya after the pack ceremony.' The Alpha clapped his hands together. 'Now let's get this ceremony started.'

Loud howls came from the audience as the Alpha turned towards us.

I looked up at the darkened sky, which contained big grey clouds. The sun had disappeared below the horizon, so it should be safe for me to return to my human form. A light engulfed me and the next moment, I was back to normal, clothes and all. Mark turned around and kissed me.

'I love you,' I told him just before he went up on stage to greet the Alpha.

'Mark, son of our deceased Beta Sebastian, welcome to the pack. Please make your way to the sacred tree to swear the oath, with the pack as your witness.'

Mark left the stage and placed a hand on the massive oak. 'I swear to become one with the pack. Its brothers and sisters are now mine. I will always put the safety of the pack first, for me and the pack are now one.'

He transformed into a wolf and howled, which was followed by the howls of other wolves in the pack.

The Alpha gestured for me to come onto the stage. My heart beat faster as I stepped up and looked down at the gathered wolves.

'Sky, witch descendant, daughter of Fergus, welcome to the pack. Please make your way to the sacred tree to swear the oath, with the pack as your witness.'

I carefully stepped off the stage and made my way towards the tree with small, steady steps. When I got to the tree, I caught sight of Mark's paw print in the tree trunk. When did that happen? I hadn't seen anyone engrave it. I placed my hand next to it and said the oath.

When I'd finished, my paw print magically appeared on the tree before my eyes. I moved my fingers over it before transforming into my wolf and howling. As the other wolves responded to my howls, my mind opened and I could hear voices inside my head. 'You are now part of the pack.' The Alpha's voice sounded in my head.

'Thank you,' I thought back as I looked towards him, and he nodded at me.

This was amazing. It was like a whole new world had opened up for me. I trotted back to where Mark was standing, and he gave me a lick on my muzzle.

'This is amazing,' I thought to him.

'Just wait until we're bonded.'

I gazed into his eyes and saw all the love he held for me. How had I become this lucky?

We transformed back to our human forms and Mark got dressed before we walked over to greet my family.

As my family left, Jax approached with Cassie and Freya. 'There you are. We were looking for you,' he said.

I turned to Freya. I wanted to thank her for what she'd given me, but I couldn't find the words.

'It is okay, my child. I know this is not exactly what you wanted, but love is a powerful tool. True love has the ability to break even the darkest of curses. Your mate bond is vigorous, and in time it may be able to overpower Hecate's shackles.' She smiled. 'Now if you will excuse me, I have other things to attend to.' She disintegrated in a ray of light.

Jax laughed. 'At least it's not just me that gets the cryptic advice.'

Cassie hit him on the arm. 'I'm sure she's just trying to help.'

'What do you think it means?' Mark asked.

Jax shrugged. 'You'll find out in time.'

Mark nudged me. 'Race you to the cabin?'

I gave him a smile before turning into a wolf once more and sprinting off.

While we were making our way to the cabin, snow came down heavily from the sky. It was magical, covering the forest in a thick layer of white. We stayed out longer than we needed. But eventually we got back to the cabin.

I shook off the snow that had gathered on my coat before walking inside and turning back into a human. I grabbed a blanket that was lying on the sofa and handed it to Mark. The cold may not have affected him as much because he was a werewolf, but seeing him completely naked made me uncomfortable.

My clothes stayed on between transformations, but I wasn't a true werewolf, so it followed different rules – probably similar to Jax, as he always had his clothes on when he turned back from a crow.

A moment later Mark came out of the bedroom wearing a pair of boxers, and we cuddled up on the sofa. 'We forgot to tell the Alpha we wanted to create a mate bond together,' I said.

Mark kissed me. 'No need. Freya already gave me her blessing.'

My eyebrows shot up. 'When?'

'After the ceremony. All we need to do is mix our blood and make love.'

I wrinkled my forehead in disbelief, and Mark wrapped his arm around me. 'Don't worry. We won't do it until you're ready.'

I considered everything he'd said. I already knew I wanted to spend the rest of my life with him. I'd known from the moment I laid my eyes on him.

I gave him a passionate kiss. 'I'm ready.'

He looked at me with love in his eyes. 'Are you sure?'

I nodded. 'I'm sure.'

A wide smile spread over his face, and he got up from the sofa and came back with a glass and a knife. 'I thought this would be the most hygienic way to do it.'

I took the knife and cut my hand, watching the blood drip into the glass. Mark did the same. We mixed it together and took a sip each before Mark lifted me up bridal style and carried me to the bedroom.

We spent the evening making love to each other, and our feelings mingled together. I could feel all the love he held for me. I fell asleep peacefully in his arms.

I was back in the fire world. Red liquid flowed along the cracks on the ground. I stepped around it, careful not to touch it, as I made my way to the volcano the creature was climbing. I shouted, but it didn't hear me. I wasn't sure if I would be able to make the climb, but I needed to try. It was strenuous, and the ground shook violently with each step I took, and the space between me and the creature grew. There was no way I would catch up with it, but I still pushed on. After much effort I finally reached the top. A stone creature lay decapitated on the ground and a horrible feeling went through me. Had the creature I'd been following done this?

I glanced around, trying to locate it. It was making its way out from inside the volcano, carrying a sword on fire. How was that possible? When it reached the top, it turned around and gave me an evil smile. My heart stopped. This was the end.

I woke up screaming, 'Someone has taken the sword!'

ABOUT THE AUTHOR

Cecilia has always been interested in writing and spent many hours writing poems and short stories throughout her teenage years. She has always had an interest in fantasy, mythology and witchcraft.

As she grew up, the writing got put on ice as she followed her true passion – Animal care. She moved from Sweden to England, where she completed her Bsc (hons) degree in veterinary nursing and started working full time at a 24 hour hospital. She later moved to Cambridge with her partner and two dogs, hoping to get a better work- life balance.

It wasn't until the lockdown came knocking on everyone's doors that she picked up her writing and fell in love with it all over again. It started off as one book, but by the time she finished the first draft of her young adult fantasy novel, she knew it would be a series.